"From page one, Catherine Mann's dangerous dark ops warriors explode onto the page to command your attention and hold your heart, refusing to let go until that last satisfying page when you finally get your breath back." —*New York Times* bestselling author Dianna Love

"Catherine Mann's military romances launch you into a world chock-full of simmering passion and heart-pounding action. Don't miss 'em!"
—*USA Today* bestselling author Merline Lovelace

"Exhilarating romantic suspense." —*The Best Reviews*

"A great read." —*Booklist*

"Terrific romantic suspense that never slows down . . . An action-packed story line." —*Midwest Book Review*

"As gripping in its suspense as it is touching in its emotional pull." —*Romance Junkies*

RENEGADE

CATHERINE MANN

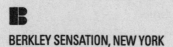
BERKLEY SENSATION, NEW YORK

THE BERKLEY PUBLISHING GROUP
Published by the Penguin Group
Penguin Group (USA) Inc.
375 Hudson Street, New York, New York 10014, USA
Penguin Group (Canada), 90 Eglinton Avenue East, Suite 700, Toronto, Ontario M4P 2Y3, Canada
(a division of Pearson Penguin Canada Inc.)
Penguin Books Ltd., 80 Strand, London WC2R 0RL, England
Penguin Group Ireland, 25 St. Stephen's Green, Dublin 2, Ireland (a division of Penguin Books Ltd.)
Penguin Group (Australia), 250 Camberwell Road, Camberwell, Victoria 3124, Australia
(a division of Pearson Australia Group Pty. Ltd.)
Penguin Books India Pvt. Ltd., 11 Community Centre, Panchsheel Park, New Delhi—110 017, India
Penguin Group (NZ), 67 Apollo Drive, Rosedale, North Shore 0632, New Zealand
(a division of Pearson New Zealand Ltd.)
Penguin Books (South Africa) (Pty.) Ltd., 24 Sturdee Avenue, Rosebank, Johannesburg 2196,
South Africa

Penguin Books Ltd., Registered Offices: 80 Strand, London WC2R 0RL, England

This is a work of fiction. Names, characters, places, and incidents either are the product of the author's imagination or are used fictitiously, and any resemblance to actual persons, living or dead, business establishments, events, or locales is entirely coincidental. The publisher does not have any control over and does not assume any responsibility for author or third-party websites or their content.

RENEGADE

A Berkley Sensation Book / published by arrangement with the author

PRINTING HISTORY
Berkley Sensation mass-market edition / January 2010

Copyright © 2010 by Catherine Mann.
Cover art by Craig White.
Cover design by Annette Fiore DeFex.
Interior text design by Laura K. Corless.

ISBN: 978-0-425-22923-1

BERKLEY® SENSATION
Berkley Sensation Books are published by The Berkley Publishing Group,
a division of Penguin Group (USA) Inc.,
375 Hudson Street, New York, New York 10014.
BERKLEY® SENSATION and the "B" design are trademarks of Penguin Group (USA) Inc.

PRINTED IN THE UNITED STATES OF AMERICA

10 9 8 7 6 5 4 3 2 1

"A Friend may well be reckoned
the masterpiece of Nature."

—RALPH WALDO EMERSON

To Joanne Rock and Stephanie Newton—both master-piece authors and friends. I have been richly blessed in knowing you both.

ACKNOWLEDGMENTS

As I write about the crew camaraderie in a military squadron, I can't help but think of the amazing support I received in bringing this book to readers' hands. I am quite possibly *the* luckiest writer on the planet to have such a stellar group of professionals around me, people who also happen to make my job tons of fun along the way. Many thanks to my savvy editor, Wendy McCurdy (organic is now one of my favorite words, and I don't mean foods!), and my long-time agent, Barbara Collins Rosenberg (thanks for encouraging me wherever the muse leads!). My deep appreciation to the super folks at Berkley who make the production process run so smoothly (and wow, doesn't the cover for this book absolutely rock!?!).

As always, my unending gratitude to my crew closer to the home front—Joanne and Stephanie for their brilliant critiques, Karen with her eagle eye for that final read-through, and of course, my air force husband, Rob, who so patiently talks me through the technical aspects of military plots. I love you all!

ONE

★ ─────────────────────────────────────

For Tech Sergeant Mason "Smooth" Randolph, a great flight was a lot like great sex.

Both brought the same rush, a sense of soaring and a driving need to make it last as long as absolutely possible. On the flip side, a bad flight was every bit as crappy as bad sex. Both could quickly become awkward, embarrassing, and downright dangerous.

As Mason planted his boots on the vibrating deck of an experimental cargo plane, his adrenaline-saturated gut told him that today's ultrasecret mission had the potential to rank up there with the worst sex ever.

The top-notch engines whispered a seductive tune, mingling with the blast of wind gusting through the cargo door cranking open. Whoever came up with dropping supplies out of the back of a fast-moving aircraft must not have stood where he was standing now. Of course, for that matter, nobody had stood in his boots on this sort of flight. That was the whole purpose of his job in an air force's highly classified test squadron.

He did things no one had tried before.

On today's mission, he would off-load packed pallets from a test-model hypersonic cargo jet, a jet that could go Mach 6, far outpacing the mere supersonic speed of Mach 1. The deck of this new baby gleamed high-tech and totally pristine without the oil and musty smell that accumulated from the history of many successful missions.

The metal warmed beneath his boots as the craft ate up miles faster than the pilot up front—Vapor—could plow through a buffet. If the plane completed testing as hoped, future fliers could travel from the United States to any point on earth in under four hours. Entire deployments could be set up in a matter of a single day, ready to roll, rather than the weeks-long buildups of the past.

No doubt, the price tag on this sleek winged sucker was huge, but for forward-thinking strategists, it saved many times over that much by shortening deployments. Of course, money had never meant dick to him.

He did care about all those marriages collapsing under the strain of long separations.

Radio talk from the two pilots up front echoed in his

headset as he checked his safety belt one last time, then raised his hand to hover over the control panel. His empty ring finger itched inside his glove. Yeah, this test in particular struck a personal note for him. It was too late for him, since his own marriage had already gone down the tubes, but maybe he could save some of his military brethren from suffering the same kick in the ass he'd endured six years ago.

Without slowing, the cargo door cranked the rest of the way open, settling into place with an ominous thunk. Wind swirled inside, the suction increasing with the yawning gape. No more time to consider how the drop shouldn't even be possible. Not too long ago, going to the moon hadn't seemed possible. It took test pilots, pioneers. All the same, this was going to be sporty.

Mason tightened his parachute straps just in case and keyed his microphone in his oxygen mask to speak to the pilots in the cockpit. "Doors opened, ramp clear."

"Copy." From the flight deck, pilot Vince "Vapor" Deluca acknowledged. "Thirty seconds to release."

Mason scanned the cargo pallets resting on rollers built into the floor. Everything appeared just as he'd prepped for this final round of flights before next week's big show for select military leaders from ally nations around the world. Pallets were packed, evenly balanced, and lined up, ready to roll straight out over the Nevada desert. Muscles contracted inside him as the pilot continued the countdown over his headset.

"Jester two-one," Vapor continued, "is fifteen seconds from release."

Mason focused on the bundle at the front of the pallet. A void of dark sky waited beyond the back ramp only a few feet away, ready to suck up the off load. He mentally reviewed the steps as if he could somehow secure the outcome. A small parachute would rifle forward, airspeed filling it with enough power to drag out the pallet. That chute would tear away, sending the pallet into a free fall until the larger parachute deployed.

"Five," Vapor counted down, "four-three-two-one."

A green light flashed over the door.

The bundle shot its mini-chute into the air behind the door. As it caught the hypersonic air, the first pallet began to move, rolling, rolling, and out. One gone. The second rattled down the tracks, picture-perfect, and then the next in synchronized magnificence as the mammoth load whipped out at a blurring speed.

Mason's gut started to ease. Next week's shindig for their visiting military dignitaries could be a huge win for the home team and move this plane into the inventory. A flop, however, could mean death to their government funding, an abrupt end to the whole project. He keyed up his mic—

The last pallet bucked off the tracks.

Oh shit. The load slammed onto its side with hundreds, maybe thousands of pounds of force. The cargo net ripped, flapping and snapping through the air. Gear exploded loose, catapulting every-fucking-where. He ducked as a piece of shattered pallet flew over his head.

"Smooth?" Vapor's voice filled the headset. "Report up."

Mason grappled for the button to respond while sidestepping a loose crate cartwheeling his way. The mesh net whipped around his leg and jerked him toward the open back. His feet shot out from under him.

"Smooth, damn it, radio up—"

His mic went silent. The cord rattled, useless and unplugged. His helmeted head whacked the deck, sparking a fresh batch of stars to his view of the night sky.

He slapped his hands along the metal grating, grappling for something, anything to slow the drag toward the back. Would his safety harness hooked to the wall hold? Under normal circumstances, sure. These weren't normal circumstances. Everything was a first-ever test at unheard-of speed.

He vise-gripped the edge of a seat. The pallet dragged at his leg. He kept his eyes focused ahead, squeezing down panic, hoping, praying Vapor or Hotwire would come back to check. His arms screamed in their sockets, and his legs burned from being stretched by the weight of the pallet teetering on the edge of the back hatch.

Don't give up. Hang on.

The bulkhead opening filled with a shadow. Thank God. The copilot—Hotwire—roared into view, his face covered by an oxygen mask, any sounds swallowed up by the vortex of wind.

Mason's fingers slipped. The weight, the force, the speed, it was all too much. "Oh, shit."

He pulled his arms in tight as the pallet raked him

along the metal floor like a hunk of cheddar against a grater. Ah damn, what about his safety harness? The strap around his waist pulled taut. An image of his body ripped in half came to mind, a snapshot that would forever stay in safety manuals to warn others of the hazards of fucking up. Not that he knew what he'd done wrong. That would be for others to decide after they buried the two halves of him in a wooden box.

Hotwire hooked his own safety belt on the run and reached. So close. Not close enough.

Mason's harness popped free from around his waist. Whomp. The air sucked at him like a vacuum. He flew out of the back of the plane at hypersonic speed, only to stop short when he slammed against the pallet, his leg still lashed by mesh. Pain detonated throughout him. Then his stomach plummeted faster than his body.

Happy fucking New Year.

Instincts on overdrive, he wrapped his arms around the pallet. The pressure on his body eased as the pallet continued a free fall downward into the inky night. His flight suit whipped against him. Images of his ex-wife flashed though his head along with regret. A shiver iced through his veins. Was he dying?

No. The wind and altitude caused the cold. Think, damn it. Don't surrender to the whole life review death march.

Either he could do nothing and pray that when the larger chute opened it didn't batter him to death against the pallet, or he could free his leg from the netting, kick away from the pallet, and use his own parachute, provided it hadn't been damaged during the haul out the back of the plane.

His options sucked ass, but at least he was still alive to fight. Getting clear of the damaged pallet seemed wisest. Determination fueled his freezing limbs. Vertigo threatened to overtake him as he kicked to untangle his boot from the netting. He jerked, pulled, and strained until yes, his leg came free.

"Argh!" Mason grunted, muscles burning.

He shoved away just as the large chute deployed. His body plummeted, pinwheeling. The pallet was jerked to a stall by the chute, tearing apart in a shower of wood and supplies. Good God, he would have been drawn and quartered.

He reined himself in, struggling to control the fall while gauging his surroundings, but the solitary void combined with an eerie silence. How much farther until he landed? If he pulled the cord too soon, he could float forever with no sense of direction, ending up lost deep in the desert.

Screw it. Better too early than waiting too long and shattering every bone in his body by not using his parachute soon enough. He reached down, feeling along his waist until he found the handle.

He yanked. Cords whistled past and overhead. Nylon rippled upward until . . . whomp.

Air filled the chute and pulled him. Hard. The rapid stall knocked the wind out of him and, damn it to hell, crushed his left nut under the leg strap.

He shook his head to clear his thoughts, no time to

piss and moan. He grabbed a riser and hefted into a one-arm pull-up to ease pressure on the strap. Ahhh, better, much better. Pain eased. His brain revved.

Now, how did that "you just fucked up bad and are now floating toward the earth" checklist go?

Canopy. His eyes adjusting to the dark, he checked the canopy, and there were no rips, no tears, not even the dreaded Mae West, where a line looped over the chute for a double bubble effect.

Visor. Little chance of landing in a tree here, so he pulled the visor up.

Mask. He stripped his oxygen mask off his face, unhooked the connectors on his chest, and pitched it away into the abyss.

Seat kit. Strapped to his butt, it contained a raft. Not much call for that in the desert. He opened the connector and ditched the raft, too.

LPUs. Life preserver units. He thumbed the horse collar LPU around his neck and down his chest, pulled the inflate tabs, and another high-pressure bottle inflated the floatie. It might cushion the landing and save a few broken ribs, although no telling what he might have already busted back in the plane. Thank goodness for the adrenaline numbing his system.

What next? Oh yeah. Steer. Damn, he was punch drunk. He reached up for the risers and grappled until he wrapped his fingers around the steering handles.

The next step? Prepare. Yeah, he was so prepared to smack into the ground he could barely see. He scanned below as best he could, checking out the sand, sand, sand, occasional bundle of desert scrub, staying clear of the distant mountains. Okay, dude. Final step.

Land. He put his eyes on the horizon and bent his knees slightly, ready to perform the perfect PLF, parachute landing fall. The ground roared up to meet him. He prepped for . . . the . . . impact.

Balls of the feet.

Side of the leg and butt.

Side of the arm and shoulder.

Complete.

Mason lay on the gritty sand, stunned. No harm in lying still for a few and rejoicing in the fact that he would live to fly and make love again. There wasn't any need to rush out of here just yet. He wasn't in enemy territory.

Although he didn't have a clue exactly what piece of the Nevada desert he currently occupied. His tracking device would bring help though. Rescue would show up in an hour or so. Maybe by then he could stand without whimpering like a baby.

He shrugged free of his parachute and LPU one miserable groan at a time. Already he could feel the bruises rising to the surface. He would probably resemble a Smurf by morning, but at least he still had all his limbs, and no bones rattled around inside him—that he could tell.

His teeth chattered, though. From the freezing cold of a winter desert night, or from shock? Either way, he needed to get moving. He pushed to his feet, stumbling for a second before the horizon stopped bobbling.

A siren wailed in the distance.

Already? Perhaps this flight experience wouldn't suck so much after all. Even bad sex could be rescued with a satisfying ending.

He blinked to clear his eyesight. Twin beams of light stretched ahead of a Ford F-150, blinding him as the vehicle approached. He shielded his eyes with one hand and waved his other arm. Ouch. Fuck.

A loudspeaker squeaked and crackled to life. "Get back down on the ground. Lie flat on your stomach," a tinny voice ordered. "If you move at all, you will be shot."

Shot? What the hell? Had he landed in some survivalist kook's farm?

But that wouldn't explain the siren. He must have drifted into restricted territory, not surprising, since they flew many of their secret test missions in secured areas. The truck screeched to a halt, and someone wearing camo stepped out. A flashlight held at shoulder level kept him from seeing the face, but he could discern an M4 carbine at hip level well enough.

He shouted, "Don't shoot. I'm not armed, and I'm not resisting."

"Stay on the ground," the voice behind the light barked.

A female voice?

Okay, so much for his PC rating today. He'd assumed the security cop was a male, not that it made any difference one way or the other. He respected the power of that M4.

Mason flattened his belly to the desert floor, arms extended over his head. A knee plowed deep in the small of his back. If he didn't have a bruised kidney before, he sure did now.

A cold muzzle pressed against his skull. All right, then. The knee didn't hurt so much after all.

"Hands behind you, nice and slow." The lady cop's husky voice heated his neck. "So, flyboy, do you want to tell me what you're doing out here in Area 51?"

* * *

Jill Walczak had a secret. But she was used to keeping secrets in her current job as one of the highly classified civilian security forces contracted to patrol the perimeter of Area 51, anonymous guards known simply as "camo dudes." With a serial killer on the loose trying to stir up the alien conspiracy nuts, she couldn't afford to relax her guard for even a second.

"Flyboy? Nothing to say?" Keeping her M4 against his head, she carefully set her flashlight aside so it illuminated his face. "Okay, then. We'll chitchat in a minute after we take care of business. I'm not telling you another time after this. Put your hands behind your back. Slowly. Grunt if you hear me."

"Got it," he growled, his discarded parachute ruffling and snapping in the night wind.

One broad hand in a flight glove slid along the

parched earth and tucked against his lower spine. His other hand started to move, inching a little too close to the flashlight for her peace of mind.

"Touch that flashlight, and I'll shoot you in the wrist."

His fingers froze.

Then he started moving his arm again, slowly, not so much as a flinch or suspicious move. Thus far he was the perfect detainee. She hoped he would stay that way.

Quickly, she set aside her weapon, locked the handcuffs around his wrists, and regained control of her M4. She was toned and trained these days, but she knew better than to underestimate the hard-muscled man in her custody. She was alone out here in the desert tonight, and she'd driven deeper in Area 51 than was normally acceptable, all because of an anonymous tip.

Was the parachuting flyboy her "something spectacular and lethal on the horizon" that would lead her to the "Killer Alien"? Four victims—one man and three women—had shown up around Area 51 and nearby Nellis AFB, three of them dead in the past year, all attacked in a manner to make it appear linked to extraterrestrials.

She shivered. Desert winter nights were damn cold and desolate. But her chill settled deeper in her bones as she thought of how her friend had died.

Jill inched off her captive and scooped up her flashlight, wind kicking sand up until it stung her face. "The time for grunts has passed. Tell me what you're doing in Dreamland."

The flyboy kept his face down, nose to the gritty ground. "I work as a loadmaster and flight engineer in the U.S. Air Force. A cargo drop went to hell, and I got sucked out the back of the plane. The heavy wind tonight must have drifted me over into the box."

The box. At least this aviator spoke the flyboy lingo for Area 51.

The man cleared his throat. "Hey, do you mind if I turn my face to the side?" His muffled voice rumbled low in the night air. "I'd rather not talk through a mouthful of sand."

"Fair enough. But just your face." She did not intend to end up like those three murdered souls, sliced like a science experiment. And around their dead bodies the killer had left an eerily undisturbed sand circle. "Slowly. Then I'll need your name."

She shifted her flashlight to his mug again. The more she kept the beam on him, the less visibility he would have in the dark to see her or attempt an escape. She swiped the piercing shaft of light over his face. The chill of darker thoughts eased.

Move over, Hugh Jackman.

The flyboy blinked fast, his green eyes glinting as she studied him more closely. Recognition tickled the back of her brain. She looked closer, taking in the smoothly handsome face. A tuft of dark hair twisted by a cowlick ramped in front as if refusing to submit to the military cut.

Yeah, she'd seen him around, all right.

The people working top secret jobs in this region

shared certain facilities as budget savers. It wasn't uncommon to pass someone in the mess hall multiple times and have no knowledge of the other person's job or even name. They'd never been officially introduced . . . until now. "Who are you?"

"Tech Sergeant Mason Randolph."

She'd heard him called a number of other things by the women dining at her table whom he'd winked at, smiled at, flirted with, dated. They'd called him names like Smooth, Loverboy, and lastly, That Jackass.

Would he remember her when he wasn't blinded by the flashlight? She ratcheted up her grasp on his cuffed wrists.

He winced beneath her. "Hey, aren't there police brutality rules against that hold?"

"Then don't move."

"No worries, ma'am. I'm a lucky son of a bitch, so we're going to be just fine." He flashed his killer smile her way, the first time he'd turned that power on her.

She was immune.

Jill eased her knee off his back, ready to haul him up. The wind howled, tumbleweed speeding past, the parachute whipping faster, lifting. Jill yanked at the flyboy's arm to pull him aside.

The nylon sheeted forward, toward her. She barely had time to blink before it wrapped around her and her captive.

She stumbled, her feet tangling with his. "Stay still."

He did, but she couldn't. Her feet shot out from under her. Cord and nylon binding them together, he fell with her, his muscled bulk sending them tumbling.

"Damn it all," he snapped seconds before they both slammed to the ground.

His body covered hers, his leg nestling between hers. Hot breath gusted over her cheek, sending gooseflesh prickling along her skin at the possibility she could be sharing air with a monster.

She forced herself to breathe anyway. He was cuffed, so she was safe. All she had to worry about was the teasing she would take at work if this part of the arrest leaked out. They were all looking for an outlet for the stress, especially with the added pressure on finding the killer and locking down security before some big shindig at Nellis Air Force Base next week. "Roll to your side, please."

"I'll try, but it would help if you freed your left boot from that cording that's lashing our feet together."

"Sure, I'm on it." She started inching her leg away.

The ground rumbled under her with an ominous reminder that anything could happen in Area 51. What the hell? She clawed at the nylon, thrashing until finally, finally, finally the parachute swooped free of their heads.

The warning rumble in the distance increased. What if Mason Randolph wasn't what the tipster had meant after all? His muscles tensed beneath her grip.

An explosion blossomed into a hazy red cloud on the horizon.

TWO

Dr. Lee Drummond liked to blow things up.

Lee had started setting fires at four after seeing dear old Dad strike a match in front of the hearth at the first snowfall. But Lee was smart, a certified genius for that matter, and quickly learned random blazes would bring serious trouble, which meant figuring out how to feed the hunger for fire legally, in a manner that didn't get a person labeled a psychopath. After receiving a PhD at nineteen, Lee had put those electrical engineering skills to use working as a civilian contractor for the U.S. military, now working in a top secret test squadron.

In an underground bunker in the Nevada desert, Lee studied the monitor, the image still rippling with shock waves from the chemical explosion in Area 51. The good doctor looked over the shoulder of the pilot in a remote control booth flying the Predator drone that had dropped the blister agent—absolutely fucking awe-some to watch work—followed by a secondary release of a trial antidote.

The antidote wasn't functioning. Already even hardy desert vegetation withered and drooped.

And here in the safe and serene little concrete bun-ker with the pilot flying and sensor operator navigating, Lee felt none of the physical effects, thanks to the spe-cialized ventilation system designed to filter out any-thing bad. The mental rush, however, was epic.

Wrangling into this operation as a technical advisor had been easy enough. Little did they know who had really orchestrated a whole mess playing out in Area 51.

The remote-controlled Predator drone circled, test-ing top secret gadgets and toys to gather toxicity read-ings. Lee pressed a hand to the headset filled with chatter from the Predator's pilot and sensor operator to the range controller back at headquarters.

"Pred seven-seven," the range controller called from his post thirty miles away, "we're spotting suspicious movement in area Bravo Two. Can you ease over that way and feed us some video?"

Anticipation tingled with a heat that could rival that mutilating blister agent they'd released in the explosion.

The pilot—Werewolf—sitting at his remote control panel, answered, "Roger control, heading that way."

From her oversized chair beside the pilot, the sensor operator monitored readings on her dials and screen. "Indicators show surface winds are one-two-zero at ten. Adjust for scan downwind from Bravo Two."

"Can do," Werewolf answered. "Coming in from downwind."

Guiding the joystick, Werewolf banked the aircraft while the sensor operator focused the camera downwind of the fire. The sensor operator had been dubbed Gucci, since somehow she managed to make even a generic flight suit look designer. The pilot and mission commander went by Werewolf. He was a hairy jackass. Enough said.

Lee stood behind them, avidly studying the screens for every nuance in case these incompetents missed something. Back in the early days here, one of the cocky aviators had labeled Lee as "Bambi." To this day ten years later, the poor bastard didn't know the case of salmonella that had put him in the hospital hadn't been an accident.

God, fliers were arrogant, and none more so than the egomaniacs in this top secret test squadron. But Lee had discovered more pointed—and entertaining—methods for taking vengeance these days.

Gucci tapped keys to zero in on an image in the far corner of one of the screens she monitored. "Check this out. There's a vehicle and two people up on that ridgeline. Can you bring us in closer?"

"Crap!" Werewolf's hairy fist clenched around the stick. "We're supposed to be studying Joshua trees, not real Joshuas. Control, Pred seven-seven."

"Go, Pred."

"There's a vehicle and two individuals on the ridgeline road downwind of Bravo Two," Werewolf said.

"Looks like it's a security vehicle, and the guard is taking someone into custody. I can't tell who from so far away."

As the Predator flew closer, Gucci zoomed in the view on the pair. She winced, her face pulling tighter than the slick blond bun on the back of her head. "Holy crap, that's Mason Randolph, and wow, is that lady cop ever kicking his ass. He's not going to live that one down."

Lee played it cool, face bland, not relaying any pleasure as the plan played out perfectly. It had taken skill weaving together two different highly classified tests to achieve the ultimate goal for tonight's little piece of justice.

Still, there wasn't any harm in enjoying a closer look. "What do you say we try out my newest toy now? Then we can hear what they're saying while you're testing the air. We'll have two methods of determining if they're in danger from the fallout."

"Roger that, Dr. Drummond." Werewolf's fingers sailed along buttons, keying in commands. He checked his data, then hit a red release button.

Fifteen thousand feet overhead, a pair of small doors opened in one of the Predator's pylons and ejected a small black ball, which fell away from the aircraft and swooped toward the earth. As soon as it had slowed down, the ball unfurled into a bat-looking shape and zoomed toward the target the sensor operator had designated.

The nanotechnology bat was designed to circle

above silently and allow the Predator to listen in on whatever was below. These nanosensors rocked. Nobody approached them, because who would want to play with a bat or spider or bumblebee?

"Bat away," Werewolf updated, "and operating normally. Audio available on button three in about twenty seconds."

The bat reached altitude and flapped its mechanical wings to begin circling the couple below, closer, closer still, until the screen filled with the image of a man in a flight suit. He broke free of the woman, hands cuffed behind him, and jumped to his feet. A parachute lay on the ground around them.

Mason Randolph. The target of this whole plan. The flyboy faced the hazy glow burning on the horizon. "What the fuck?"

"Damn it," the lady cop ordered, raising her weapon, "hold your position while I radio in."

"My plane!" Mason's voice came out harsh and strangled as he nodded toward the pluming cloud of smoke, damn near oblivious to the threat of an M4 carbine. The horror on his face spoke volumes more when he seemed unable to scavenge for more than a few words. "My crew!"

Ah, Mason had thought the explosion was a crash of his hypersonic jet. Lee hadn't considered that, but it was a nice little something extra. The bastard deserved to hurt. Lee had done some earlier work on that project as well and knew firsthand how damned important that plane was to Mason.

And about the woman? Innocents shouldn't suffer, but sometimes collateral damage was unavoidable.

The ginger-haired guard released her hold on Mason's shoulder. "Stay put, and I'll find out what's going on. Know, though, that I will have my gun trained on you at all times."

Mason didn't even seem to register her words. He just stood stock-still, scrub brush rolling over his boots to tangle in the parachute.

The radio inside her truck squawked loudly through the open door. "Base to Unit Five, please report."

Keeping her gun level, she backpedaled to her vehicle and reached inside for the radio. "Unit Five is on freq. Over."

"What is your location, Unit Five?"

"Range road one-twenty at klick nine. I have an aviator in custody who parachuted into the region. Then something blew on the horizon, something big. Was there a crash? Over."

The radio crackled for a couple of heartbeats. "No crash reported. The explosion is a mishap in Bravo Two. You need to get the hell out of there now."

The female in camouflage jolted at his words. "Damn it all, Bravo Two is where they do chemical testing. That smoke undoubtedly contains some bad shit."

No kidding.

Mason sagged with obvious relief. Relief? Mason had to be the first person on record happy to hear his skin might melt off at any second. He must be awful damn tight with that crew of his. Too bad he couldn't have suffered for a while longer.

The bat monitor swooped lower, closer to the chick. "Confirm you said in Bravo Two."

"Roger," the voice on her radio responded. "I repeat, get the hell out of there with your extra baggage. Head the opposite way on range road one-twenty and turn south at road nine. Don't stop until you get to gate eleven. Wait there for hazmat. We have a hazmat truck and crew en route to meet you for decontamination."

The camo dude eased one hand free and pulled the ranger wrap on her neck up over her nose. The cloth protected breathing during heavy winds whipping the sand around. Right now it seemed pitiful defense against lethal toxins.

"I'm on my way directly to gate eleven." The cop tossed her radio back into the truck and sprinted toward Mason, whipping a bandanna from her pocket before she screeched to a halt beside the flyer. "Hold still. I'm going to tie this around your face."

"A gag isn't necessary," Mason countered, back to his regular cocky self, apparently still riding the high of learning his crew hadn't buried their plane nose-first into the desert.

Dumb bastard didn't even appreciate how close he'd come to dying. If that cop hadn't been out there— where no one normally would have been—Mason's insides would have curdled the same way all the vegetation around them soon would. His good-looking face would be disfigured with blisters.

"Be quiet," the no-nonsense cop snapped. "I'm trying to protect your lungs, but if that's a problem for you?"

"Just do it." He bent his knees slightly so she could reach to secure the bandanna. "Any idea what they're pumping into the atmosphere today?"

"I'm the one who asks the questions. Now move toward the truck."

"Yes, ma'am," Mason called over his shoulder, bandito look complete. "A woman who likes to be boss. Totally hot."

The spy bat plunged closer, following the truck's progress toward a hazmat truck far on the horizon. Lee studied the screen, savoring every moment to feed this hunger until the time came next week to destroy Mason Randolph's life.

Publicly and permanently.

* * *

"Please remove your clothes and toss them onto the ground."

Stepping back out of the truck, Mason heard the "get naked" order from the man in the hazmat suit, the mask muffling the voice Darth Vader style. While stripping down in the January-cold desert night sounded crappy, he had a serious issue with launching his own radioactive fashion line for the new year. Given the heightened security because of that killer on the loose, he suspected this might take longer than normal. He just wanted to clean off whatever he'd been exposed to and get back to work figuring out what the hell went wrong on tonight's flight before next week's high-profile gathering.

His job was everything to him. In fact, he'd been forced to sacrifice everything for it—his family, an inheritance, and finally, his wife. Hopefully tonight he wouldn't be giving his life.

The pair of hazmat workers in white suits opened a side panel on their van. The high-speed ride with the lady cop had been silent and tense. She'd parked him in the backseat, with his hands still cuffed, and peeled rubber in the abandoned desert, nothing but cacti, scrub brush, and a big fat moon. He probably had a concussion now, too, after slamming his head against the roof from all the ruts and holes she'd four-wheeled over until they met up with the hazmat van hauling ass toward them.

"Hey, ma'am," he shot over his shoulder to the camo cop, "it's kinda tough for me to get undressed with the cuffs on. Wanna take care of these?"

"Of course." She tucked behind him as one of the hazmat workers began unrolling a water hose. "But realize these guys change nothing for you. If you make a move for my gun, you will be shot."

"Got it. The guys in the space suits will not save me. Although I have to admit I think we have bigger concerns right now."

"Ya think?" The keys jingled as she worked the lock, and then his hands were free.

He shook the circulation back into his fingers. "Time to boogie."

The large van idled behind the lady cop, with an isolation chamber waiting to swallow them up for transportation to a hospital. Mason untied both his boots and kicked them free. His survival vest went next, landing on the ground with a puff of sand. He'd been this route once before over in Afghanistan, when a suspicious canister exploded in the middle of their compound courtyard. The event had been blood pressure spiking for him—not to mention for his ex-wife, who'd been talking to him on the phone when the Klaxon had blared. The Afghan instance had been a false alarm.

This time, they already knew chemicals were most definitely involved.

Mason yanked down the long zipper on his flight suit, shrugging his shoulders free one after the other. He should be freaking out right about now for fear of his balls perpetually glowing in the dark, but he was too caught up in the relief from learning his crew hadn't crashed. He'd survived a hellish plummet to earth. And as a bonus, the cop had apparently decided against popping a bullet through his skull.

A hose-down sounded like small potatoes.

He shucked his flight suit in what had to be record time and jerked his T-shirt over his head as he toed off his socks. Wearing nothing but his boxers, he kicked the rest to the side to be collected and burned.

He thumbed the waistband of his shorts and turned, just as icy spray from a water hose slammed into his chest. He stumbled back a step before planting his heels in the gritty earth. His teeth chattered twice before he could steel himself to the cold. Oooh-kay, apparently the boxers stayed.

One of the spacemen directed the nozzle, while the other guy worked the controls on the side of the truck. The dude with the hose swished the spray back and forth between him and the cop. The water battered his skin, the bitter night air turning downright frigid. No worries about his balls glowing just yet, because he was pretty damn sure they'd retreated deep inside his body in search of warmer territory.

"Turn," the spaceman ordered.

Mason pivoted on his heel. The shower pummeled his back, and he dug his toes deeper into the sand, a shallow pool swelling around his feet. He glanced to the side to check on Madame Cop.

He forgot all about anchoring himself in place and stumbled forward a step. Holy Venus de Milo in a sports bra. The woman beside him had a smoking-hot body. Thank goodness for the cool spray of water, or he would be one embarrassed hombre.

She danced in the shower of water, long legs graceful even under the force of a power hose. She raised her arms overhead for a more thorough sluice. Her full breasts shifted ever so slightly under the stretch of green spandex.

Water glistened on her skin, refracting from the truck lights. She might be busty, but she was also lean and toned, which made sense, given her job. She had to pin guys his size, after all.

She pivoted and faced him full-on for the first time since she'd stepped from her vehicle, not that he'd been able to see her then because of the way she'd blinded him with her flashlight. Something about her seemed familiar, but he couldn't place where with her face still cast in shadows.

Turning her back to him, she presented a pert butt in green cotton hipster panties. Her deep red hair turned nearly black with saturation as the water worked it loose to stream down her back.

Now was definitely not the time to think of how good her curves had felt against him when they'd tangled up together in his parachute.

The spray from the hose dwindled, and the second spaceman opened the back of the truck. Mason tore his eyes off the woman before she caught him gawking like an adolescent nube. They had bigger concerns, for God's sake,

Shaking water from his arms, he sprinted toward the sanitized vehicle. He heard splashes behind him and realized his cop companion was a step away. He stopped short to let her enter first.

"Th-th-thanks." Her teeth chattered. "Nice to see your mama taught you some manners."

His Junior League mother had been big on manners. His smile went tight. "Just checking out your rear view."

"What a tool," she muttered as she grabbed a rail to pull herself up and into the silver metal cavern.

He followed, keeping his eyes off her underwear and perfect backside, because in spite of his own ribbing, he had been taught better by his socialite mother. Mason sat on the metal bench across from the lady cop. The door slammed shut and hissed with a decontaminating seal, leaving them alone together in a cavern bathed in the glow of the red lights lining the ceiling. He snagged one of the thin, metallic space blankets to pass her and draped another over his shoulders. Slowly, his skin stopped burning from the cold.

How flipping ironic to be so cold his skin felt like it was being stabbed everywhere by fiery needles. Or could that be the effect of the chemicals? He shoved the fear away to be dealt with later, since there wasn't a thing more he could do about it now.

But what about her? Should he prep himself for a hysterical meltdown now that the initial crisis had passed?

She'd seemed tough enough while grinding his nose into the dirt. Still, she had to be scared shitless right about now. He tried to search her face, but the dim red lights still made seeing her face difficult. Although he couldn't miss the way she shivered inside her blanket, from cold or fear or going into shock he couldn't know for sure, but better to err on the side of caution.

He'd always found distraction to be the best cure for the shakes in a crisis, and she'd already shown her vulnerability. "So, do you come here often?"

She hugged her blanket tighter. "Pardon me?"

"What's your sign? What's a nice girl like you doing in a place like this? I'm new in town, could you give me directions to your place?" He rambled through the cheesy pickup lines as the truck jolted forward, waiting until . . . yeah, he could already sense the fire crackling back to life inside her.

"How juvenile, like your underwear," she muttered softly, although she must not have said it too softly to have been heard over the revving engine.

"Apparently you didn't think much of my cartoon boxers. Damn shame. Valentine's Day is what? Only a few weeks away?"

"Six weeks."

Like he couldn't count. But hallelujah, he had her talking. "What's wrong with a man wearing some cupids and hearts in preparatory celebration of the holiday of love? I thought your gender longed for males who won't forget Valentine's Day."

She snorted, but at least her teeth had stopped chattering. Irritation was better than fear or hypothermia. Hopefully he could keep her distracted long enough for them to find out whether or not that toxic explosion had wrecked their DNA for life.

"Ah, you prefer your pickups to be more straightforward." He thrust out his hand. "Hi, I'm Mason."

"You told me earlier." She ignored his hand while keeping her own buried in the folds of her blanket.

"And you are?"

"Not interested in chitchat or pretend pickup games to pass the time."

"I guess that's a big fat nope to telling me your name."

Camo dudes were notoriously closemouthed. They even went to extreme lengths to avoid having their photos taken by tourists or the press. But it wasn't like he wouldn't find out her name eventually.

She leaned back against the metal seat, eying him suspiciously as the truck jostled along the desert, siren wailing. "How can you be so oblivious to what's going on around us? To what just happened with that toxic explosion? At this very minute our insides could be festering into a genetic cesspool."

"Lady, twenty minutes ago I thought my crew had crashed." The hell of that moment rolled over him with a fresh wave of nausea that outweighed even the prospect of his own personal DNA septic tank. He knew they would have been every bit as upset in his position. In fact, his squadron buds were the only ones who would give a shit if something happened to him. His ex-wife, Kim, had already remarried, and he barely spoke with his parents since turning his back on the family legacy at eighteen. "Everything else pales in comparison."

Surprise glinted in her eyes, then something nice and soft. He wished he could tell their color, but the red light messed with everything.

"I'm sorry, Sergeant. That must have been terrible for you."

"Damn straight." He'd been sure Vapor and Hotwire had crashed and died, and that somehow it was his fault because he'd screwed up with that airdrop. He still couldn't figure out what had gone wrong with the pallets, and if he didn't uncover the flaw or mistake, he risked worse happening next go round. Talk about a downer notion.

Lighthearted beat serious any day of the week. He eyed the prickly woman across from him, a mega-hot, prickly woman. "Do you know karate? Because damn, your body kicks butt."

Any signs of sympathy faded from her eyes, and she shot him a withering look. "No, I do not. And no, you may not have a quarter to call your mother since you promised to tell her when you met the woman of your dreams."

His mother likely wouldn't answer a call from him anyway, but no need to wade in those stagnant waters of how he'd disappointed his family.

Mason clapped a hand over his heart, foil blanket crackling. "Somebody bring me a bandage. I just scraped my knees falling for this lady."

"Sergeant Smart-Ass."

"So they tell me." Yeah, he knew himself pretty well, the good and the bad. However, he still didn't have a clue where he'd met that sexy voice before, but he intended to find out.

Right after he figured out why his test flight had gone to shit just in time to land him in the middle of an explosive situation.

THREE

Jill towel-dried her hair in the Nellis Air Force Base hospital bathroom while mentally listing all the ways she could find out more about Tech Sergeant Mason Randolph and what he was really doing in that specific restricted portion of Area 51 last night. Could he really be the Killer Alien? Her skin burned until she could almost feel the steam rising from her wet hair. She certainly had plenty of time to interrogate him covertly, since they were stuck in quarantine together.

After arriving at the base just at sunup, she'd been transferred by a female tech into a glistening white chamber, where she'd ditched her blanket and underwear in a toxic waste bin. The tech had hosed her down again then handed her a paper robe. Jill then gave what felt like gallons of blood before going into a larger quarantine room with two gurney beds. She hadn't expected to want another shower, but something about the whole scary night left her needing some good old-fashioned hydrotherapy.

In the bathroom connected to the sterile chamber, Jill reached for the pile of surgical scrubs and tugged the green shirt over her head, itchy to finish here and get somewhere she could access her work computer. She needed to check in, but she was denied visitors until the military gave the okay.

She stepped into the drawstring pants and started combing through her wet hair. So far no big chunks fell out, thank goodness.

No one had told her what she'd been exposed to and likely never would, given the secrecy level of Area 51. She understood the risks that came with her job and gladly accepted them, now more than ever, as she had been drawn into the local police investigation to find the serial killer. Most thought she'd dug in for the career advancement, and that was okay by her. She needed to downplay how much she burned to avenge her friend's death. Personal connections to victims were frowned upon.

Jill slipped her feet into the flimsy plastic flip-flops and opened the steel door. Voices flooded through, and she stopped half-in, half-out. Apparently her quarantine mate, Tech Sergeant Mason Randolph, could have visitors—as long as that person stayed on the other side of the large glass window.

Mason stood barefoot in a hospital gown in front of the framed pane, pressing the Talk button on the small

speaker box. Behind him were two stretchers and a
wall of medical gear for dispensing oxygen and taking
vitals. Other than that, the space was an empty, sterile
wash of white and silver. She couldn't hold back a grin
at the incongruous image of such an obviously virile
man in a wraparound gown and spiky wet hair, the
whole getup giving him a Peter Pan appeal.

"God, Colonel Scanlon," Mason said to the older
man on the other side of the window, "things just went
to shit up there. I honestly thought I'd checked the
weight balance on the casters, but apparently not. No
excuses."

She tucked more covertly against the half-open door
to listen. No need to feel guilty. Her job presented her
conscience with a free pass on eavesdropping while
Mason chatted with a lieutenant colonel wearing a
flight suit and Buddy Holly glasses. Right now, she
was flying solo. She was learning what she could about
an unscheduled parachute into the middle of an already
suspicious toxic test. That also made her wonder again
who'd given her the tip to look there in the first place.

"We're just in the early stages of investigating the
incident," the colonel answered cryptically, "but I expect we'll have everything cleared up by next week's
shindig."

"What do Vapor and Hotwire have to say?" Mason
clasped his hands behind his back, keeping the hospital
gown closed and somehow managing to still look macho.

The gaunt colonel, silver flecking his temples,

leaned against the wall. "You know I have the utmost faith in you, but I can't give you the details of their individual versions just yet. We have to keep everything separate for a while at least. Not knowing protects you."

"Of course. Protocol and all."

"Don't worry about the flight for now." Scanlon smiled, more of a grimace really, but it crinkled the corners of his eyes. "Just enjoy your time lounging around here. We'll spring you from this place and get you back to work before you know it."

"I hope so."

"I've got some feelers out for more info on that explosion. So far, it's sounding like a straight-up blister agent test."

Only a blister agent? Her skin started tingling at just the thought.

Mason didn't appear fazed in the least. "I appreciate your help."

"No problem. It's what we do for our people." The colonel checked his watch. "I need to head out. I'm visiting Captain Tanaka, too, while I'm here. Everyone at work sends their best."

Mason plucked at the hospital gown. "I'll bet they're just sorry to miss the opportunity to see me in a dress."

"They already offered me tickets to a hot new show at the Bellagio if I snap a photo with my cell phone."

"I'll bet they did," Mason quipped. "And hey, Colonel Scanlon, I appreciate your coming by."

"No problem," Lieutenant Colonel Scanlon answered as he backed a step away. "I'm just glad you're all right. Take care now."

Scanlon pulled his hand off the speaker button and turned to leave.

Jill gripped the door. How Mason could take this all so lightly blew her mind. Could that be a sign of a darker disdain for human life?

Even though one of the victims had been male, they still suspected the killer was targeting women. It appeared the man might have been a boyfriend who got in the way.

Mason had lady-killer—the Romeo kind, anyway—written all over him. The times they'd crossed paths in the area mess hall, he'd tried to pick up her female friends and workmates. Never her though. When she'd watched his act for the third time, she'd made a point of broadcasting off-limits vibes.

Now she had to get close to him.

Mason shifted from one bare foot to the other but didn't turn around. "You can come out now."

Jill winced, releasing the bathroom door to hiss closed. "You knew I was here that whole time?"

He pointed to the glass window. "I can see your reflection."

Damn it, she should be more careful. The people back at headquarters were counting on her. The families of those victims—Lara in particular—counted on her. Her boss had to already know what had shaken down in the desert, and he would expect some concrete info from her once she got the all clear from the doctors.

She stepped closer. "I didn't want to interrupt."

Her eavesdropping hadn't told her much anyway, and neither man relayed anything telling with his body language. The colonel couched everything with curt professionalism, and the playboy here covered his emotions with charm. Did he realize she'd been listening out of more than curiosity?

Mason turned to face her with a megawatt smile. "How come you get pants and booties? Did you bat those pretty eyelashes at somebody around here?"

Pretty? Would he have flirted with her so outrageously back during her overweight high school days? "Are you up to date on your political correctness training, Sergeant?"

"I'll trade with you. My dress for those pants. You don't even have to give me the shirt."

"Not a chance. Get your own." She couldn't resist glancing down at his legs, dusted with dark hair and . . . holy crap! "What happened to your leg?"

She stared at the bruise wrapping around his ankle and up his calf in all the colors of the rainbow.

He hefted himself up onto the gurney, somehow managing not to expose anything embarrassing. "That little mark is just a by-product of my parachuting screwup. It's only a sprain. The flight doc said he'll wrap it later when he finishes up with a page to the ER. I'm damn lucky this bruise is all I have."

"Doesn't it hurt?" The wound at least backed up his story about being sucked out of a plane, which would mean the "surprise on the horizon" had been what?

Someone else in the desert? Or a sick joke to land her in the path of a blister agent? "Can't they give you something for the pain?"

"Painkillers are for sissies."

"What a load of macho bull." She hopped onto the edge of her gurney, hitching one leg up to cuff the scrub pants so they wouldn't drag the floor.

He nodded toward her. "I think they sent us into the wrong bathrooms. Those scrubs are so loose on you they must have been meant for me."

"Or maybe you pissed off one of the nurses around here."

"Not a chance."

"What a tool," she muttered.

"So you've said."

A door hissed open, and a nurse wearing a surgical mask over her mouth and sterile white clothing entered. With brisk efficiency, she took Jill's vitals, then Mason's, making notations on the charts, then rehanging the info on the beds. Mason grinned at her. The woman's blue eyes twinkled over her mask.

Jill fisted the paper covering until it crackled in her grip.

Once the door swished shut behind the nurse, Mason eased off the gurney and started limping around the room. "I applaud your dedication to your job."

"Pardon me?" She smoothed the paper, inspected the pillow and blanket, and wondered if they actually expected her to sleep in here with him tonight.

Mason stopped by the table of instruments and

picked up that thing doctors used to look inside ears. He brought it to his eyes and inspected the room. "Following me all the way in here to keep watch."

"Not funny. Put down that, uh, thing. You're going to get us in trouble." Great one, Jill. Like a serial killer would be concerned about censure over playing with the hospital equipment.

Wait. She stiffened. Were there scalpels in here? She glanced through the window to check, and yes a nurse stayed parked at the observation station. Not that Mason actually fit the profiler's pysch report, something she would be reviewing again the minute she got back into her office.

"It's an otoscope."

"Thanks, Dr. Randolph."

"I'm most definitely not a doctor." His jaw tight, he set the otoscope back on the tray, picked up a tongue depressor, and flicked it into the trash can in a perfect two-point shot. "I bet you didn't chew gum in school when you were a kid."

"And I bet you stuck it under the desk."

"Guilty as charged." He punched the light controls, adjusting the levels from dim to bright again and again. "You don't have to worry about me running away." He plucked at the hospital gown. "The breeze on my backside is a serious deterrent."

"I'll have to remember that next time I'm trying to detain someone." She grabbed her blanket and pondered the best way to pump him for information about the flight.

He abandoned the buttons, leaving the lights on dim as he limped toward her. "You should have listened to me when I told you there was no reason to worry about me being there. We could have left right after you found me. Then we might not have ended up here."

"Remind me again what you were doing?"

His face blanked for a flash before he turned his back on her to tinker with the blood pressure machine. "I told you already. My flight went bad, and I had to parachute out. I can't say more than that until the incident investigation is complete. You should know that, Nancy Drew, from your snooping around during my conversation with my boss."

All right then. He wouldn't be talking. She would simply have to use the time to study him and hope to get a read off him from more subtle clues that would be valuable later. If he wasn't involved in anything, maybe he'd seen something on his way down. "Sit, before you hurt yourself worse."

He leaned on the edge of her gurney. "Why don't you like me?"

"Who says I don't like you?" She forced herself not to inch away and most definitely not to look overlong at the cowlick along his forehead. He definitely wouldn't have given her a second glance in high school, back before she'd found her mentor and her mission in training to be a cop. "I don't even know you well enough to form any kind of opinion one way or another."

"Come on. It's obvious you've got something against me."

She sat upright again. "The prospect of spontaneously combusting into flesh-scarring blisters makes me a tad cranky."

"At least it's not boring in here."

"Speak for yourself."

"Fair enough." He punched her pillow back to fluffy status. "Having you here keeps this from being a snooze fest for me. But I'll leave you alone so you can get your beauty sleep. Not that you need it."

"Save your charm for the nursing staff. I'm not tired." She pointed up to the small TV screen mounted on the wall. "Maybe we should just watch television."

"Talking to you is more fun." He hitched up onto her gurney. "So you're actually a camo dude. Or would that be dudette?"

"I thought you were going to let me sleep? I'm a security cop"—who just happened to be tasked with the special duty of protecting the highly sensitive boundaries of Area 51—"and you have absolutely no respect for personal boundaries."

"Sorry. You said you weren't sleepy." He stood again. "Back to my question. You're a security cop who happens to work around—"

"Nowhere." Damn, he was pushy. Was he just curious, or did he have a darker motive?

"I've just never seen a woman in that, uh, job that doesn't exist guarding nowhere."

She pulled her blanket over her legs and flattened her pillow again. Silence swelled, broken only by the *shoosh* of the air purification system. "I guess that makes me all the less conspicuous then, if you're not expecting me. If that were my job, which it isn't." She tucked her damp hair behind her ears. "How about let's discuss your job for a while?"

"Touché." He commandeered the remote control and settled back on his gurney five feet away. He swung his swollen ankle up, propping it on a wadded blanket.

"So, is that a 'no' to discussions about why you were parachuting into the middle of nowhere and what you may have seen on your way down?"

His smile faded. "It was dark, and I was more concerned about not shattering my legs when I landed."

"Sucks to be you." Sucked to be her, too, since she obviously wasn't going to learn squat about what really happened. The military was so uptight about this whole incident they weren't even letting her use a phone until morning.

"I don't know. The day turned out not so bad after all." He fluffed his pillow and leaned back on his side, propped on one elbow. "You're entertaining."

"You sure do know how to charm a woman."

"I never could charm you in the dining hall."

What? "So you do remember."

"You thought I didn't?"

"You didn't say anything."

"Neither did you. But honestly, how could I forget the way you savored the yakasoba special and soft-serve ice cream while looking down your nose at me?"

She really hated it when people commented on her

eating. Not that she intended to clue him in on how to push her buttons. "About your flight—"

"Shhhh . . ." He pressed a finger to his mouth, his lips the perfect balance of fullness without being girly. "Remember the little green men. The walls have ears. If we're not careful, they might beam in and abduct you for their medical experiments."

Her fist twisted in the blanket. Could his mention of alien killings be coincidental? She forced her voice to stay level and opted to shoot straight for the pink elephant in the room. "Don't you think that remark is in bad taste, given the recent Killer Alien scare?"

"You're right," he conceded without a blink. "I must have lost sight of how much fear it's stirred around here, since I was half a world away for all of November and December."

She stored away that nugget of information to confirm later. If he'd truly been out of the United States for that time frame, then he had an unbreakable alibi for two of the murders. It wasn't like he could just jet back to Vegas from across the world in a couple of hours.

The kick of relief she felt over the possibility of his innocence unsettled her. She should be disappointed to learn the lead may have taken her in the wrong direction yet again. She reached to punch the light control down another dimmer notch and lay back on her pillow.

"Jill?" Mason's voice slid across the room like a smooth shot of good liquor over her tongue that made a person close their eyes to savor it all the more. "Thanks for not blowing my head off back there in the desert last night."

"You're welcome, Maso—" She stopped short, her nerves going on high alert. "How did you find out my name?"

He jabbed a thumb toward the end of her gurney. "I peeked at your chart while you were in the bathroom." He sprawled onto his back, adjusted the blanket, and turned on the tiny TV before she could even think of a comeback.

Why would he bother nosing around in her chart? He could have just been obnoxiously curious in the same way he'd played with the otoscope, and honestly there wasn't any harm in him knowing her name. The camo dudes preferred anonymity, but it wasn't required. Nothing would stop her from her mission, a deeper job than cruising the perimeter of Dreamland for overzealous tourists who'd attempted to sneak into restricted territory.

She was out to catch a serial killer, someone they suspected hid in the bowels of the most secret military facility in the world.

FOUR

★

It was his twentieth wedding anniversary, but Lieutenant Colonel Rex Scanlon didn't need to worry about remembering to buy his wife her favorite candy or cologne. He'd already purchased the flowers, and tonight after work, he would deliver them to her grave.

Rex stepped out of the military hospital elevator and followed the numbers and arrows printed on the wall, leading him toward Chuck Tanaka's room. The flowers for Heather should stay fresh in his car. He'd picked up the bouquet of her favorite daisies from the grocery store on his way to the hospital. It was all too easy to remember exactly when she died, since it had happened on their anniversary. How damned ironic the number of times he'd forgotten the date while they were married. Now there wasn't a chance in hell the day would go by unrecognized.

But first, he had another member of his squadron to visit now that he'd finished up with Sergeant Randolph.

A young airman in fatigues pushed a cart full of half-empty food trays past, the rank smell of mass-produced meals clogging the air. God, he hated hospitals and the memories they kicked up. Heather may have gone quickly, but the short time he'd spent outside her room in the ER felt like a lifetime as he'd waited to hear why his wife, forty-one years young, had suffered a heart attack. He'd expected the doctor to come out and explain that they needed to be more careful, eat better, exercise more, reduce stress.

Instead, the ER physician informed him they were very sorry. Heather had died. They'd tried to bring her back but weren't successful. Blah, blah, blah. The rest had blurred in his mind as he struggled to face a future without his wife. A future as a single father of twin boys just finishing up high school.

Rex stopped in front of Tanaka's room number and swiped his arm under his nose in hopes of diluting the antiseptic smell.

A chaplain in fatigues stepped out and pulled up short, holding the door half-open. "Oh, excuse me, Colonel. Captain Tanaka is a popular fella right now."

"He already has another visitor, Chaplain"—he glanced at the name on the uniform to refresh his memory—"Hatch."

Yeah, he would have remembered the guy's name if he didn't spend so much time hiding from him.

The chaplain tucked his day planner under his arm. "He's allowed two visitors at a time. They probably wouldn't even complain if he had more. Everyone likes Captain Tanaka."

Rex's neck itched. He considered leaving and going straight to Heather's grave, but he would only have to come back here again, which would mean wasted time when he had a suspicious in-flight incident to deal with. "Tanaka's a good guy. Have a nice evening, Chaplain."

He cut the conversation short. Chaplain Hatch probably had a busy schedule, too.

All about efficiency, he could hear Heather's laughing voice in his head. He could imagine her lifting his glasses off and leaning to kiss him, hear her whispering, *I like that best how particularly efficient you are in the bedroom* . . .

He cleared his throat and thoughts. Time to focus on Captain Tanaka and the airman's recovery. Rex tapped on the door, the light pressure nudging the already cracked door open wider.

Tanaka had a lady visitor.

Good. The guy deserved some female TLC. The women had always gone for the Hawaiian's charm and what Heather had called Tanaka's exotic appeal.

Tanaka lay in bed, the head of the mattress upright, his leg in a cast from the latest surgery. Nearly every bone in Tanaka's body had been broken while he was held captive in Turkey last spring by a sadistic bitch bent on torturing military secrets out of service members. He faced a long road to recovery, but thank God he was still alive to recover.

Doctors couldn't predict how much mobility he would regain. This could be it for him, but he was alive, and he had all his limbs and his brain, when too many others weren't as lucky. Still, standing here seeing one of his people suffer, feeling like he'd failed this young man, Rex didn't much see the luck.

Tanaka looked up sharply, then smiled. "Hello, sir, come on in. You remember Livia."

Livia? Livia Cicero? No way in hell.

She turned from the edge of the bed to smile.

Oh shit. It most certainly was.

"Well, hello, Colonel."

There was no mistaking her sultry beauty, made all the more striking by her dusky Italian complexion. Her shoulder-length black hair, sleek and straight, brushed her shoulders. But her mouth, that he remembered most. Who could forget her temperamental, diva, pain-in-the-ass mouth?

He stepped deeper into the private room. "I hadn't realized that you two know each other." Tanaka had been a captive when Livia started the tour. "Italy is a long way from Las Vegas."

He'd met the Italian pop star when he'd been transporting USO performers overseas. The diva had been a regular thorn in his side the whole time, although no amount of prima donna behavior warranted being caught in the crossfire of an attack launched on the USO group. All that aside, what the hell was she doing here, dolled up in her low-cut spangly tank top and overlong peasant skirt belted with some kind of absurd wrestling champion–style knockoff?

Her smile flashed as bright as the rhinestones cinching around her waist. "Nowhere is too far away to visit this special hero."

Tanaka elbowed up higher, his sweatsuit rather than pj's attesting to how the hospital had become a home for him. "After Livia recovered from her injuries from the attack on the USO group, she stopped by to see me in one of those 'rock star visits the troops' moments."

Rex felt a stab of guilt at the mention of that explosion in Turkey where people like Livia had been injured. "That's nice of Ms. Cicero to take time out of her busy career."

Her glistening red mouth curved into a practiced smile, lips that had blown a pouty kiss for her first album cover. "I did not get to finish my tour with the USO troupe, so I am here to spread goodwill," she said, her voice throatier than he remembered. She adjusted the flow of her skirt over her legs. "I was actually already coming to this area next week with a British general."

Next week's gathering of foreign ally military leaders? The general should have notified them of his Italian "guest." Bringing someone from a country not on the list raised a red flag in his head. "You're dating a British general?"

She shrugged. "He's a friend of the family. It's nice publicity for both of us to be seen together. And the visit gave me the perfect opportunity to look in on another dear friend while I am at a loose end—"

"Loose ends," Rex corrected automatically, even though she possessed an overall fluency in English. Only through idioms and her sexy accent did her nationality show.

"Yes, yes, loose ends." She nodded, fluttering her perfectly manicured nails through the air.

Tanaka scratched his knee just above his cast. "She's looking into performance options in Las Vegas."

"Shhhh." She tapped her full lips. "My agent says that is a secret."

Laughing, he winked at her. "Sorry about that, but if it's such a secret, why did you tell me?"

Her face went somber. "You're obviously a very good secret keeper."

Tanaka had proven that during his weeks in captivity. The air went darker and thicker than the antiseptic smell coating the air.

Rex moved closer, stopping at the foot of the bed, where crutches rested. "Ms. Cicero, how are you doing since the accident?"

"I am well." She sat straighter, her skirt a bold

psychedelic splash of color against the stark white linens.

"Glad to hear it."

"You sound as if you do not believe me. If you wish, check me over, Colonel." She paused to inch her flower-child skirt up provocatively. "I will be glad to show you any healing injuries."

Yeah, this was the same troublemaking woman he'd met last spring. "I'm sure they're lovely legs, but I'll pass. We wouldn't want to give Tanaka over there a heart attack."

She cocked her head, long chandelier earrings brushing her shoulders. "Thank you for the sweet compliment."

"It wasn't a compliment."

"I know." Her smile broadened.

He'd considered her high-strung, and he still did, but that didn't stem the guilt over her being hurt on his watch. If-onlys were a pain in the ass, but he couldn't stop his thoughts.

If only he'd found Chuck sooner.

If only he'd discovered the mole faster.

If only he'd insisted those damn entertainers abandon the tour the minute he'd smelled trouble.

Except it hadn't been his call to make.

She patted Tanaka's hand on the bed rail, gripping the metal bar as she rose slowly. "I need to go. You enjoy your visit with the colonel."

Livia leaned to kiss the airman's broad forehead, her

tank shirt hitching up and revealing a creamy patch of skin along the small of her back. The tiniest edge of a tattoo peeked out, but not enough for him to determine the design.

Rex blinked twice and averted his eyes, but not soon enough to avoid something stirring inside him, something he'd been too grief-numb to consider in a year—heat. And he resented the hell out of the fact, because it reminded him that even if in some strange universe he could reach out and touch this woman, it wouldn't be as good as what he'd lost.

Livia straightened from the hospital bed, her shirt sliding back into place. Rex stepped away, opening the door to speed her exit.

He stayed silent, holding the door wide, as she gathered the crutches. Hey wait. The crutches were hers?

Rex clamped his slack jaw shut. He'd assumed . . . Ah hell. He was off his game today. It had to be because of Heather, certainly not due to some flirtatious woman who toyed with men for kicks.

He cleared the door as she passed, fanning a wave.

"Good-bye, Colonel."

He watched her thump-thumping down the hospital corridor. She had on two shoes, no cast or braces that he could see. It must be something to do with her left knee, bent and bearing no weight.

He didn't think that her injuries in the explosion could have been worse than what he'd been initially told. Surely if there had been more to her accident, the star-hungry paparazzi would have reported it.

Must have been something that happened afterward—a simple sprain maybe, probably from rehearsals.

He turned back to what had really brought him here—a morale visit to Chuck Tanaka. "So she comes to see you often?"

Damn it. So much for forgetting about Livia and focusing on Tanaka.

"She came to visit me back at the start when I was still pretty messed up, said she felt bad about what had happened to me."

"None of it was her fault."

"I understand she wasn't to blame, but apparently she feels guilty about some outing where she left against security's advice."

She had come close to blowing the whole undercover operation when she left the American air base in Turkey against lockdown orders. "I'm sure she's here out of more than guilt." Rex was done talking about Livia. "So, Captain, what's the next step with your rehab?"

"The docs say I'll be out of here tomorrow."

Tanaka didn't look ready to leave.

"That's great news."

"I'll have outpatient rehab for a while, until, well, until I stop getting better. With some determination, I should be back on a surfboard by summer." His stubborn jaw set, Tanaka stared at the cast on his leg, swallowed hard, then looked back. "Straight up, they don't know if I'll fly again."

Rex gripped the end of the bed and kept the sympathy off his face that Tanaka wouldn't welcome. Pity sucked ass.

From the first look at Tanaka after they'd rescued him from his brutal captor, Rex had suspected Tanaka's flying days were done. No one could take a beating that bad and come out whole again, inside or out. But that didn't mean Tanaka was finished, damn it. "We do a lot of things in our squadron that don't require flying. We have need of your skills and knowledge. There's a place for you as long as I have a say."

"Thank you, sir." Tanaka nodded, but the shadows in his eyes said well enough that nothing could replace the sky.

"No thanks needed. Just doing my job and making damn sure you do yours. The air force has a lot of money invested in you." He clapped Tanaka on the shoulder.

"Roger that, Colonel."

A light tap sounded on the door. Tanaka winced. "That would be my physical therapist. He's running late today because of some emergency. Gotta admit, I almost hoped he wouldn't show. The dude's a real sadist, but he's persistent and seems to know what he's doing."

"I'll let you get to it then." Rex backed toward the door, mission complete here, although his day was far from over. He had a crash investigation gearing up and a testing project on temporary hold, racking up lost dollars by the second.

But first, he had an anniversary date to keep.

* * *

The next morning, Mason slipped on his shades against the piercing Vegas sunlight in the hospital parking lot.

He hadn't slept much during his night in quarantine with Jill Walczak. In fact, he hadn't slept much the night before that with the Area 51 landing mess. At least he'd been released from the hospital with a clean bill of health, as had Jill, who was walking alongside him through the sliding glass doors and into the parking lot.

From behind the protective shield of his sunglasses, he studied the reserved woman beside him. He couldn't figure her out, and he'd made it his mission to be damn good at figuring out females after he'd missed the boat so soundly with his ex-wife. Given Jill's red hair, he expected a fiery temper and close-to-the-skin emotions, but she was too good at hiding herself behind that prim and huffy mask. She definitely wasn't his type, yet something about her pissed him off and turned him on all at the same time.

He paused at the end of the hospital porch overhang, scanning the lot for where his pal David "Ice" Berg would have dropped off his truck for him. He should be sprinting across the lot to his ride, which sure enough, was conveniently parked just to his right, next to a blue minivan. Yep, he could go now. He should go now.

Ah hell.

He wasn't going anywhere yet. "So, Jill Walczak, can-do cop, you don't think much of me, do you?"

"My opinion of you doesn't matter." She turned away and sat on a bench. She still wore hospital scrubs, as did he, rather than waiting around for someone to bring clothes from home, which meant she likely didn't have anyone.

He would leave in a minute. He couldn't get into his truck anyway, since his path to the driver's side was blocked by a mom who'd parked her double stroller behind her minivan while she buckled in her other kids. No sweat. He wasn't due at work for another hour.

As much as he burned to clear his name of any screw-up with that flight, he couldn't walk away just yet, not until he figured out a way to shake free of this damned annoying—tenacious—attraction to a woman who obviously considered him pond scum. "Guess I'll see you around the cafeteria at the soft-serve ice cream machine."

She put her hand above her eyes to shield them from the glare of the desert sun as she looked around. "Somehow I managed to get by without speaking to you before. I'll persevere again."

"You know there are those who say ignoring a guy is the best way to get his attention." And damned if those people weren't right.

She fixed him with an assessing stare. "Then by all means let me shower you with compliments, you handsome piece of man meat."

He liked a woman with grit. "Are you always this crabby?"

"Nope."

He hooked his elbow on the back of the bench so he could face her. Or rather he could if she would turn toward him again. "I take that to mean you do have some kind of grudge against me."

She stared pointedly at his hand only an inch away from her shoulder. "I make it a habit to avoid men with notched bedposts."

"I know for a fact that you have never seen my bedroom." He didn't move closer. He didn't need to. He could see the goose bumps of awareness rising on her arms. She'd thought about his bedroom, and now that had him imagining her there. "Because, believe me, if you'd been there, I would remember."

She rolled her eyes and snorted.

"Damn, lady, that was a good line."

"Whatever."

Maybe if he could tease her into a smile or a good mood, they could move on to some kind of acquaintance/friendship status, because no matter how smoking hot Jill Walczak might be, no way in hell did he go anywhere near complicated women. And without question, Jill was more complicated than solving a Rubik's Cube in the dark.

Time to change tactics by going with no tactics at all, just straightforward honesty. He was a little rusty at that strategy. "Do you need a lift? I have my truck here if you're waiting around for a cab. A couple of buds from my squadron dropped it off for me."

"I've got a ride. He should be here any minute now."

He? "Great."

So much for his theory about no one bringing her clothes.

The foot traffic picked up, repeated swooshes of the automatic doors admitting and expelling a couple of doctors in uniforms, a nurse pushing a patient in a wheelchair. Out in the parking lot, the minivan mom had just finished strapping in most of her brood while the toddler in the front of the stroller squirmed and screamed. No wonder Mom wanted to keep his noise out of the van as long as possible.

He grinned. Give 'em, hell, kiddo.

His smile faded as he stared at the little rug rat. Sometimes he wondered about his decision to stay single after his divorce from Kim, since that meant he would never be a dad.

Sighing, Jill finally turned to Mason. "You don't need to stay with me. I'm okay. If I have any more questions about your parachuting accident, I'll get in touch."

"Sure. Whatever. I'm not waiting around." Just hanging out keeping her company until her ride arrived. What the hell was up with that? He needed to get his head in gear for the crash inquiry he faced in an hour. He'd racked his brains through the night and couldn't come up with anything more than he'd told the boss initially. Hopefully by the time he checked in today, they would have figured everything out and be back on track for next week's big show.

Time to punch out. He scratched his hand along his jaw, still bristly from the crappy disposable razor they'd given him to use. "Before I go, I want to say thank you."

"Thank you?" Her green eyes blinked wide.

Green. Holy crap, they were green. He'd wondered back in the hazmat truck, and now he knew. They were light green, like an apple, and damn, wouldn't that come across as the most unsexy comment ever? Your body is like Venus, your hair so whispery red my hands itch to feel if it's as soft as it looks. And your eyes remind me of apples.

Of course she had no idea how very much he liked apples. "Thanks for arresting me, except for the cuffing part, which I could live without, since I'm not into kinky, oh, and I'd have rather bypassed the knee in my kidney. I thought for sure I would pee blood this morning, but I'm digressing here."

"And you have a point to telling me this?"

He hitched his sore ankle onto his knee to ease the throbbing and shrugged a kink from his neck, maybe a result of his tussle with a pallet in midair or possibly from the stress of nearly getting gassed to death. "I'm grateful you were out there in that corner of the desert with your radio handy to call for speedy help. If I'd hung out in that crap from the explosion for much longer, I wouldn't have been walking out of the hospital with a clean bill of health today."

And he wouldn't have been able to return to work

and find out what the hell went wrong with that flight. Only by solving that mystery could he save the same from happening to some other tester down the road. And the next guy might not be so lucky.

Damn. Flirting with this woman suddenly seemed like the lamest thing of all to do. He could show up to work early and get a head start on the meeting.

Mason stood. "That's all I wanted to say. If you're sure your ride's on the way, I guess I'll make your day and push off."

Jill actually laughed. "Thanks, and yes, I'm sure he's on his way." She glanced up at him. "Good luck, Sergeant."

"Good-bye." What was it about this woman that tugged at him? She wasn't his type at all, so serious, not to mention able to see through his bullshit.

Mason fished his keys from his pocket—thank you again, Berg, for having the foresight to leave the extra set at the front desk, since everything on him had gone into a decontamination bin. He stepped down off the curb.

Ouch! Shit. His ankle still hurt like a son—of a gun.

He shook off the pain and started forward, more carefully this time, toward his Chevy truck parked just to his right. The mom still hadn't cleared her stroller away, since now she was trying to settle the crying baby while the toddler pitched all of his many bribes out onto the asphalt.

Another engine revved off to the side, one with

some serious muffler issues. He checked left. A beat-up, rusty sedan roared in front of the hospital, gaining speed, bumping two wheels onto the sidewalk, heading toward him. Toward Jill. Toward the screaming toddler just to his right restrained in the double stroller.

And he had only a few seconds to figure out how to save them all.

FIVE

"Jill! Get behind the bench!"

What the hell? Jill barely registered his words, but the unmistakable authority in his tone sent her feet moving on instinct until she found herself in a crouch behind the concrete bench. From her peripheral vision, she caught sight of an elderly couple huddled a few steps to her side behind another bench.

Mason was sprinting full-out along the sidewalk toward a minivan. Only seconds ago, he'd been limping. Now he ran with undeniable athleticism. Adrenaline had a way of numbing anything. His muscles bunched and strained against the green scrubs.

A roaring sounded behind her, the growling car coming closer. She leapt toward the elderly couple behind the other bench just as a rusty sedan scraped along the concrete seat. Sparks flew from the screeching metal.

The bench held.

Rock bits spewed in the air, bit at her skin, even as exhaust fumes choked her. The vehicle regained traction and peeled rubber along the patch of sidewalk, just where she'd been standing.

It careened back into the lot and plowed forward. Through the rear window she had an unobstructed view of the car speeding toward Mason. Oh God.

But wait. An unobstructed view? Where was the driver?

She tore herself from behind the bench and raced after the car—not that she had any chance of catching up with it.

Just ahead of the car, Mason scooped up a huge stroller in a bear hug. He leapt into the air, twisted at the last second, and landed on his back. Bits of loose asphalt sprayed from the ground as he skidded.

The car whooshed past him and into a telephone pole. A woman screamed. Her hands flailing, she rushed toward Mason and the stroller.

The toddler, who was strapped in, giggled.

Jill kept running full-out, only a few steps, only a few seconds. Everything had happened so quickly. "Are you okay?"

"I'm fine." He eased the stroller to the side and upright in a smooth move that left her blinking. The mother pushed past and unbuckled her child.

"Omigod, omigod, omigod!" She scooped her son

into her arms, tears streaking down her face as she kissed his curly little head and babbled, "Thank you, sir, thank you for saving him."

As the adrenaline let down, Jill realized how he'd summed up the situation with lightning-fast reflexes, keeping her safe while trusting her to act rather than simply tackling her, somehow determining who was in imminent danger.

It would have been easy to believe the car was heading for the elderly couple instead. Mason had chosen correctly. She understood well from work how tough it could be to make the right choice sometimes. She also knew how hard it was for some men to believe in a woman's training, even when the guys were pros, too. But he had trusted her.

Her attitude toward Mason shifted ever so slightly.

There were people behind them—she heard curses, footsteps running away, a woman speaking with 911. Jill extended her hand to Mason.

A blast echoed. She jerked back. Mason sprang to his feet.

Flames erupted from the crashed car about ten yards away.

The ground rumbled, and a hubcap clanked to rest beside her. Jill flinched, and the toddler burst into tears, his siblings peering out of the minivan with wide eyes. Good God, she and Mason had experienced two explosions together in less than forty-eight hours. Had the world gone nuts?

Mason darted forward again, the bright morning sun

dancing off the flames. Damn it, she wasn't standing around and watching this time.

"Wait, Mason," she shouted, running after him. "What if there's a secondary explosion? Stop!"

He closed in on the burning vehicle. "I've got to check on the person driving."

"There wasn't anyone behind the wheel!"

"Maybe the driver passed out." He shielded his eyes from the heat with his arm and peered through the passenger window. "There could also be somebody else in the car, maybe in the back."

She inched forward carefully. "I'll check the back. You get the front."

Jill moved in closer. Heat from the flames scorched her skin. She peered through the jagged broken glass into the backseat. "Empty."

Mason backpedaled from the front. "No one here either. Let's clear the hell out."

He hooked a hand around her elbow and yanked her alongside as he hoofed it to the clustering crowd. His vise grip nearly lifted her from the pavement as he propelled her until they stopped by a lamppost.

Jill sagged against the cool metal, gasping for air. "How could no one be in the car?"

Mason scratched the back of his close-shorn head, favoring one foot by bending his knee. "The little green men sure are busy lately."

"Not funny. Terrorism?"

"Honest to Pete, I'd rather it be the little green men." He nodded toward the approaching security police.

"Either way, you and I aren't going to be saying good-bye anytime soon after all."

* * *

Watching Jill wrap up her statement to the security cop, Mason didn't know what the hell was going on, but he didn't like it.

Somebody had drawn a bull's-eye on his back, and Jill Walczak had almost been caught in the crossfire.

He didn't believe in coincidence or even a funky notion of fate. Facts told him he'd nearly been killed three times in two days. Somebody was gunning for him, and he had no idea who or why. Yet.

The security cop tucked away his PDA, crisp camos, and blue beret attesting to his attention to detail. "That'll be all for now, ma'am, but we may be calling you again for more information. You caught a lot of important nuances that could be helpful in figuring this out."

Jill nodded, her ponytail swishing. "That's my job, too."

The cop nodded. "I'll be in touch if I have any questions."

Yes, they definitely would be speaking again sometime soon. But first Mason needed to check in at work. Factoring in his top secret mission into any suspicions could be tricky.

She turned to Mason, a frown wrinkling her brow. "I guess this is it then."

Maybe. Maybe not. That depended on how his instincts about this latest incident played out once he'd checked in with his boss. "Thanks again for saving my ass out in the desert."

She opened her mouth, but whatever she was going to say was drowned out by the growl of a poorly tuned engine. His instincts already on alert, Mason tensed.

Jill smiled. "My ride."

He turned quickly to look. What kind of man would she be drawn to? A vintage Mustang convertible rumbled toward them, but not the beloved kind of vehicle kept in pristine condition and housed in a garage. This old Ford, top up, sported a dirty, torn roof and blue paint sun faded out to dull silver. If he wasn't mistaken, the hood was spotted with an abundance of bird poop.

The brakes squealed as the Mustang slid to a stop. The driver's side door creaked open, and cowboy boots hit the ground. With a duster and a panama hat, the guy wouldn't be missed in a crowd.

His face wore the desert-weathered look of man around sixty. Probably not a boyfriend. This must be her father.

Not that it mattered who he was.

The driver cruised to a bowlegged stop beside Jill. "What the hell trouble have you gotten yourself into this time, girl?"

She stepped in for a quick hug. "Thanks for the sympathy."

"You don't like sympathy." He kept an arm around her neck and rubbed his knuckles against her scalp. "Glad the aliens didn't scoop you up."

"Me, too." She leaned into the hug for a second before stepping back. "Phil, this is Sergeant Mason Randolph. Mason, meet Phil."

Mason thrust out his hand. "Nice to meet you."

The old character thrust out his hand to shake. "Yost. Phillip Yost. But you can just call me Phil."

He shook hands with . . . Yost? "Yost?"

But Jill's last name was Walczak. Shit. Was she already married to someone else? He hadn't even considered that possibility. Dumb ass. His skin felt too tight for his body. He absolutely never messed with another man's wife, an unbreakable rule.

"I'm her uncle, in case you were wondering."

"An honorary uncle, actually," Jill hooked arms with Phil Yost, "but I don't think about it, except for those times other people notice."

Yost's smile glistened as brightly as the shark tooth dangling from the black cord around his neck. "No need to get fired up, Gingersnap."

Mason couldn't resist. "Gingersnap?"

She scowled. "Say it once more, and you'll be eating sand again, Sergeant."

"Yes, ma'am." He gave her a half salute. She got hotter by the second.

"Good-bye, Sergeant." Presenting him firmly with her back, she walked toward the rusting Mustang.

Damn, she had sass to her ass that matched her ornery personality. She'd almost been "slimed" into a genetic mutant and run over by an alien-possessed car in the span of about thirty-six hours, and she didn't even seem fazed. His ex—most of the women he'd dated—would have been totally freaked. Hell, most of the guys he knew, too. He had to admire that.

Mason looked at the sedan, smoke still rising after the fire department had doused the flames. The heat simmered low now, like the insidious sting in his leg where the rope burn still ached a reminder of how life could catch you unaware in a flash.

* * *

Rex Scanlon gunned it down the squadron main hall.

He'd made it past the one-year anniversary of his wife's death and even made it into the squadron early the next day. Time to turn the page and move on. Too bad somebody had forgotten to inform the yearlong knot in his chest to go away once he'd placed the flowers on Heather's grave last night.

He would work past it just as he'd done every day since his wife's death. Rex ushered the two Predator crew members into the small briefing room where three of his crewdogs waited. While both the chemical test and the hypersonic jet mission were tasked by his squadron, they shouldn't have come anywhere near each other that night. But thank God his spy drone crew had been slated to gather data. Now they were able to provide extra visuals on Mason Randolph's landing.

Most of the time, juggling so many diverse test projects could be a headache. This time, it had worked to their advantage.

In the briefing room, pilots Vince "Vapor" Deluca and Jimmy "Hotwire" Gage were giving Mason hell over the rolling car incident.

Vince leaned his elbows on the long table and gestured with a doughnut. "So, my brother, you get tired of testing airplanes and switch to remote control cars?"

Mason rocked back in his rolling chair. "Seems damn dumb to run myself over."

Jimmy cracked his knuckles. "Ah, but you got to save the girl while going all macho for her."

Mason held up his hands, scraped and raw. "I can think of much better ways to catch this woman's eye that wouldn't involve blistering my skin while checking out a burning car. Besides, she's a cop, one of those sneaky camo dudes. She can pretty much save her own ass."

"Good point," Jimmy said. "Women appreciate it when you recognize they're strong, too."

"Camo dude?" Vince paused chewing his glazed jelly doughnut.

Rex cleared his throat. Mason's chair creaked upright as the three men stood.

"At ease." Rex gestured for Werewolf and Gucci, two other aviators from his top secret squadron, to follow him inside. The small conference room was filled with a long table, cushioned chairs for comfort during long-ass meetings, and a TV/DVD combo mounted into the ceiling for videos and telecoms. "We're including the pilot and sensor operator from the Predator flying during the incident. I thought they could shed some light on the whole accident, since they watched from a bird's-eye view."

He didn't even want to consider what kind of hell this squadron would have been going through if Mason had died in that in-flight accident or on the ground from overexposure to a blister agent burning up the inside of his lungs. This squadron had experienced some close calls over the past year and a half he'd been in charge, but he'd never lost a plane or a man. Even thinking about the possibility made him itchy. Stats told him he'd covered all his bases, then covered them again until he couldn't remember what sleep was beyond a catnap.

He couldn't think of anything else to double-check. But he'd learned long ago there was more art than science to this job.

Werewolf clapped Mason on the back. "Glad to see the Ghostbuster mobile didn't take you out this morning."

Gucci took her seat. "Any word on that incident, Colonel?"

Rex stepped behind the podium while everyone else settled in a place at the long table. "There are no terrorist groups claiming responsibility as of yet, and the security cops said there wasn't a bomb present. The engine itself exploded. The vehicle was simply one of the remote models we use in range testing."

Werewolf pressed, "Those aren't supposed to drive willy-nilly around populated areas. What was it doing in a congested hospital parking lot?"

"The SPs are questioning a sergeant from transportation about that as we speak. He has all the paperwork in order for parking it there last night, complete with the proper authorizing signatures." Rex scratched behind his neck, right over the kink twisting tighter by the second. "Apparently it started driving when there was some kind of brief power outage."

Mason straightened in his chair. "Except?"

Rex gave up on the knotted muscle. Again. "The major who supposedly signed the order couldn't possibly have done so, given he was playing putt-putt with his kids."

Werewolf held up his hands. "Okay, hold it right there. Who the fuck gets time off to play putt-putt with their kids these days? That's reason enough to make me suspicious of the guy."

Vince thumped him on the back. "Jealousy is an ugly emotion, my brother."

"But we're talking putt-putt here," Werewolf said, as if describing a week on a Caribbean beach.

What a sorry state when they started jonesing over the possibility of a free day to play miniature golf. They loved the job, believed in the mission, but there just weren't enough people to complete all the test projects in a regular forty-hour workweek. If they didn't do it, it didn't happen, which meant more people could die overseas because they didn't have the best equipment. Deployments would last longer with less efficient options. More civilian casualties could rack up when even one was already unacceptable.

And he wasn't talking about just the best planes or tanks or intel, but biochem gear, flak jackets, weapons. This list was long and far from complete.

So yeah, dreaming about sunscreening up with a hot date on the beach would have to be put on hold for now. They couldn't dream bigger than an evening away at a two-bit park, and he couldn't afford to feel guilty about overworking his people.

"Gentlemen and ma'am." Rex gripped the edge of the podium. "I'll do my best to schedule our next squadron brief at a putt-putt palace or perhaps even a water park. Now, can we get back to the business at hand? We don't have answers on the crashed car today, and I'm afraid we're not going to get top priority from the security police on that. They're maxed out working with local authorities on the whole Killer Alien scare."

The room went silent. No smart-ass comments ricocheted around now. Three killings linked to the base was nothing to laugh about. "If we're done with jokes, we need to debrief the in-flight incident and see what we can put together from what others observed."

Vince scrubbed a hand along his shaved head. "Boss, there really isn't much to say. I reviewed the telemetry data, and we were within fifty feet of the planned altitude and only a tenth of a Mach under speed."

Jimmy leaned forward, fists clenched. "The winds were well within limits, too. If the PhDs remembered to carry all their naughts and whatnot, then this should have gone like clockwork. Right, Vince?"

"Roger that. We finished up our quick-look report, and it has all the numbers in there. The problem has to be either bad math from the eggheads or some kind of equipment failure. The contractors are going over the aircraft inch by inch to try to find a point of failure. It's a hurry-up-and-wait game." Vince spread his hands and sighed. "Basically, sir, all we've got for you is a heaping helping of jack shit."

Rex pinched the bridge of his nose under his glasses, then tucked them in place again. "Sergeant, do you have anything to add?"

Mason stood again. "Now that I've had time to deslime my brain, some things have come to mind worth noting. The camo dude—Jill Walczak—wasn't cruising the perimeter. She was miles deep into Area 51."

Rex glanced down at the chart for referencing. "Not unheard of or out of her jurisdiction, but certainly unusual." Still . . . "It wouldn't hurt to look into what she was doing there."

"That's what I was thinking, sir."

"Especially in light of next week's gathering. Anything else?"

"Well, sir, actually, there is." Mason hesitated briefly before continuing, "I don't want to sound paranoid, but it sure seems like I have a bull's-eye on my back with the in-flight incident, the blister agent scare, and a car gunning for me, all in two days. My gut tells me something's wrong."

Rex searched the sergeant's face for signs of stress and just found hard frustration. "I can see why you would feel that way. There's a lot of luck and gut that goes into this job. It bears listening to when the mojo's not with you."

"My thoughts exactly."

"I can always get another loadmaster for the final two flights before the big show."

Mason's shoulders went back defensively. "No, sir. I'm fine. I simply thought the coincidence worth mentioning."

"Absolutely. It's always better to talk through all scenarios. With that in mind, let's see what our Pred buddies can bring to light."

The Predator pilot popped a DVD into the player. "This is all the footage we caught. We can't look up, of course, so we didn't see our man Smooth until he drifted into view."

Rex had already reviewed the footage in his office, but even so, seeing Mason lose it when he'd thought his crew died hit him in the gut all over again. Even stalwart Jimmy Gage cleared his throat.

Vince leaned over and gave Mason an exaggerated goofy-ass hug. "Love you, too, my brother."

Low laughter eased the tension. Rex fast-forwarded to footage of Mason and the lady cop getting hosed down by the hazmat team, which, as expected, stirred the laughter louder.

Werewolf clutched his gut, chuckling. "Nice boxers, dude."

Jimmy leaned toward Mason. "When does she get to meet your parents?"

Mason stayed quiet for once.

Vince popped the last of his doughnut into his mouth. "Sheesh, somebody is touchy."

Rex let their ribbing play out for a few minutes, a part of the whole squadron unity he used to be a part of before rank and position separated him. "Nice to know you take your work so seriously, gentlemen—and ma'am."

Gucci held up her hands in self-defense. "Don't lump me with these bozos, sir."

"Understood." Rex shut down the video feed and wrapped up the meeting. As the aviators filed out, he gestured for Mason to stay behind. "How are you doing physically?

"Not too bad sir." Mason subtly shifted his weight to one foot. "Sore, but otherwise okay."

"How's your cranium? You want to talk to someone?" This kind of near death experience could mess with a flier's head long-term if they didn't sort it out up front. The air force had first-rate shrinks on staff with specialized training. "I'll set that up. I think in your position, I might want to hash through a few things with a neutral third party. Get away from all this macho bullshit and spill it."

Mason's jaw jutted. "Is this because of what I said about the bull's-eye?"

"I would say the same to anyone." True enough.

"I think it's all good with me. I may be checking my six o'clock a bit more often, but I'm not ready for a straitjacket yet."

"All right, but I will ask again." No doubt Mason was worried about admitting any perceived weakness impacting his career. It would take a while for all the new views on the acceptability of getting help to soak through the ranks. "You can be sure there is no foul from my view if you take me up on that offer."

"Thanks sir, I appreciate the concern, but that kind of help is for people who've been through something like Chuck." Mason shifted the weight off his injured ankle. "I tried to stop by and see him before I left the hospital, but I heard he checked out. How did he seem when you saw him?"

"He seemed good. He said something about his physical therapist being a real sadist, but apparently the guy worked a miracle, since Chuck is out of the hospital."

"That's great. Really great. Hopefully you won't have any of us to visit at the hospital again."

God, he hoped that was true. "And this camo dude cop you spent the past couple of days with in there, what's your take on her?"

"Tough, professional . . . prickly."

"Guards from her unit are supposed to patrol the border of Area 51 and stop overeager tourists from trying to sneak in. You were well past the border."

"She *said* she saw me parachute in and came to help."

Mason's recounting sounded logical. Still, something seemed off. "It was mighty damn dark, which makes me think she must have been close to see you. What do you think could have been her real motive?"

"My guess? She's pulling extra duty like most cops around the base, tightening up security before next week's big show. Then there's the serial killer scare."

Or she could have been snooping. "It's tough to tell sometimes if we're following an instinct or paranoia. It's best to err on the side of our intuition." Something he'd learned the hard way when he hadn't listened to his gut a year ago when they'd shouted at him to spend time with his wife. "You're the logical choice to check out a bit more information on Jill Walczak."

SIX

★ _____

Lee Drummond charged down the main hallway in Mason Randolph's test squadron, rounded a corner, and slammed smack into someone stupid enough to try to juggle coffee and a BlackBerry. Scalding-hot java splashed from Gucci's paper cup onto Lee's blouse.

Gucci jumped back to avoid getting burned. Lee wasn't so lucky. Pain fired deep.

"Oh God, Dr. Drummond, I am really sorry." Gucci tucked aside her BlackBerry and pulled three neatly folded tissues from the sleeve pocket on her flight suit. "I would dab it for you, but that would be, uh, rather awkward." Gucci waved toward Lee's shirt.

Damn it. Lee plucked at the fabric, rage steaming hotter than the drink. This was her favorite silk blouse, and now it was likely ruined. Just because she was a PhD engineer didn't mean she had to dress like a nerd. She spent a lot of time and money on her clothes.

Of course, she'd learned to expect the misconceptions. When most people read her byline on scholarly pieces—Dr. Lee Drummond—they assumed she was a man. It wouldn't have occurred to anyone that the young genius PhD who'd written groundbreaking papers pioneering new ideas in explosives could actually be a female—Ashlee, actually.

Lee took the tissues and blotted the pink silk. "I can take care of it myself. Thank you."

"I'll have it dry-cleaned for you." Gucci threw away her cup in an industrial bin. "That looks like an Ann Taylor."

"It is." Lee sniffed back some of her anger. At least somebody had noticed her clothes. Anger cooling faster than her stinging skin, Lee reminded herself why she was here in the first place—because of Gucci.

The rumor mill had it that Werewolf and Gucci had been called into a closed-door briefing. No such invitation came Lee's way when they should all be desperate for her opinions about the incident two days ago. Her ire heated up a notch again.

She might not be an active duty aviator in this squadron, but by God, she was a civilian contractor for them, with the highest level of security clearance. They *needed* her. "How did the meeting with Colonel Scanlon go?"

Gucci blinked fast, tucking to the side to let other foot traffic in the hall pass by. She ducked her head and lowered her voice. "You know about the meeting?"

"I was consulted beforehand. It's my equipment, after all, but I had a prior appointment and couldn't make it over until now."

"Oh, right, of course you're in the loop. We weren't able to add anything new, though. The whole in-flight incident really has them stumped."

Good. Lee suppressed a smile. "That's too bad."

Mason didn't have a clue, and he wouldn't, right up to the time she ruined his career in the middle of next week's high-profile gathering. She hadn't gotten this much satisfaction since she was nine years old in high school and realized she could pay back the girl who'd beaten her in the race for class president.

Lee wadded the tissues in her hand. "Is there any fallout from local authorities?"

"There doesn't appear to be a problem, although I think the colonel's a little concerned about why that camo dude was so deep in the testing range."

A simple phone call with an anonymous—and false—tip about the serial killer had sent Jill Walczak running. "Security's not something to mess with around here, that's for sure."

"Amen, sister." Gucci pulled out her BlackBerry and glanced down, reading. "Hmmm . . . Gotta run. Hey, if the coffee stain doesn't come out, let me know, and I'll get you a new shirt. Ann Taylor's even having a sale right now, so I could buy you two for the price of one." Gucci smiled apologetically. Genuinely.

"Not necessary. It was an accident."

And lucky for Gucci, she'd taken the time to be sincerely nice. Not that an apology would have saved the high school class president from her injuries. Lee had been too young back then to understand the difference between good people and bad people when she'd rigged a science experiment to bubble acid out of a test tube, scarring the pretty new class president's arm.

Things were different now. She was wiser, more mature. She had a code. She lived by logic these days. Only those in the wrong deserved punishment. If ever someone deserved to pay, it was Mason Randolph.

And Jill Walczak? The lady cop had proved useful once. Perhaps she could be useful again for dealing with another increasingly infuriating problem.

* * *

Sitting at her corner desk in the trailer offices, Jill opened a fifth computer file to go along with the four other records on victims of the serial killer—one woman attacked, three people murdered in the past year—outside of Las Vegas. All mutilated. Sometimes she wondered why she'd decided to go into law enforcement. She'd expected less gore and more intrigue in switching from the police department to contracting with the company that hired camo dudes.

So much for expectations. She shoved aside the half-eaten bag of baked barbecue chips.

This latest murder had only been discovered an hour ago. The press hadn't even caught wind of it. Yet. So

far the media coverage had been mostly local. This
latest killing would send the whole thing national, in-
viting copycats from all over everywhere.

She scrubbed a hand over her gritty eyes, not that
she expected to wipe away the image or feel any better
rested. Body number four had been discovered while
she was in the hospital. The murdered female had been
dead for less than two hours when discovered just before sunup, when she and Mason Randolph had been
pretending not to know the other was still awake in
quarantine.

Now she wouldn't even need to check his flight log.
He couldn't be the perp, since she could attest person-
ally to his location during this new, fourth killing. She
tamped down twinges of relief over his innocence. She
needed to get her priorities in order. A woman was
dead, a military wife and mother of a young child.

Her boss had alerted her to the file on victim number
five the minute she'd walked through the door. Now
Thomas Gallardo paced around the double-wide trailer
that housed their main office deep in the desert. They
had smaller, single-wide outposts for housing surveil-
lance equipment and space for an occasional coffee
break, since they were so far removed from any fast-
food row. She ate most meals in the truck, however. As
the only female in a so far predominantly male profession, she didn't want to be seen as slacking off.

Thomas paused by the table with a coffeepot and
two microwaves. He'd trimmed his hair into a super-
short buzz cut as his hairline started its journey back-

ward. The overall effect was of a man confident in him-self, no hiding behind a comb-over. "The freak is really ramping up on the violence."

Jill clicked through the file to the first photo, even though she'd already studied it so hard she'd burned the image into her brain. A dark-haired woman in her late twenties lay in her backyard, eyes wide in a death stare. Her sleek pink workout suit was slashed, her wounds administered post mortem just like the others. "She also had the same nail-sized fatal wound penetrat-ing her temple."

That detail had not been released to the public.

"That's the only consolation I can find in a case like this. At least the victims die fast before he mutilates them."

Her finger circled the photo on the screen, along a pattern in the desert backyard where landscaping rocks had been swept away to create the signature swirls around her corpse. Only by the third killing had they made the connection with those rings. They'd gone back and reviewed photos from the earlier crime scenes, and sure enough, the round pattern had been left every time, growing larger. "How many tips have we received on her murder?"

"We stopped counting an hour ago. I moved Rhonda to one of the outlying trailers and transferred all calls to that number. The nonstop ringing was driving me batty. I hear that downtown they're getting ten times as many."

Just what this area needed. A killer on the loose who seemed determined to stir up every alien conspiracy

loon, which left authorities wading through an astro-
nomical amount of crap looking for a lead. "There's no
way we have enough manpower to investigate all of
them in any timely fashion."

"We'll pass everything along to the local sheriff's
department like I did with the other three killings, and
keep an eye out for what we can."

She minimized the file, her screen saver rippling
with the ocean waves of an island paradise she'd never
seen in person. "I want to see copies of the notes on all
the calls."

"Sure. It'll be your lost sleep, not mine. Actually,
you'll have the afternoon free, since I don't have a vehicle for you yet. The truck you were driving when you
stumbled on that flier has been repoed by the air force.
They said once they're sure it's been decontaminated,
we can have it back."

"I'm sorry for the inconvenience. I know we're already short of vehicles this month." They seemed to be
suffering from an outbreak of mechanical issues, so
much so that their in-house mechanic was being
quizzed.

"We're pulling some of the older Jeeps out of retirement. We should be fine as long as there aren't any
high-speed chases." He held up a set of keys. "Have a
nice evening shift."

"I'll try." She clicked off her computer and snagged
the keys from his fingers. The newer trucks definitely
had better pickup than the older Jeeps with a couple
hundred thousand miles on them.

"This Mason Randolph guy, do you think he could be our killer?"

"He says he wasn't even in the country when victims number three and four died, and of course he was with me in quarantine during the fifth crime."

"Okay, sounds like he's in the clear. All the same, go ahead and document his alibi in case this fifth case turns out to be a copycat." Thomas hesitated in the doorway. "I just hate to think about you taking down this sick bastard all by yourself."

She tamped down resentment over the implication that she was more vulnerable as a woman. Mason hadn't doubted her strength for a second—a surprise strength she'd found when she'd started jogging alongside Uncle Phil her senior year in high school. "I'll be careful."

"I'm just glad you're all right."

"Thanks, boss. Me, too."

There had been a time she called him by his first name, back when they'd both worked for the local sheriff's department. She'd even considered dating him. Ten years wasn't that much of an age difference, after all. But then he'd transferred to this job and been promoted outside her realm.

He stayed planted in her path, crowding her space. "Next time, call it in before charging off on your own. And before you get your hackles up, this has nothing to do with your being a female." He leaned closer. "I don't like the idea of any of my people out there without backup."

She struggled not to back away defensively. That

would only draw attention to an awkwardness she hoped was only her imagination. "Will do, boss."

The sound of tires crunching gravel in the parking lot snapped his attention. Thomas looked over his shoulder, giving her the chance to step past.

He backed up just as the front door opened in the reception area, security buzzer sounding to announce the new arrival. Mason Randolph walked into the lobby, skimmed his fingers over the empty secretary's desk, and stopped to wait by a framed grid map.

Her stomach knotted. What the hell was he doing here?

"Mason?" she called from behind him. "Is there news on the crash at the hospital?"

"Hello, Jill." He swept off his blue air force hat. "I'm afraid not." He turned to Thomas. "I'm Sergeant Mason Randolph, the guy responsible for keeping her in quarantine last night."

"Thomas Gallardo," he thrust out his hand. "Jill Walczak's boss."

Thomas and Mason shook hands, Thomas assessing and Mason seeming as laid back as ever. Did the guy get worked up over anything? If he started playing with the equipment here—a vest, ammo belt, and radio hanging on the wall—Thomas would blow a gasket.

A memory flashed of Mason's raw pain and his hoarse shout when he'd thought his crew died in the desert.

Thomas rocked back on his heels. "What was it you were doing out there in the first place?"

"Like I told your camo cop here, I was flying a regular old cargo drop, and things went to hell. I got caught in some crosswinds and landed where I shouldn't have."

"That's what she said."

Did Thomas question if she'd told him everything? Did he suspect her?

"Your people sure are Johnny-on-the-spot. Walczak here showed up as I was still kicking free of my parachute."

"Lucky for you, given what happened with that explosion. Blister agent, right? Sure wish we could get more details from your base."

"Sorry to have tied her up with a hospital stay." Mason neatly dodged answering the question.

"I'm just glad we have her back safe and sound."

Thomas's cell phone rang. He glanced down at the number and winced. "I need to take this. Nice to meet you, Randolph."

Once Thomas retreated into his office full of coyote skulls and cacti, Mason turned toward Jill. "It's almost suppertime. How about we get something to eat?"

A dinner date? "You're kidding, right?"

"I'm hungry. It's the end of the workday, so you must be hungry, too. We both almost got hit by a truck this morning. Seems to me like you would want to know how that happened as much as I do."

He had insider info? That was a mighty big bone to waggle in front of her, and she could see from his eyes that he knew how much he tempted her, damn it.

Still, she could hold her cool. "You're not asking me out on a date?"

He shifted closer, his green eyes narrowing. "Do you want me to?"

She sagged back against the secretary's desk. "Now I know you're kidding."

He scooped up a photo cube from the desk and flipped it in his hand. "I've had a shit week, and I really need to turn it around."

"I'm working tonight." She held up the keys.

"Tomorrow then?"

She wondered what he really wanted. Without question, he had some hidden agenda. Talking to him would make sense, but on her terms. "If you don't mind being a third wheel, you can join me and Phil for dinner out tomorrow night."

"A threesome, huh?" He grinned wickedly, setting the cube back on the desk, his arm an inch away from her hip.

"I was just getting to the point where I could tolerate you." She flicked a hard glance at his arm then looked back in his eyes again. "Don't blow it."

He smoothed his handsome face into somber contrition, a look totally negated by that stubborn cowlick ramping his military short hair up in the front. "Thank you kindly for the invitation to join the two of you."

Maybe Phil could tap into his old camo cop skills and help her get a read off Mason—while helping her keep her distance. "Yes, I'm supposed to meet him af-

ter he finishes up his shift." She jotted down Uncle
Phil's new work address. "Meet us here."

"Will do."

She searched his face for what he really wanted and
found . . . nothing. The man shielded his emotions well.

What else did he have hidden inside his mind that he
worked so hard to let no one see? He might have side-
stepped all suspicion as the serial killer, but Mason had
secrets she hadn't even begun to tap. And if she wanted
any chance at figuring out what was going on at night
in Area 51 while the rest of the world slept, she could
do worse than aligning herself with an air force sergeant who didn't miss a trick.

SEVEN

"Trick or treat," Mason shouted along with his crewdog pals as they stood on the doorstep of Chuck Tanaka's apartment. This homecoming had been a long time coming and deserved celebrating.

Chuck leaned on one crutch, standing in the entranceway to his new first-floor place, labeled moving boxes lined neatly along the wall. "Trick or treat? It's January, you morons."

Mason hitched the two bags of groceries more securely in his arms as he angled sideways past Chuck, careful not to bump the cast on his pal's leg. "January, huh? Guess we'll have to unload all this junk here then."

Gucci and Werewolf trailed behind holding sacks of cupboard staples and premade meals. Vapor and Jimmy brought up the rear with their girlfriends in tow, everyone draping their jackets one at a time along the arm of the brown leather sofa. Mason had planned to bring Jill along, an idea that hadn't panned out, but at least she'd agreed to dinner tomorrow. He would have liked to see how she interacted with his crew. That could have given him some additional insights for the colonel—

Ah, damn.

Who was he kidding? The woman intrigued him, and he wanted to see her again. He never had been particularly smart when it came to females. Something he would be wise to remember the next time he was on the receiving end of one of Jill's carefully rationed smiles.

Chuck backed out of the way, his crutch and one good foot in a gym shoe thud-thumping an uneven gait. "Leave it to Vapor to make sure no one goes hungry."

Vapor unloaded his bag on the counter—mustard, hot sauce, buffalo wings, pretzels, and doughnuts. "Don't thank me." He clapped Mason on the shoulder. "This was our buddy Smooth's idea. His contributions are those frozen things he stored in Tupperware."

Chuck's eyes narrowed, lifting a container labeled baked ziti. "Are you trying to poison me?"

Mason opened the freezer and wrenched away the best freaking pasta this guy had never tried. "I like to cook. So sue me."

He hadn't regretted turning his back on his parents' millions, but he sure as hell missed the family chef. With limited funds, Mason had figured out how to make his own favorites from scratch. He'd even hand-made the pasta while trying like hell to purge a certain Gingersnap from his mind.

A noise sounded from deeper in the apartment.

"Oops." Vapor held up his hands, a pilfered dough-nut in one large fist. "Uh, you've already got company. We'll scram."

Chuck leaned against the kitchen bar stacked with paper plates and bottles of Gatorade. "No need. That's my physical therapist, checking the workout gear in the spare room."

Footsteps sounded from the hall a second before a lanky guy in a navy blue windsuit came into sight. Chuck waved him over. "This is my PT guy, Garrett Ferguson, does contract work for the base hospital. He's been checking out all the new toys in this spe-cially equipped apartment to make sure they work right." He gestured behind him further. "And you al-ready know Annette."

A slim woman in a baggy dress entered the living area, long dark hair shielding her face. She swept back her brown mane, and Mason recognized her.

Mason tried to place a name with the face . . . and then it came to him. "Annette Santos, right? You used to work contract with us."

"Now I have a real life working normal hours, thank you very much. I was even able to get the afternoon off to help Chuck come home." A denim hobo bag swung from her arm, the contents spilling over the top. Heavy dark eyebrows and her light accent were attractive enough, but they didn't hold the same firepower for him as Jill's clipped way of speaking.

Thank God Annette had been here for Chuck. Now that Mason thought about it, Chuck had never mentioned any family back in Hawaii. For them, the squadron filled that void. Or it did for Mason anyway. Since he'd left home at eighteen, the once-a-year phone call from his folks at Christmas—while unfailingly polite—was hardly the stuff of Hallmark cards.

Jimmy's girlfriend, a local orchestra conductor, plumped a pillow on the sofa. "Nice digs."

Annette elbowed Chuck lightly in the side. "He needs a decorator."

Vince dropped onto the couch, the big lug sinking in deep as he propped his feet up in front of the wide screen television. "Looks to me like he's got all the important stuff. We'll have to hang out here on game days."

Mason took in the generic apartment floor plan, two bedrooms, the door to the spare now open and showing pristine new workout equipment.

Chuck leaned back against the wall, standing on one foot. "The building has an indoor pool and a gym, but this here doesn't close up at night."

The physical therapist—Ferguson—passed him another crutch. "Don't overdo. Stick to the pace."

"That's rich, coming from you, you sadist." Chuck took the second crutch and propped it against a chair.

Annette stopped beside him, tucking her shoulder

under his arm in a way that could be intimate or could be simply supporting. "Push yourself too far, and you'll set back all your hard work." She arched up to kiss his cheek, still slightly hollow and sallow beneath his darker skin. "I have to go. I'll call later."

Chuck squeezed her against his side in a one-armed hug, his dark eyes shifting to her. "Thanks again, beautiful. You're the best."

"Enjoy your guests. No need to see me out." She waved over her shoulder. "Nice to see everyone."

The front door closed quietly behind her.

All eyes shifted toward Chuck, but no one asked the burning question about the woman who'd just left.

Mason didn't see the need for silence. "I didn't realize you and Annette were an item."

Vince stretched his arms along the back of the sofa. "Rumors have been flying all around the squadron that you're seeing the Italian singer."

"You dog!" Werewolf slugged his arm. "You're using this R & R to your advantage."

"Yeah, that's me, a freewheeling bachelor." Chuck plowed his hand through his jet black spiked hair.

"So which is it? Friend or girlfriend?" Werewolf leaned toward the physical therapist. "You've seen more of him than we have lately. Any good gossip to share?"

Ferguson shook his head. "Patient-therapist confidentiality."

Laughter rumbled through the room at his none-too-subtle dodge.

Chuck collected the second crutch, some of the fight slipping from his face. "Annette came by the hospital. She was attacked a few months back and needed someone to talk to."

Attacked? Holy shit. Mason leaned forward. "What happened?"

Chuck's eyes narrowed. "Someone mugged her on her way into her apartment, roughed her up badly enough she spent a night in the hospital. She wasn't raped, thank God, but the incident, the feeling of being so out of control, screwed with her mind all the same." His face went tight and gaunt. "She needed to speak with someone who could relate."

Chuck would definitely fit the bill. He'd taken a helluva pounding during his captivity. He bore outward marks even now with his limp and a scar that slid up into his buzzed short hairline.

Straightening, Chuck plastered his lighthearted look in place again. "So do you want to crank up the widescreen television and help me eat some of this food?"

No one questioned the mask. Mason understood as he knew the rest of them would, too. "Sure, I'll fire up the grill."

"I don't have a grill."

Mason clapped him on the shoulder. "You will as soon as we unload it from the back of my truck. Welcome home, brother."

This was his family. It was enough. It had to be.

* * *

Rex Scanlon didn't stop by the club for a drink with the crewdogs anymore. Even thinking about it made him sick to his stomach. All those lost minutes could have been spent with Heather if he'd just gone straight home. She'd told him she understood the whole crew bonding process.

Okay, she hadn't always been totally cool with it. He smiled to himself. Sometimes she'd been downright pissed off after all week with their hellion twin boys, so he'd spent the weekend draining all that energy from his kids while Heather read in a hammock. His smile faded.

Now his house was stone quiet since the boys started college. The sons—who he used to be so close to—had spent their Christmas break at a friend's ski cabin.

He pulled into the driveway of his stucco house, identical to all the other Southwestern architecture in the neighborhood. He hadn't cared much where he lived when he'd moved out of base housing after Heather died.

Rex shut off his fifteen-year-old Jeep Wrangler, the headlights slicing away. He probably should have just stayed at the office, but he was hungry, and the snack bar held little appeal. He'd already burned out on everything there. So he'd come home to finish off the take-out Chinese left over in his fridge.

He slammed the door shut, the cold desert night wrapping around him. It was about time he cleared

Heather's boxed things out of the garage so he could park inside. He would get around to it—sometime.

The moon played hide-and-seek with the clouds between two mountain peaks, casting dreamlike flickers across the porch until he could have sworn he saw Heather sitting on the front stoop waiting for him. He stopped dead. Was he losing it? He'd held it together all year, tough as hell, but he was functioning. If he'd been deluding himself, he needed to get off flying status. Fast. He couldn't risk the lives of the people he led.

He blinked again, and his vision cleared. Sure enough, there was a real person on his porch, but it wasn't Heather.

"Ms. Cicero."

The Italian diva rubbed her hands together for warmth, crutches propped against the step. "Colonel."

"What are you doing here?"

"Your manners are just as lovely as I remembered." Her Italian accent was more exotic in the dark of night, although her English had improved in the months since they'd met. "As for what I am doing here, I was waiting for you, of course." She hugged her bright orange wool jacket closer around her, her legs swallowed by wide-legged jeans tonight. He still had no explanation of what caused her limp.

He stopped beside her, hands jammed in the pockets of his leather flight jacket. "You shouldn't be out here alone. Haven't you heard there's a serial killer on the loose?"

"A killer?" She shivered. "No, I had not heard. But you are here now, so I'm safe."

Yeah? And who would protect him from this international rock star who, for some bizarre reason, had decided to track him down? "How did you get my address? I'm not listed in the phone book."

"I asked my agent." She flicked her silky black hair away from her face.

"Gee, and all this time we've been paying top-level security personnel and secret service when we should have consulted music industry agents instead."

"Your residence isn't a state secret, is it?"

He exhaled long and hard. He didn't have the energy for this—for her. "Could you please do me a favor?"

"What would that be?"

"Don't waste my time or yours with the flirting."

"You certainly do think well of yourself if you believe I am here to flirt." She waved a manicured hand. "Please stop towering over me and sit."

He hesitated.

She patted the spot beside her on the otherwise empty stoop. "I need to rest my knee before I leave."

Her knee. He'd guessed correctly at the hospital. He wanted to ask her how she'd injured it, but that would prolong their conversation. He wasn't going to sit beside her, but he could see where looming over her was overdoing things. He leaned back against the stucco wall, crossing his booted feet at the ankles.

"Thank you," she said softly, then her spine went straight, and she exhaled, her breath puffing a light fog in the cold dark. "I came to say I am sorry for any trouble I caused to your people while we were with the USO in Turkey."

"Thanks."

A small smile teased the corner of her lips. "You are not going to tell me it was not my fault."

"It wasn't your fault."

"You lie."

"I don't lie." Except in the line of duty working in a top secret job, but that didn't count. He prided himself on his integrity and stuck to the truth. "Sounds like you're suffering from some guilt. That's your issue, ma'am. Not mine."

"Ma'am?" She tucked her hands into the sleeves of her silly orange coat. "Isn't that a little ridiculous given I am . . . how much younger am I than you? Or is there a problem with me asking your age?"

"It's rude, but that's never been a concern of yours before." Damned if she wasn't every bit as blunt as him. "I'm forty-two."

"Fifteen years older than I am. Not so much." She hugged her knees, the sides of her arms pushing her breasts closer together, just visible in the vee of her coat.

"Calling you ma'am is a product of my military training, nothing to do with age."

"Why not call me Livia?"

Time to end this before she made a fool out of both of them. "Cut to the chase."

"Excuse me? I am not familiar with that phrase."

"It means get to your point. Why did you come to see me?"

She stood slowly, her hand falling on his arm to brace herself. She eased one foot up off the ground, no doubt favoring her knee, but the effect still had the look of a vintage film star, crooking a leg in the middle of a kiss.

Except they weren't kissing, just sharing the same few inches of air. "Perhaps I find you interesting."

"Perhaps you find me unavailable."

"You certainly are that, even though you wear no ring." Her brown eyes went darker with sympathy. "I am sorry about your wife."

He didn't like it any better when Livia went soft. "Right. Thanks. And you're here because . . . ?"

Her gaze locked on him for two more gusty breaths before she pulled away and leaned on the wall next to him. "Actually, I am here to find out how things really are for Chuck. I don't trust that he is being honest with me."

"You want to know about Chuck?" Now wasn't that a kick in the ego? He'd been worried about her hitting on an old guy like him, and she had the hots for one of his young crewdogs.

"I just said as much, did I not? I'm worried about him and what will happen to him now that he is out of the hospital."

Chuck deserved happiness more than anyone. He did not need some diva nymphet leading him on. Rex angled closer to crowd her, and yeah, he knew it was intimidating, but he had a point to make. "Don't fuck with Chuck Tanaka's head. He's been through enough."

When she'd left the base in Turkey and endangered their whole dark ops mission with her high-profile kidnapping, authorities had determined she was simply reckless. Base security had watched her a little more closely since she wasn't an American, but no one had seriously considered whether she could have a darker motive for ignoring orders.

Yet here she was again, connected to another sensitive military project, and this time he wouldn't be as easily persuaded her reasons were a hundred percent innocent.

* * *

The next evening, Mason pressed the brake on his truck as he pulled into an empty parking spot outside the Atomic Testing Museum. Not what he'd expected when Jill gave him her uncle's work address.

Hopefully tonight would be more fruitful than his frustrating day at the squadron with no answers to what caused the in-flight debacle. They had checked and rechecked data and flight tapes and any damn thing they could think of. The contractor couldn't find a mechanical malfunction either. Without answers, they were faced with two options.

One, fly the final two test runs with an additional loadmaster on board for more observations. If those flights went flawlessly, chances increased that somehow he'd simply fucked up. They would cross their fingers and continue with their demonstration next week.

Or two, they could just scrap the drop altogether and simply show off the plane and its speed. Certainly it was impressive enough on its own, but without the proven ability to off-load goods, a big part of the oomph would be lost in their part of the presentation. Years of work wouldn't mean dick.

Slamming his truck door closed, he spotted Jill a couple of car rows down. Leggy and curvy, she was serious pinup material in her jeans and a turquoise fitted jacket.

Her silver studded heels surprised him. He'd pegged her for a more earthy type. Not that he was arguing with a woman in heels and pouty, slicked lips.

He was so screwed. Maybe it was a good thing after all that her uncle was coming along for dinner.

Mason pulled his focus back in tight on his reason for being here. To find out more about a certain sexy camo cop.

Mason stepped ahead to hold open the door to the museum. Jill gave him a passing half smile as she walked by. "Glad you could make it, Sergeant."

She strutted away, long legs eating up space. Maybe this was just her personality—brusque. That fit with what he'd observed of her in the mess hall. His eyes dropped to her heels again.

Unzipping his leather flight jacket, he followed her into the Today and Tomorrow Gallery toward a clump of elementary school–aged kids with happy birthday goody bags dangling from their fists. Phillip Yost stood by a piece of the Berlin Wall serving as a tour guide— or a docent, as his mother would have said.

A dozen or so kids with birthday party name tags stickered to their shirts were listening to his story about watching the wall fall. To hear the guy tell it, he'd actually been there.

Yost clapped his hands together. "Well, kiddos, that concludes our party tour. Now make sure to ask your moms and dads to come back here so you can take a longer look around."

"Hey, Uncle Phil, over here." Jill waved to catch his attention.

Yost pulled his volunteer ID lanyard with the museum logo from around his neck and angled through the crush of kids ripping into goody bags full of candy. "Thank goodness you're on time. I'm starving to death." He stopped short when he saw Mason and cocked his head to the side. "You brought company."

"Hope it's okay if I butt into your plans."

"Completely okay. In fact"—Yost clapped him on the shoulder—"I'll gladly pick up the tab for your meal. You and Gingersnap here are bonded through a near death experience."

Mason kept his face blank. The old guy shouldn't know about the desert incident. Between her job and his, what happened was classified.

Come to think of it, what had Jill told him about why she needed to be picked up at the hospital?

Yost kept nodding. "Yeah, you did a damn fine job at keeping Jill from being flattened by the Casper mobile."

Ah. Mason gave himself a mental head thunk. "No need to buy my meal for that. All I did was shout. She took care of herself just fine."

Yost hooked his thumbs in his pockets and rocked back on the heels of his rattlesnake skin boots. "I taught her everything she knows about self-defense. Glad you noticed. We can argue about the tab later over dinner."

Mason jabbed a thumb toward the museum sign. "Cool way to spend your retirement."

"Honest to Pete, these kids are tougher to corral than any crooks I used to chase. Did she tell you I used to be a cop, too? She takes after her uncle," he rushed on before Mason could answer. "I taught her everything I know. She's carrying the torch, and I'm keeping busy here and with my dogs."

Yost had been a cop? Interesting.

The older guy jabbed a thumb at an image from the first nuclear bomb test. A mushroom cloud formed in the desert, shock waves rippling away in circles propelling sand outward. "This is what the future is about. Who controls it? Will they harness it or exploit it? This could be an answer or an end."

"You sound like some of the people I work with."

"Must come from living here so long."

Jill ducked her head between them. "Hey, Uncle Phil, is your shift over or not?"

"I'm a volunteer. There's no punch card now that I'm not a cop anymore."

The older man snapped his fingers to snag the attention of a college-aged girl wearing her tour guide name tag. "Alexus, can you take it from here and make sure they're all picked up by parents?" He pressed a hand to his lower back. "My sciatica's acting up again." He turned to the kids. "Old back injury from chasing a truck full of drug runners across the desert. Would have caught them, too, if they hadn't shot out my front tire and sent me crashing into a Joshua tree."

Alexus's eyes went saucer wide. "Really?"

"Hell no. Even the kids don't fall for that one." Yost shook his head. "My back does ache, but that has more to do with the fall I took that time I hydroplaned on a surprise puddle of puppy pee."

Mason chuckled. "Definitely not as cool a story."

Jill bumped her shoulder against Phil's. "You men can be so juvenile sometimes."

"It's in the DNA," Phil said as he walked Jill toward the exit and opened the door. "Everything boils down to protecting the cave, kiddo."

She glanced back over her shoulder. "You're joking again, right?"

Mason stepped into the parking lot, lights flickering off and on in a fickle fight with the sinking sun. "My pal Jimmy dislocated his jaw playing volleyball. By sundown, rumor going round the base was that he'd taken a rifle butt to the face dealing with insurgents at the gate."

Yost shrugged into a jacket. "I sure as shit have some better stories than that for real. Just can't share them because they're still classified." He stopped by his beat-up Mustang. "Although if you get enough drinks in me tonight, boy, you'll learn what desert secrets are really all about."

EIGHT

Sitting in Uncle Phil's car outside the Little A'Le Inn, Jill watched Mason park his truck four spaces down. She had half expected him to be a no-show back at the museum, and now here they were, at Uncle Phil's favorite local hangout. She felt more than a bit juvenile insisting they take different vehicles.

Now that she had ditched her annoying defensiveness, she realized if they'd ridden together, she could have used the time to question Mason. She couldn't keep her thoughts from running full force into lip-lock with the sexy loadmaster when she needed to focus on discovering how to stop a twisted bastard from taking more lives. A sicko who could be anywhere, even here. Given all the victims' ties to the military, the killer could be drawn to a place like this simple corrugated building, a popular hangout for base personnel as well as tourists.

Jill slammed the passenger door. As Uncle Phil ambled over to Mason, she scanned each face heading in and out. Uncle Phil swore by the food at this small but packed hangout in the middle of nowhere, technically listed as the tiny town of Rachel, Nevada, near Las Vegas. Cars filled the lot, angling willy-nilly, a nearby patch set aside for RVs parked and plugged in.

Shivering, she pulled her skimpy jacket closer, mentally kicking herself for choosing her wardrobe tonight for looks rather than practicality. Her toes numbing in her pumps, she joined Mason and Phil, already gabbing away about constellations visible this time of year. She trailed a step behind as they brushed past a woman who was overdressed in comparison to the casual campers and military-looking personnel in civilian clothes.

Jill resisted the urge to compare her jacket with the woman's wardrobe. The confident female had the kind of look Jill had ached to have back during her chunky high school days. No carroty red hair for this lady. Her sleek brown mane was clasped back in a classic, chic ponytail, and she wore black leather knee boots with a red skirt.

The woman nodded toward Mason, recognition flickering through her golden brown eyes. "Sergeant."

Mason nodded back. "Good evening, Dr. Drummond."

Jill looked back over her shoulder at the retreating woman, then back at Mason. "She's a doctor?" The woman was chic *and* smart? Some people sure got lucky in the genetics sweepstakes. "Is she one of your flight surgeons?"

His boat shoes crunched against gravel. "Actually no, she's a civilian contractor who, uh," his gaze darted away for an evasive second before he continued, "she works for our testing unit."

"Doing what?"

"She's an engineer."

Uncle Phil whistled low, rubbernecking to catch another peek. "She sure doesn't look like any engineer I've ever seen. The ones I've met all have their heads in the clouds and wear pocket protectors."

Jill swatted his arm, nudging him along. "You should know better than to have preconceived notions about people."

Her conscience pinched, and she glanced at Mason. Hadn't she made snap judgments about him based on his looks and what others had to say about him?

Phil tore his eyes away from the doctor. "I would have thought she was a coed."

Mason paused at the glass door, his breath fogging into the cold air. "Word has it, she was a wonder kid genius who went to college before the rest of us had finished junior high. She's been working for the air force since she was about twenty, which I guess must make her around thirty."

He guessed? Mason hadn't thought about Dr. Drummond's age? It didn't seem he'd thought much about the woman at all, regardless of how attractive she was.

And that little realization had absolutely nothing to do with finding a serial killer. So much for getting her head back in the game.

Phil waggled his eyebrows. "It's those hot leather boots that make her look like a sorority girl. Don't you think, Mason?"

"No comment, sir." Mason shoved open the bar door, holding it for Jill and Uncle Phil.

Voices, laughter, clanking bottles, and the low bass thrum of the jukebox swelled out and wrapped around her, sucking her into another world. Jill stepped over the threshold into the muggy room. No matter how many times she came here, she was always reminded of that bar from the first *Star Wars* movie, the place where Han Solo hung out drinking with all the aliens while funky music twanged around them. This place was definitely a universe away from the rest of the planet.

Jill tucked into the line waiting for a table. Off to the side, the bartender, who looked more like ZZ Top turned surfer, leaned toward a tourist with a camera around his neck. "You've got your grays and the greens. The grays are your most common breed of aliens. About seventy-five percent of the ones we've seen out here fall into that category."

The elderly tourist angled forward with avid eyes while his wife clicked cell phone pictures of Area 51 memorabilia on the wall. "Gray, as in the short, androgynous-looking ones? Sort of like a washed-out Teletubby, right? My grandkids watch those things. They love 'em."

The seasoned bartender—Aaron—sketched on a napkin, while the other guy setting up drinks raced to and fro behind him. "I guess you could put it that way. But they're not to be confused with the short, nongrays that are more white and childlike looking."

"What about the greens?" the wife asked, capturing an image of an alien mannequin in the corner.

Aaron took another napkin to continue his "artist" renderings. "Reptilian like, but not totally, though. The grays, now, they're humanoid. Then there are the Nordics, which are quite intriguing, since they look human, too. It sure lends credence to the possibility that our form isn't from Earth. Or maybe they interbred with us somewhere along the line."

Uncle Phil snorted and mumbled, "*Rosemary's Baby.*"

Aaron glanced up. "I heard that, you old desert rat."

"Sorry." Phil inched toward the bar. "But you know I'm a cynic."

"We're used to unbelievers around here." He passed Phil a longneck bottle of beer.

Mason stepped ahead of Phil, only favoring his injured ankle slightly now. "Aaron, I'll get him to stop that kind of talk if you'll move us up in line."

"Consider it done, my friend. Hey, Gina? Some help here, please." He snapped for a waitress's attention before shifting back to his tourist audience. "You got a whole bunch of other sightings that are robotic or even mistlike. Nothing's beyond the realm of possibility. It's a big universe out there . . ."

No doubt Aaron would earn some extra bills stuffed in his tip jar, not that any of these folks were about the money. It was all about the thrill, the buzz, being a part of something that never grew boring.

While Phil sidled to the jukebox, Jill followed the waitress through the press of bodies toward their table in back. She glanced over her shoulder at Mason. "You know Aaron?"

"We're kindred spirits of sorts."

Jill looked back and forth between the aging surfer with a questionable floral fashion sense and the smoothly handsome Mason. "You'll have to pardon me if I miss the connection."

"You really need to stop thinking so literally. The guy's got an interesting life story. He bucked the family landscaping business, bought an RV, and headed for the West Coast. He ran out of money here, got this job, and twenty years later, he still lives in that same RV with his surfboard strapped to the top."

"Sounds like a real character."

Mason held out Jill's chair for her with more of those old-school manners she found oddly charming.

"He's happy, meeting his bills while doing something he enjoys. That's the measure of success in my book."

A middle-aged waitress with a six-month-old fried perm stopped at their table. "Hey there, Sergeant."

"Hi, Gina." Mason took his seat under a poster print advertising a 1950s flick called *Cat-Women of the Moon*. "How'd your daughter do on her science project?"

"She got an A and an invitation to participate in the science fair." She cocked a hand on her hip, her T-shirt hitching up to display her pierced belly button above her low-rise jeans. "She's already written you the cutest little note to say thanks. We both really appreciate it. I know next to nothing about junior high–level thermodynamics."

"No problem. I enjoyed it." He smiled nicely, not flirtatiously at all, as Jill would have expected. His eyes even stayed firmly off the patch of bare stomach. "She really didn't need much help, just some pointing in the right direction."

"Thanks all the same." Gina pulled a pencil and order pad from her jeans pocket. "I assume you want the usual?"

"That would be great. Thanks."

Jill set aside her menu, not having a clue what she wanted on any front tonight. "I'll have whatever he's having, and get the same for Phil."

The blaring song from an old Kiss album faded, a Willie Nelson tune cranking to life. Phil settled into a seat with a slow creak of his cowboy boots, his chair closer to a movie poster for *Devil Girl from Mars*. "What did you just order for us?"

Mason passed the menus to the waitress. "An avocado and tomato sandwich on foccacia bread."

Phil's eyes went wide. "You're fucking with me, right? That isn't even on the menu."

"They make it up special for me here. If you hurry, you can catch Gina before she places the order."

"Nah, not worth the effort." Phil grabbed a fistful of peanuts from a bucket in the middle of the table. "Are you gay?"

Jill gasped. "Uncle Phil!"

Mason tipped back his chair. "What if I were?"

Could the whole player act have been a smoke screen? She assessed him across the table and . . . Nope, that was one hundred percent heterosexual interest in his eyes as he stared back at her.

Jill swallowed hard. "If you were? I wouldn't have to worry about you hitting on me."

Mason winked, nudging her foot with his. "Keep worrying, gorgeous."

Phil pitched the peanut hulls onto the floor under his chair, as was standard protocol in the joint. "I've never met a guy who would admit to eating a froufrou sandwich like that, much less do it in front of a female."

Mason rocked back in his chair beside her, and damn, he made boat shoes with no socks look hot. Then she saw the bruise on his ankle and remembered how he'd run full out on that sore foot to save a toddler. "I like what I like. If we're lucky, they'll add papaya slices to our order."

"I'll pass on that. It might mess with the bouquet of my beer." He lifted his longneck. "I might give these guys a hard time, but we all ought to thank these folks for keeping the alien buzz going. Some people are so willing to believe the hype, they'll attribute anything to an ET sighting. At the museum today, I even heard a tourist vowing he saw some freaky fast spaceship that night my Jill landed in the hospital." His squinty old eyes narrowed tighter. "Now, that wouldn't have anything to do with what the two of you were doing out there in the desert, would it?"

Mason tugged out a napkin from the metal dispenser. "I believe people see what they expect to see. I also think folks are in a frenzy with this latest killing I heard about on the radio."

Phil drained a quarter of his beer. "Since you're both sitting here, I'll take it then that you and Jill weren't sucked up into an alien craft and tortured?"

"Do we look traumatized?" Mason waved between himself and Jill. "Although you may want to check out the cow population, just to be sure. I hear they're chewing the grass in a labyrinth pattern."

She went still. He wasn't the killer. She'd determined that much. But why the reference to alien markings when that had been kept secret from the public? Coincidental given that patterns in the grass were also generalized folklore for aliens? Probably, but still eerie in light of those very real file photos she'd seen. They'd been able to keep the dirt pattern out of the news again, but for how much longer? "You know, boys, I understand your macho need to make light of serious things so you feel more invincible, but quite frankly, I find these jokes of questionable taste, given those poor dead people."

Mason winced. "My apologies. Chalk it up to the warrior habit of making light to keep ourselves from freaking out in a tight situation."

"Sorry, Gingersnap. We men are pigs sometimes." Phil leaned back to make way for Gina to set their orders in front of them then rested his elbows on the table again. "You have to realize we old folks have been a part of this alien culture for longer than you can even remember. We've seen some spooky shit over the years. There was a time when people gave serious credence to the Majestic 12 theory."

Okay, that was a new one to Jill. "Majestic 12?"

"Also known as M12 or Majority 12 or a number of other names. It was a supposed code name for a secret group formed by the president himself back in the 1940s. It was made up of military leaders, scientists, even folks from the government. Their job was to look into UFO sightings. This was just the first of many government groups that have supposedly participated in cover-ups over the past few decades."

Phil leaned on his elbows, farther across the table. "Any of these military folks in here could be one of them." He pointed his sandwich toward Mason. "Even you."

Mason simply smiled, draped a flimsy paper napkin over one leg, and ate his sandwich. Jill resisted the urge to swat Phil on the back of the head. He certainly wasn't holding back tonight. All the same, she appreciated the way Mason didn't seem to judge eccentrics like Aaron, and Uncle Phil, even. He simply accepted them for who they were.

Phil finished off his beer. "If you ask me, I think you military folks just screw with the locals sometimes so they don't know which end is up when you decide to pull off something for real."

Mason swiped his napkin across his face. "You must spend a lot of time on the Internet."

"Got my own satellite connection out at the ranch." Phil stuffed the sandwich into his mouth and chewed. "Hmmm, not bad," he said with his mouth full. "Eat up, and I'll show you who else likes to screw with the tourists."

* * *

Was Mason actually screwing that mousy lady cop?

Lee sat in her Lexus outside the tiny metal frame restaurant and monitored the continuous flow of people in and out. She'd come here to check on a possible link to mess with Mason but had been surprised to see him walking with Jill Walczek into the little tin building. How much longer would they stay in there? Mason's truck was still parked in its spot, and she hadn't seen him or his dinner companions leave.

Was Mason bored or desperate? She only had to consider that one for a second. The man was never desperate, so he must be at loose ends. She could almost sympathize. She hated boredom almost as much as she despised how unfairly some people treated her. Arranging for that remote controlled car to blow had been blessedly easy for someone as smart as her, and it *had* sparked some interesting reactions. Mason's behavior had exposed some weaknesses for her to exploit.

Apparently getting naked with the lady cop in the

desert and then watching her nearly get run over had left an impression on Mason and Jill, enough so he'd actually been introduced to the woman's daddy figure. Lee sipped her vitamin water then carefully wiped a napkin along the rim before setting it in the holder. She could see why Jill would chase down Mason, but why was he taken with her?

Lee scratched her fingernail back and forth along the label on her vitamin water. Jill wasn't ugly, but she wasn't remarkable either. She had nice hair, a little on the orange side. She had definitely worked out to make the most of her figure, but other than that, the woman didn't do much to maximize her best features. Yet Mason didn't seem able to take his eyes off her.

Her nails dug deeper into the drink bottle. He'd shown a new weakness at a time when Lee had a problem. Now she just had to figure out how to fit those two new variables into her plans, which were fraying along the edges.

The Killer Alien was a copycat. The first victim— the one who'd lived—had been Lee's work. The bitch Annette Santos had actually thought she could get away with claiming joint credit for a test project they'd worked on. Or rather one Lee spearheaded, *created*. Annette had only done some grunt work research. Lee's fingernails popped holes in the plastic covering her vitamin water until the shredded wrapper peeled away.

But she had made Annette pay, and in a way that couldn't be traced to her. She glanced up at the circular silver alien charm dangling from her rearview mirror, a charm she sometimes wore around her neck. The markings in the sand had been inspired. So much so that some freak with an alien fetish had locked onto the whole circle swirl and made it his own.

Of course it had to be a man. Everyone knew the statistics. Serial killers weren't women. *She* wasn't some psycho.

Hopefully she could use the man's gruesome crimes to take care of some business on her own, undetected, and cast suspicion on their local nut job murderer, rather than have him somehow lead them back to her. So far, the killer had chosen victims all related to the base, which would prove helpful in drawing police attention to Mason.

And Jill Walczak? Lee centered her charm again . . . *precisely*.

Jill would be the perfect victim for the next serial killing, one that would also point directly to Mason as the perp.

NINE

Mason eyed the GPS on his truck windshield and thanked God it was functioning out here in the middle of the desert mountain range, because otherwise they could very well get lost going back. He certainly wasn't counting on the navigational skills of the drunk old man beside him shouting out directions. Since Phil had been wasted before Mason finished his avocado-tomato foccacia sandwich, they'd all piled into Mason's truck.

"Turn by that crooked cactus there," Yost barked, then burped.

Crooked cactus? Good Lord, it sounded like something out of a black-and-white movie. At least the kooky guy offered up a distraction from the sweet scent of Jill sitting between them.

Something had shifted between them in the restaurant, and he wasn't sure what. He'd only been shooting the breeze with Yost when he'd realized she was looking at him with a new intensity.

The truck jostled over the rocky path, nudging her toned thigh closer to his, before she pulled away.

Cranking the steering wheel as they passed the twisted Joshua tree, Mason looked at Jill sitting between him and Yost. Her eyes darted left, right, on the windshield again, her hand grazing her waist over her gun strapped in place.

Mason dipped his head. "What's the matter?"

Her hand stayed lightly against her weapon. "After our conversation back at the restaurant, I can't help but think about the serial killer, especially when we're so far from civilization. Until he—or she—is caught, there's no need to be reckless."

Yost waved a drunken hand through the air. "Ah, there are three of us. We're not just one defenseless woman caught with her hands full of groceries as she struggles to open her front door."

Jill gaped at him. "Damn, Uncle Phil, do you always go around thinking of scenarios for catching a woman unaware?"

"I think maybe," he mumbled, "I read something like that about one of the killings in the papers. Been following it. The old cop in me can't help but eat up the details. Got anything you want to share, girl?"

Jill jerked a thumb toward Mason. "You could fill him in on what the press says about the ongoing investigation, since he's been out of the country for the past couple of months."

"Ah." He leaned forward, eyes gleaming as bright as the dashboard lights. "Then you missed the frenzy ramping up. It was my girl here who caught the similarities in some unsolved cases. She started tracking details this fall in hopes of catching the guy."

Mason shot a quick look at Jill, surprised. He hadn't realized she was this involved in the investigation. What else didn't he know about her?

He looked back out the windshield. "Five attacks as of yesterday, four of them dead, right? I heard it on the radio on my drive over for supper. Some local woman. They haven't released her name yet."

"Damn." Yost shook his head. "This area is already so crazy with alien conspiracies, it doesn't take much to freak people out. Stop here."

Mason braked and put his Chevy in park in the middle of a patch of desert that looked much the same as everything that had come before. He turned off the radio but kept the engine and lights on. Moonbeams glinted off silvery rocks bleached white over years of exposure to the sun. Mason stepped out of the truck and met Jill and the old guy at the back of the truck.

Phil lowered the tailgate. "Some folks believe it's some kind of ritual killing for a cult, and they're using the alien scare to cover their tracks."

Jill thumbed her gun again. "Not a very original thought, if you ask me."

The older guy hitched up to sit on the tailgate. "Valid point. From what I'm hearing out of my prior contacts, it appears each of the nabbings have been while the person was alone." He leaned deeper into the truck bed for the bag he'd retrieved from his trunk and tucked there before they'd left the bar. "Since most of them are females, I'm guessing the one male victim must have been a guy who stumbled into the wrong place at the wrong time."

Jill jumped up to sit next to him. "That seems to be how things are pointing. The guy's just so damn clean about the killings. Even with this latest murder, there's virtually nothing to go on. We're all praying we get a break in the case before he strikes again."

"Amen, Gingersnap." His grim face softening, he pulled a battery-powered strobe light from the duffel and turned to Mason. "About those alien sightings. Back in the day, some of us camo dudes would hang out in watchtowers and fuck with the locals. We would flash lights in the sky and amplify everyday noises over a megaphone. You'd be amazed how worked up conspiracy nuts can get over repeated clicks of a lighter or the slow, squeaky release of air through a balloon. We even made the paper with that one."

They sounded like his kind of guys. Noticing Jill's slight shiver, Mason eased off his leather jacket and draped it over her shoulders. "Ah, a close encounters sort of moment."

Jill stiffened under his touch but then gathered the

jacket closer around her, tucking her hands in the sleeves. A bitter wind rolled over them, but his sweater provided more than enough protection with the added heat of being this close to her.

Phil was too busy playing with his oversized flashlight to notice the coat exchange. "We may have inspired a movie or news story here and there to kill time on a boring desert night. Pretty soon the military realized there was a big payoff in these rumors. Secrecy wasn't as big a concern if you had an alien story scapegoat." He turned off the light, the beam cutting short. "People are more cynical these days. Damn shame. Life was a lot more fun back then."

Jill rested her head on Phil's shoulder. "That's one of the things I've always loved about you, your ability to find the fun in anything."

He snapped the light on and off three times before swooping it across the mountainside. "Why bother living if you're not going to enjoy the ride?"

Jill's laugh filled the desert void.

Mason looked at her appreciatively. Damn, but he liked this woman.

Phil jerked the spotlight in a haphazard circle against the desert horizon. "Once, a while back, we took one of these, covered it with purple cellophane, and shone it on that mountain over there. Next thing you know, shops were selling T-shirts with bright purple rays shooting from a flying saucer." He looked at Mason, his eyes suddenly cold sober. "I imagine some of the stuff you fliers do will fuel stories for decades."

"Hmmm." Mason offered up a noncommittal grunt. Even if what the old guy said was true, that didn't mean anyone in the military could confirm it. "I would imagine so. You know we're probably in more danger of being shot for trespassing by a pissed-off rancher."

"Do you two want my secrets or not?" Phil clicked off the spotlight. "Or maybe I should be asking you, my new friend. Do you allow this sort of thing to continue to divert attention from tests? Or to divert attention from the aliens?"

* * *

Jill searched out the truck window for anything to divert her thoughts as she drove alone with Mason down a dimly lit street after they'd dropped Phil off at his place. The sleepy desert neighborhood where she lived had mostly turned in for the night.

She hugged his jacket around her shoulders, chilled from her thoughts as much as the night air. "Thanks for the ride home."

"You're right that backtracking to pick up Phil's car would have wasted a lot of time," he conceded, even though he still seemed surprised that she'd agreed. "And Phil was in no shape to drive himself or anyone else."

"He's not a drunk, but he does have his longneck moments."

As a keen observer of human nature, Mason hid a

canny intuitiveness beneath his slick exterior. It was the kind of quality that made the best investigators, and it intrigued her on any number of levels. Jill wondered how he had gained such skills.

Of course that could be said about a number of aviators who worked around here, and truth be told, she had no reason to suspect he had anything to do with the serial killer. She should say good night and move on.

Should. But couldn't. Not yet. "I like you, Mason Randolph."

The dashboard lights sparked off the glint of humor in his green eyes. "The surprise in your voice could be insulting."

"Good thing your ego can take it."

He laughed softly as they rolled past the small stucco duplexes, homes old enough to show their age without gaining the quaintness of a historic neighborhood. Sort of like his truck, older but well-loved. His Chevy had been a surprise. She'd expected him to drive some sort of chick magnet sports car.

Mason slowed over a speed bump. "Are you ready to pony up why you initially disliked me on sight?"

Was she? She had to be honest with herself that she'd climbed into his vehicle with him for a reason beyond her job. The attraction she felt around him had gone beyond his perfectly sculpted features to something deeper inside him. "Maybe I just have a problem with guys with double-digit notches on their bedposts."

"We've already established you've never seen my bedpost. And since a savvy cop like you knows better than to listen to uncorroborated gossip, I think your problem with me goes deeper."

Jill took a bracing breath. "My mother went through quite a few men after my dad died."

"Deadbeats?" His face creased with sympathy.

"Actually, no. For the most part they were really great guys." And she'd grieved every time one walked out the door for good. "I can't fault Mom on her impeccable taste or her ability to attract quality men. Most of them even fell in love with her. She just couldn't love them back. I know it sounds like I'm dissing her, but I really do love my mom. Flaws and all, she loved me and did her best." She shrugged. "She just never could get past her need to have a man to validate her enough to form a real relationship with anybody else." Including her own daughter. "After a while I learned it was better not to get too close."

"Something you did until it became a habit to keep your distance."

"Wow, you're really good with the empathy." She tried to make light rather than let those damn nice words of his sink in too deeply. "No wonder the women fall into your bed."

Oops. Had she really said that?

His eyes went sleepy-lidded for an assessing heart-beat before he looked back at the road. He didn't answer, just kept driving.

"Uh, turn here." She pointed to the left. "Mine is the duplex at the end of the cul-de-sac." She scratched along a patched tear in the upholstery. "Sorry if I got defensive there."

"I'm cool with being told to butt out."

"More like back off just a little." Seeing the way his shoulders filled out the white cabled sweater offered up enough temptation for one night. "I'm sharing here, not opening my whole life up. Which I guess proves your point about my keeping distance." She flexed her toes in her silver-studded pumps. "I really got close to her third husband."

He eased down the brake until the truck stopped in front of her duplex. Mason hitched an elbow on the steering wheel and turned toward her with undiluted attention. "Tell me about him."

"You've met him already, actually."

The frown cleared from his face. "Yost? Uncle Phil. Of course."

What was it about this guy that had her babbling so much so fast? "You've got to be sick of hearing about my crazy childhood."

He tugged a strand of her hair, lingering at the end to toy with it. Toy with her? "I'm interested, or I wouldn't be here."

Interested? "Don't waste your pickup lines on me. I'm not falling for your typical smooth act."

He released her hair. "That's a hefty assumption you're jumping to."

"Your reputation with women has nothing to do with assumptions or even simple gossip." She couldn't stop the defensiveness. "You forget I've seen you in action in the mess hall."

"I am who I am. I live life my own way while doing my best to make sure any decisions don't harm someone else. Maybe that's why I like Uncle Phil." His seriousness unsettled her far more than his smile. "Tell me more about him."

She could end this conversation by getting out of the truck, but for some reason, she wanted to linger, explore this unexpected connection between them. "He was a cop who lived for working security out here. Some unsubstantiated rumors tainted his reputation, so he took an early retirement and started giving tours at the museum."

"Where's your mother now?"

"In San Diego with husband number five. The woman has quickie divorces down to an art. When— and if—I ever get married, it will be forever."

His green eyes darkened for a hint. Then the shadows were gone before she could figure out what he was thinking.

"Yost stayed here, though, in spite of everything."

"He says nothing will run him away from where he grew up. He seems to enjoy his volunteer work at the museum, and he runs a kennel out at his ranch. He periodically goes to the pound and rescues dogs about to be put down, then trains them for anything from security detail firms to an elderly person needing a companion." She stroked her door handle. "Thanks for dropping him off tonight and for bringing me home."

"My pleasure."

She met his stare, held it, and when he didn't move to step out of the truck, she wondered if maybe, just maybe he would lean closer to kiss her. Her mouth went dry. She bit her tongue to keep from dampening her lips. Still, he didn't move, and she sure as hell wasn't going to throw herself at him.

"Good night, then." She slipped off his jacket, opened her door, and stepped out just as Mason rounded the hood of the truck to join her. Of course he would be the type to walk her to the porch. He had a way of making old-fashioned manners seem nice rather than over-the-top.

The desert night felt all the colder without his jacket. She followed the split in the walking path to her porch on one end, identical to her neighbor's at the other end of the duplex. She stopped at the Spanish-style wrought-iron entry gate that closed off her small rock garden beyond the stucco arch. A soothing fountain bubbled from a large terra-cotta pot streaming water down a pile of rocks. Three cacti of varying sizes sprouted from the stones.

Jill turned to face Mason. "Thanks for an, uh, interesting evening."

"No need to thank me for anything. The plans were Phil's, not mine."

"You didn't judge Phillip. That means a lot to me. Maybe even enough for me to reconsider some of my hefty assumptions."

He flattened his palm against the stucco arch, his arm

right beside her face. "Hey, how can you not like a man who tapes purple cellophane to a spotlight and gets more press than some high-tech piece of machinery?"

She laughed. He laughed. And the sounds tangled up between them in their solitary pocket of space. He stared at her again.

His head lowered.

Only an inch, but enough to telegraph his intent to kiss her while giving her time to refuse. She didn't say a word because yes, he was coming toward her. Instead, she slid her hand to his chest, warm, even though he must be cold in just jeans and a sweater with only a simple T-shirt beneath.

His head dipped toward hers, slowly, deliberately. He brushed his mouth over her, his eyes still open, searching her eyes for as long as she could keep looking back. Then sensation surged through her, and her lashes slid closed.

His hand slid from the arch, his knuckles skimming along her cheek. She was so far outside her comfort zone with this man. She took risks in her job on a regular basis, but she kept her relationships safe, little chance of getting her feelings trampled, something that had happened more often in high school than she cared to remember. The past should be the past. She didn't want to be locked in some adolescent time frame, but damn, some wounds ran deep, catching a person unaware at the most inconvenient of times. And that was enough of thinking. She intended to take charge of the moment and feel.

She clutched a fistful of his sweater, her thumb tracing along the corded pattern. Mason palmed her spine, low and firm, deepening the kiss until the hard planes of his body, the taste and texture of him, the scent of warm leather imprinted in her memory.

Right now, she couldn't remember all the reasons why she'd thought he was bad for her. She could only feel the heat pumping through her, tingling, tightening her nerves to a peak. The low groan in the back of his throat told her just how into the moment he was, too, a heady, heady notion.

His fingers plunged into her hair, cupping the back of her scalp in a seductive massage. She sagged back against the arch, and he followed along with her, sealing their bodies closer. She slid her hands along his sweater to explore the play of muscles along his chest. Her fingers climbed around and up to his shoulders, savoring the way his muscles jumped and bunched in response to her touch.

God, this was spiraling out of control quicker than she could have expected, and she'd already expected him to be damned good. He tasted like papaya and *man*. Her resistance was fading fast after an evening of surprising peeks at Mason's depth. He wasn't the caricature ladies' man she'd allowed herself to believe, but beyond that, she didn't know much about him.

He eased his mouth from hers, and she stifled the need to moan a protest. She needed to be strong, because now it would come, the push for more. He would roll out some Romeo suave ways that would douse the heat tingling along her nerves.

Mason brushed his cheek against hers, his late-day beard a seductive abrasion. His fingers continued their gentle circles along her head, and she could have sworn his hand trembled slightly.

"Good night, Jill." His breath steamed over her ear before he stepped back.

Good night? He was leaving? Not pressing for more? Surprising to say the least, because she didn't doubt for a second that he wanted her. She'd felt the intimate hard evidence clearly enough when they'd been body locked together.

She braced a steadying hand against the arch, the world shaky under her feet.

"Night, Mason." She pushed open the creaky iron gate, blinking to clear her eyes and regain her balance.

She kicked a stray landscaping stone back into the garden. And then another stone. Why were so many disturbed? The sensor-activated security lights flickered on. Mason still warm at her back as he waited for her to make it inside, she slid her key halfway in the lock.

The hair prickled along the back of her neck, her cop senses on alert.

Her front door slipped open before she even twisted the dead bolt. Oh God, someone was in there. Or someone *had* been there. She knew without question that she'd locked up earlier. She was relentlessly professional about her safety.

Mason's hand clamped on her shoulder. "Back up. Now."

Jill stumbled against him. She needed to get her head together, call the cops, and assess the situation. As she backpedaled away, her eyes fell on the rock garden, now fully lit. Her stomach roiled. More than just a couple of rocks had been kicked aside.

Someone had swept away a whole section to create an unmistakable swirl in the sandy earth beneath.

TEN

★ ———————————————————————————

Jill couldn't move, could barely even process what she was seeing in her patio garden. She'd reviewed the same dirt swirl in crime scene photos hundreds of times. But she'd certainly never expected to see the serial killer's signature at her own home.

"Hey, Jill?" Mason pulled her arm. "We need to call the police."

"I am the police." Well, sort of. She didn't work for the police department anymore. Her jurisdiction as a contracted security force extended only to the acreage surrounding Area 51. Still, she couldn't let a murderer just walk away if he was in her duplex. He could even be in there harming someone else.

But Mason was right. She couldn't face someone so sadistic half-cocked—and she definitely couldn't let

Mason go in unaware. She would have to warn him and make sure he fully understood the danger.

Jill pointed at the dirt swirl in her garden. "That's the serial killer's signature."

"Shit." Mason stepped between her and the front door.

She tugged her cell phone out of her purse, her gun still in her other hand. Jill thumbed seven on her phone and waited through two rings.

"Gallardo," her boss barked from the other end of the line, his voice gruff from sleep.

"It's me. Jill. Send someone over to my house ASAP. There's been a break-in, and it looks like it could be our serial killer."

"Damn it, Jill," Gallardo snapped from the other end of the line, now sounding completely awake. "Get the hell out."

"I *am* outside, and I'm with Sergeant Randolph. I'm armed and watching the premises."

"Good. Good," he said so loudly that Mason could undoubtedly hear. "Both of you get back in the car and wait. Do not, I repeat, do not go inside without backup, and I don't consider Randolph legal backup."

The line went dead.

Mason's jaw jutted forward. "There's not a chance in hell I intend to let a serial killer get away if he's in there. I'm not your regular tie-wearing civilian. What does your boss think I do for a living?"

She agreed with him, up to a point. "But you're not armed."

"Says who?" He reached under his jeans leg to pull out a knife. Had that been strapped to his leg all night? "I'm going in first. Don't argue. We don't have time. Seconds count."

She couldn't argue with that, especially not when she knew full well the level of this killer's brutality. She would check on her neighbors after clearing her place.

"Let's get moving." Her heartbeat stuttering in her ears, she followed Mason. He moved with stealth through the stucco arch, past the disturbed rock garden, and nudged her door open. Thank God, the older hinges didn't creak like the gate.

She blinked fast to adjust her eyes now that they were away from the streetlamps. Her living room was dark, as she had left it. Only a night-light in the kitchen cast any illumination. The tiny plug-in miniature teacup didn't do much to give them a visual edge.

Her tiny kitchen and dining area appeared empty. *Breathe. Don't forget to breathe.* If there was somebody lurking inside, he must be in the computer room, bedroom, or bathroom.

Mason stepped through the living area and into the narrow hall. The carpet absorbed all sound of footsteps. Of course, the same would apply for anybody else trying to sneak around.

A thud sounded behind her. She spun around fast. A teapot rattled on top of the corner curio cabinet. The light inside flickered on and off.

A second thump sounded, followed by the muffled

sound of a couple laughing, and she realized the noise had come from the other side of the wall—the other duplex.

Mason turned back toward the hall leading deeper into her home. As they approached the three doors, he glanced back at her again, a question in his eyes.

Jill checked around her. The computer room door was closed as always. The bathroom door was wide open. Her bedroom door, however, was half open. She generally left it wide like the bathroom door.

She pointed at her bedroom. Mason nodded. They eased closer, angling sideways to peer inside.

A dark-clad body loomed over her dressing table.

Her skin burned and pulled tight. Adrenaline was kicking in, without a doubt, but it surged so hard and fast it hurt.

Dark clothes and a stocking cap tugged low, he was riffling through her jewelry box. If he was looking to make a quick buck to make up for not finding her home, he was going to be sorely disappointed.

Jill leveled her gun and stepped forward. A board creaked under her foot. The intruder looked up sharply, tensed.

He bolted toward an open window she knew darn well she'd locked. He'd set up his escape route.

Mason charged after him. The dark figure dived headfirst through the window. If he made it through, he would have a winding maze of streets in which to lose himself. Mason's long legs closed the gap between them.

He grabbed the intruder's feet and heaved him back into the room with a grunt and an oof. The two men appeared evenly matched in size, but Mason had the upper hand in slamming the guy's face to the floor. Jill kept her gun pointed up, watching for the moment he might need help, and she needed to be careful not to shoot the wrong guy in the process.

The intruder twisted and flipped, somehow managing to get on his side. Mason powered a punch forward. The crack echoed through the room as bone met bone. The guy's head snapped back against the carpeted floor. His very *thick* skull, apparently, since he only shook his head, barely stunned. He didn't seem to have a weapon, and for some reason Mason had opted not to use his knife.

The dark-clad man bucked against Mason's restraining hold while reaching, grasping.

Jill slammed her high heels on the man's thick wrist. He screamed, his body doubling up.

In a flash, Mason flipped the guy to his stomach and ratcheted his hands up high behind his back. "What the hell were you doing in here?" He pumped the restrained hands up higher. "Answer me, damn it."

"Stop, stop!" The man in dark clothes went limp. "I'm not fighting back. Don't hurt me. I'm not fighting, man."

"You sick jerk." Mason peeled away the guy's stocking mask to reveal a male in his twenties, sandy hair and scared-as-hell blue eyes. A total stranger. "They're going to take you apart in jail after what you did to all of those people."

"What are you talking about?" His eyes went wide, fear fading to confusion. "I just wanted to find some money for a meal."

"You can try that line on the cops when they arrive in about sixty seconds."

"No, really." His words tumbled out faster and higher with agitation. "The door was open, the lights off, like it was practically begging me to help myself, so I came inside. If you're stupid enough to leave your place open like that, how can you blame a guy for checking things out?"

Jill knelt to his level, her gun in plain sight. "You're not in any position to call someone stupid."

"Sorry, sorry, really, lady, let's take it down a notch. I'm cooperating."

Jill glanced at Mason. "I always lock my door."

He nodded. "I figured as much. Money for a meal, huh? More like cash for a fix to pacify you, since your original plan didn't work out."

"Does it really matter, dude?"

Hell yes, it mattered. In fact, it was the difference between finding a serial killer and a two-bit bum. But why would the serial killer leave his signature in her yard without attacking or sticking around? Feasible. In fact, he could have done the same to countless other women who didn't report it, because before now, no one other than the cops knew about the signature move.

If it wasn't this guy, could the real killer have been watching her and Mason from the minute they'd stepped out of his truck, when they'd kissed? Even the possibility made her nauseous.

It looked like the serial killer was still out there and now he had her address.

* * *

Mason stood outside Jill's entry gate while the cops encircled her duplex. Neighbors clumped in small groups in their yards and on the street corner. Thomas Gallardo—Jill's boss—was speaking with local police. He'd pulled up five minutes after the cops.

The intruder was restrained in the back of a police cruiser, waiting to be taken to the station, where they could begin picking apart his story to determine if he told the truth about finding the place open. If he was the serial killer, then he was a damn good actor.

Of course, that was the whole point.

And to think Jill could have stumbled in on the guy alone if they hadn't ridden together. If they hadn't stopped to talk. And more.

No time to think about that now. Mason checked his watch. Oh one hundred. He had exactly two and a half hours to wrap this up and get home before he busted crew rest—the mandatory twelve hours downtime before any flight. He couldn't afford for anything to go off course in flying this next test mission for the hypersonic jet. He had two flights, both of which needed to go flawlessly before they could present the craft to the visiting generals.

That didn't mean he could just bail on Jill. "You really think this could be the serial killer? I'm assuming it has something to do with that pattern in your garden, since that was when you freaked out."

She eyed the press, then the small groups of people in bathrobes, one of whom must have called the media. "I did not freak out. Much."

"There's no shame in that. Whoever this dude is, he's not someone to toy with."

"I agree, and yes, the pattern in the garden has significance. You're going to hear anyway, so I might as well tell you. It appears at every scene. We were able to secure the crime scenes before the press arrived, but someone leaked a CSI photo from the latest killing. So it's not like it matters if somebody snags a snapshot of my garden."

"*You* had this information? I would have thought the investigation for these cases rested with the sheriff's department, not to someone hired out by a security agency."

"Since all of the victims have a tie to the military in this area, we've been on a higher level of alert."

"It makes sense to use all trained eyes available." He reached into the cab of his truck, pulled out his jacket, and offered it to her. "Is that why you were so deep in the desert the night I parachuted out?"

She hesitated for a second then took the coat from his outstretched hand. "I can't talk about details, but suffice it to say I get to hear about more going on than I normally would, which leads me to do things that wouldn't usually fall under my purview."

"If those marks in your garden mean what you said they do, then the killer has figured out just how involved you are in hunting him down."

A dry gust of wind rolled through, and she burrowed deeper inside his jacket. "I shouldn't have told you that about the markings, but I wanted to make sure you understood who was probably waiting inside. I may take heat for it, but I stand by my decision. Regardless, I can't let up now. The second victim—Lara—was a friend of mine."

Lara? An unusual name he'd only heard once before, here in this area. It couldn't be the same person. But still, why not ask. "What is her last name?"

"It's public knowledge, so it's okay for me to tell you her name was Lara Restin."

The oomph went out of his knees, and he leaned back against his truck. "Damn it. I knew her, too."

"You hadn't heard what happened to her?" She sounded suspicious.

"I told you I haven't been up on the details. I didn't know her well, but I know who she is—who she was. Damn," he said again, the enormity of it blindsiding him after an already off-kilter night.

She leaned on the truck beside him, almost touching, her presence comforting even without contact. "It sucks you in, doesn't it? Putting a real person's face on the crime."

He had too many faces in his head since he dealt

with life-and-death stakes on a daily basis. He couldn't do his job, go to war, and walk away unaffected. But maybe—given her profession—she understood that better than most.

Understanding her job, however, would only carry him so far. He didn't give a shit that she carried a gun. That didn't mean he planned to leave her alone here. He had a little longer before he had to hit the road. "You shouldn't stay here."

"I know."

"You do? No arguments about independence and how you're trained?"

"Not a one. If this killer targeted a man who was a black belt in karate, he's a sadistic bastard." She clenched her fists. "But why pick me to scare? There are plenty of others involved in the investigation, and it's not like I have a direct link to the military."

"You wear camos, and you work around Area 51, the alien playground."

"I guess you have a point."

"So where do you intend to stay?"

"Phil is the logical choice, and honestly I think it may be time for me to borrow one of his dogs—a really big dog."

"A guard dog would be an excellent idea, wherever you stay." He scratched behind his ear. "I'll drive you there. I have time before my crew rest kicks in."

"Crew rest?"

"For a flight. It's my job. I do work every now and again."

"So I've seen." She nudged his foot gently with hers. "Is your ankle okay?"

He flexed his foot and held back a wince. "Almost as good as new. I don't even need to tape it anymore."

"You're a speedy healer . . ." Her voice trailed off awkwardly. "If it's really not too much trouble, I'll take you up on the offer of a ride. And thank you for not pressing me to stay at your place."

"As much as I'd like to think I'm a damn good kisser, I don't expect one kiss is going to automatically lure you into bed."

"Is that what you're after?" Her eyes looked defenseless for once. "An affair with me?"

"Honestly? I don't have a clue. You've pretty much blindsided me since you pulled up out there in the desert after my accident, and you haven't let up for a second since."

"Wow"—she crossed her arms defensively—"you really are good. Almost too good sometimes, Mason."

She didn't believe him? Now, wasn't that a kick in the ass.

Gallardo motioned for Jill, interrupting whatever answer he could have rolled out.

Jill hugged herself tighter, her eyes skirting away from him and to Gallardo. "If you're done with me here, boss, then I'm going to stay with a friend."

Gallardo nodded. "The cops seem to be finishing up, and I certainly don't have anything else to ask tonight. I think staying with a friend is a wise idea." He grinned. "Unless you want to come hang out at my place with my wife and three kids?"

"Not a chance would I risk bringing anything like this to your family's doorstep."

His smile faded. "Good point." He clapped Mason on the shoulder. "At least I know you're safe with this guy. I assume he's who you're staying with?"

Jill chewed her lip.

Mason stepped into the breach. "And you know this because—?"

"We ruled you out as a suspect—for that matter, we ruled out a number of people on the base—because you weren't even in the country when some of these crimes occurred. Obviously you can't be in two places at once or jet back and forth in a couple of hours."

And just as Jill had her hold-back information, he had things that he couldn't discuss without breaking a half-dozen laws and landing himself in jail. Of course, he knew he was innocent, so it actually didn't matter that his alibi was bunk, since the new technology he worked on could have him around the world in a blink.

But what about other suspects they may have erroneously scratched off the list?

* * *

Lee watched Mason Randolph with Jill Walczak by the curb, cop cars strobing lights over the sleepy neighborhood. Enough people had poured out of their homes so that no one would notice her.

Just as she'd expected, they'd ended up back here and found her little "gift" in the garden. She'd walked around inside for a while, curious about why such a mousy woman caught Mason's eye, but there hadn't been anything extraordinary to offer insights. She'd considered burning the place down—she was an expert, after all, in how to rig electronics to explode and could have incinerated the place in a beautiful fire no one could have ever traced to arson. In the end, even as much as she enjoyed the heat and beauty of flames, she'd opted for a more subtle approach. The petty thief had been a surprise bonus. At least some of her plans were coming together well . . .

Mason and Jill had their heads close together with a new intimacy, gained from their lip-lock, no doubt. Would Jill go home with him?

Lee made a mental calculation of the odds and decided not. If nothing else, Mason wouldn't want her left alone tomorrow, and he had a flight. Most likely Jill would go hang out with that weird cop stepfather of hers. A logical assumption.

Lee took comfort in her ability to reason under stress. She was in control, damn it. She wasn't some stalker, camping out by her prey for hours while wearing adult diapers to keep watch. She reached for the ignition, confident events would continue to roll out as planned even after she left.

Jill and Mason were snagged in the web of attraction, and fighting it would only make things sweeter when Lee made her move. For now, they were putting together the clues she'd left for them. The game was more fun that way. Life was definitely getting more interesting tonight.

Lee put the car in drive, her hands trembling ever so slightly with excitement. If Mason was half as smart as he thought—and he must be to work the types of jobs he did—then he would figure out his connection to all the dead people. If only there was some way to watch the reaction to that revelation. But the signs would come soon enough. He would be in and out of briefings with local cops and security police on base. The people he cared about would have protection.

But "protection" only offered her more options. She could already see the way this would play out, given the research she'd done on Phillip Yost. She'd been denied the satisfaction of a blaze, but there were other ways to toy with people until the time was right to end the game. If her calculations were correct—and they always were—Jill would have a specially trained dog very soon.

And pets only provided Lee with another tool to punish the deserving.

ELEVEN

★ ──────────────────────────────

Rex Scanlon had a really bad feeling about this flight.

He set the hypersonic cargo jet on the release heading. The last time this had been attempted, things had gone way wrong, and Mason Randolph had almost died. Rex was going up with the crew this time in the pilot's seat, overseeing, hoping like hell he could prevent a repeat of the accident.

Vince "Vapor" Deluca was flying copilot beside him, while Smooth oversaw the back with Jimmy "Hotwire" Gage offering an extra set of hands and eyes in case things went to shit again.

Peering out of the windscreen, Rex marveled at how normal it looked from up high. You'd think going this fast would look different, but unless the plane was close to the ground for something to gauge off of visually, this was just like flying in an airliner. Too bad this wasn't a craft that needed a lot of stick and rudder from the pilots when it operated at hypervelocity. Computers and autopilots were required to keep such a fast-moving aircraft on the straight and level.

They were only a few days from unveiling this hypersonic jet to a select few in the international community. And one of those generals would have a particular Italian pop star on his arm during social hour.

He forced his hands to relax inside his gloves and glanced down at the time remaining on his center screen just as Smooth keyed the radio. "Sixty seconds to release."

Rex thumbed his own microphone to speak to the cargo deck. "Everything good in the back, Smooth?"

"Cargo in the green and ready to go. Of course, I thought that before."

"We're gonna stick to the script," Rex shot back. He knew this was a time for business, and they needed to stay focused. Especially for Smooth. His accident on the last flight could very well lead to mistakes on this one, unless he did this exactly as they planned and trained. "Ready for the doors?"

Smooth's voice came back all business this time, "Roger pilot, back end is up on one hundred percent oxygen, and you are cleared to open the doors."

Vapor punched a button on the screen, and the back hatch rumbled. He gave a thumbs-up and reported, "Doors show open, thirty seconds to release."

Rex acknowledged with two clicks of his mic and scanned to make sure they were on heading and on airspeed. He activated the radio. "Control, we are in the green and ready to release. Do we have a green range?"

The range controller answered, "Roger, green range, cleared to release."

Vapor began a countdown from ten seconds, toward release. ". . . three, two, one."

Rex had to force himself to breathe. No matter how many flights he logged in, he never lost sight of the fact that this could be his final one. How different this aircraft was from the ones he'd started flying twenty years prior. In the old days, they were all full of gauges, switches, blinking lights, and crappy seats that left you aching for days. This beast had only five computer screens and very few other instruments, although the seats didn't seem to have made it into twenty-first-century technology.

The radio clicked. His muscles tensed.

Smooth's voice came over calmly. "All pallets are gone. Release appeared normal. Cleared to close the doors."

Relief burned along his scalp inside his helmet. He would worry later about the fact that they still hadn't uncovered the near-fatal glitch from last time. Right now was about celebrating victory. Vapor punched a button, and the doors closed, leaving the aircraft silent.

Rex said, "All releases nominal. No problems."

Years had gone into working toward this moment. And he would have no choice but to rethink the final unveiling of the plan. Now he had to worry about people in his squadron who may or may not have been tied up in the current murder spree, since apparently the alibis some of his people had provided wouldn't hold up in reality because of the secrets inherent in their missions.

It appeared some of the alibis used could be false if the individuals had been deployed working on this aircraft. Their schedules had been kept hush-hush, even from family, so no one would know how quickly they'd traveled across oceans.

Thank God he'd tapped Mason to spend time with the camo cop. She seemed to have an inside track in this investigation. Lives depended on the secrecy of his job—but with a serial killer on the loose, lives were at stake in another arena as well. Choices were rarely clear-cut for him, but what a damn mess.

He couldn't imagine that any one of the men or women in uniform who worked for him could be responsible for those brutal killings, but bottom line, he couldn't risk it. He'd started clearing security channels just before takeoff. With luck, once he landed, he would have the okay to talk to authorities.

He couldn't reveal details of specific dates of test flights or travel schedules, but he could work with investigators to ensure everyone they'd cleared was in fact unavailable. Tricky, but doable.

One task at a time. For now, he had a flight to complete. He couldn't assume everything was flowers and rainbows just because the cargo drop had gone well. "All right, intrepid airmen, time to get this puppy on the ground. Smooth, is everything still good with you in the back?"

"Roger that, sir. Everything's tied down and ready to end this flight."

"Roger that. Vapor, get us clearance back to the field, and I will slow us down." Not an easy task in a plane that could go this fast. He pulled back the throttles while Vapor called for clearance.

"Control, we are slowing and requesting clearance direct to base."

"Roger, you are cleared to descend to flight level two-five-zero and turn right to zero-three-zero. We have some civilian traffic just north of the range that we need to let pass before you swing around. Why don't you strangle your lights for a couple of minutes?"

Vapor turned off their exterior lights. No need to have an airliner full of people see something whiz past their windows at Mach snot. Rex kept pulling back the throttles until they settled in at a very normal-looking 400 knots. He tapped Vapor and pointed at the airspeed on the screen.

Vapor nodded, his helmet freaking huge on the guy's big bald noggin, and keyed the microphone. "Control, we are at 400 knots and flight level two-five-zero."

"Roger that. Lights back on, and please squawk three-two-two-one."

Vapor's hands flew over the screen. "Lights configured and squawking three-two-two-one."

"Radar contact twenty miles north of the field, cleared straight in."

"Roger, that," Vapor answered. "Hey, Smooth, you certainly are doing a bang-up job at keeping a close-up eye on that camo cop. Anything we should know about, Romeo?"

Smooth keyed up. "And why should you know about it?"

Jimmy Gage chuckled over the airwaves. "Actually, our Smooth here has been going through a dry patch in the dating world. I just thought it was because of all the TDYs, but now that I think about it, he mentioned crossing paths with her in the mess hall. Maybe he's been waiting to make his move."

He dimly registered his crew bantering back and forth. It had been—what?—over a year since Heather died, since he was able to be a part of that easy conversation among a crew. The death of his wife hadn't just ripped his heart out, it had alienated him from these guys far more than the differences in rank ever could.

Rex lined up on the field and began to slow further. At 200 knots he called, "Flaps."

Vince moved a handle on the control panel and reported, "Flaps in transit."

Rex continued to slow, setting up for landing. At 180 knots he called, "Gear."

Vince moved another handle, and the gear settled down below the aircraft. "Down and locked, three green. So what was that about Smooth's declining love life?"

"Since you asked," Jimmy answered, "I can't recall him dating anyone since Erin Murphy."

Vince shook his head and whistled low. "God, that poor woman."

Smooth snorted. "Gee, thanks for the compliment, brother."

The airwaves went silent for a stretch of static before Rex asked, "You haven't heard about Ms. Murphy, have you? I can't believe the cops haven't questioned you, since you're in her recent past."

Smooth clicked his mic. "Sir, I'm getting a bad feeling here."

Vince shot a quick look at Rex before saying, "Smooth, prepare yourself. Erin Murphy is dead. She was killed outside her apartment."

Rex wished he wasn't stuck strapped in this seat unable to do a damn thing for Smooth. He understood full well that moment of crushing loss, the weight of knowing someone you'd cared about was gone forever. It had taken him a whole year for thoughts of his wife to recede enough where his knees didn't buckle out from under him every time he thought of her.

Silence popped and snapped over the airwaves again before Smooth answered. "Colonel," his voice thudded through, heavy and dark, "we need to talk."

* * *

Jill needed some answers.

Sitting at a stark table with six chairs, she looked around the vault room, underground at Nellis Air Force

Base, and figured she wasn't going to find any clues on the bare walls. She didn't know what to think of the turn of events.

Two hours ago, an official car from Nellis had pulled up at Uncle Phil's. A nondescript guy in a dark suit had flashed ID from the air force's Office of Special Investigations and informed her she needed to come with him. The brusque agent only said it had to do with the Killer Alien and that at this time, it was best not to speak with anyone else. Beyond that, he wouldn't answer anything, not even about the guy who'd broken into her place.

She'd freaked for a second, wondering if "suit guy" was the serial killer with forged credentials. But his partner driving the car had equally good credentials, and the vehicle bore an authentic government license plate. Just to test things, she'd insisted on bringing her work gun, and they hadn't argued. The whole encounter had been so surreal she could have half sworn she'd really been swept up into a sequel to *Men in Black* with two men in suits, one of whom could have been Will Smith's even hotter cousin.

Now, instead of researching crime data on the Internet over a bagel, she waited in the vault room with the OSI guy and his partner. At least he'd owned up to a name, Special Agent Barrera. But everything else apparently had to wait for the rest of his *guests*—

The vault door clicked, then hissed louder than the vent recycling air. Her stomach rumbled for food, the bagel long gone, and she hadn't eaten anything else in hours. Not to mention, it really sucked being dragged out in ripped jeans and a Hello Kitty T-shirt that was a hundred years old. God forbid she keep anything in her life that wasn't kick ass, or her rep as a tough girl would be shot for good. She would just have to brazen it out while displaying a bow-wearing cat on her chest.

The vault hinges gave an exaggerated groan that set her teeth on edge. If tentacles wrapped around that iron portal, she was feeding the darn thing Agent Barrera.

Mason walked in wearing his flight suit, followed by his squadron commander and her boss, Gallardo. Her eyes zipped back to Mason. He didn't have the same ready grin as the man she'd met back in sector two-five-zero that night he'd fallen out of the sky. His brows were drawn back in a grim, determined line. Still, she relaxed for the first time in two hours, seeing him.

Oh, right, and seeing her boss, too.

Agent Barrera slid slickly to his feet and gestured to the empty seats. "Thank you for joining us on such short notice, Miss Walczak. I believe you're already acquainted with Lieutenant Colonel Scanlon and Sergeant Randolph."

"Yes, sir. Has there been any word about the intruder you arrested in my home?"

"I'm sorry, ma'am." Barrera's deep brown eyes slid over her with a brief flash of compassion. The weary circles under his eyes were darker than his chocolate-brown skin and attested to how much overtime he'd put into this investigation. "We realize you've already had an upsetting couple of days. So far, it appears he's telling the truth. There's even footage from a security camera of him entering your place, and he didn't spend any time in your garden. Although oddly enough there is a patch of missing footage from before he arrived, like somebody messed with the tape. Looks like we have a techno-savvy villain on our hands."

Her garden, where she'd found the killer's alien-like signature she wasn't supposed to have told Mason about. She glanced at Gallardo for direction on what to say.

"They already knew about the dirt swirls. Their intelligence is in contact with local authorities. You were lucky this time, Walczak."

She relaxed a little, but not for long. Mason's tense shoulders broadcast that something bad was coming. When had she grown so attuned to nuances in his body language? Jeez, spend one night with a man wearing a hospital gown, and apparently she became an expert on him. And there had been that toe-curling lip-lock . . .

Agent Barrera leaned closer as if suddenly trying to make friends with her. "We believe we have uncovered the reason you were targeted."

She sat up straighter.

"Our link is thin"—Barrera paused, glancing at Mason then back—"but it appears all the victims had a connection to Sergeant Randolph."

A chill settled in her chest. "What's the connection?" she asked, looking at Mason.

"Connections, plural," Mason answered. "I didn't

put everything together until this morning when I heard another victim's name and realized I knew both people. In checking with Agent Barrera to confirm all the names, well, I knew all of them."

What a hellish realization that must have been for him. She was tortured over knowing Lara, only *one* of the murder victims. She couldn't imagine if five of her friends had been attacked so viciously. "How? When?"

"The woman who survived the attack, Annette Santos, worked in the same office with me two years ago. I heard that Annette was attacked a while back, but I didn't make the connection to the serial killer." His fists went white-knuckled. "The second victim, the first known to die, was Lara Restin, a nurse from the base hospital." He looked at Jill. "As you know, I dated her a couple of times."

Agent Barrera pulled a pencil and pad from inside his jacket, all PDAs and cell phones having been checked in before they entered the vault. "Why did the two of you break up?"

"Nothing traumatic. She decided after a couple of dates that it wasn't going anywhere for her, so she broke it off. I still can't believe—" He looked away, clearing his throat. "The third victim, Craig Walker, played intramurals with me, baseball, but not on the same team. Definitely a thin connection at best, since at some point I've played intramurals with nearly everyone on this base."

Scanlon nodded for the first time, his easy support

of his men obvious to her, even if she hadn't been privy
to all of the guy's words to Mason back in the medical
facility. "True enough. The same can be said for the
fourth person, Heidi Green, who worked at the base
barbershop. We all went there at some point."

Mason scrubbed a hand over his head, his hair
askew from what appeared to be helmet head. "Heidi
gave a great cut but never talked much. She wasn't
there when I went in last week, the day after I got back
from a TDY. I didn't ask."

Scanlon tapped beside Barrera's pad. "There was no
reason to assume anything other than it was her day
off. But now suddenly Jill Walczak has a suspicious
break-in with somebody leaving this signature mark
like the serial killer did. When Sergeant Randolph
pointed out the connection, we decided it was time to
inform the OSI."

Jill's mind raced with possibilities. She considered
the notion that they could be looking for a whacked-
out, jealous woman—a strong possibility, without question. Still, serial killers were almost always men, so
they needed to explore both sides of the gender issue.
"Could it be a boyfriend who got pissed off or a husband? Wasn't the fifth victim married?"

Mason's eyes were cool. "I don't date married
women. She and I saw each other before she hooked up
with him. We met when she worked in the commissary."

"Sorry, didn't mean to insult. What about some guy,
already unbalanced, who could have assumed his wife
was having an affair?"

Agent Barrera's eyes narrowed. While he kept his silence, he obviously wasn't missing a beat. Jill knew firsthand that sometimes people relayed more when you just let them talk.

Mason clasped his hands together so tightly his arms flexed and bulged inside his flight suit. "I don't know what the hell's going on, but I couldn't let you just wander around out there."

They'd been looking for the common link among the victims since they'd identified the similar killing pattern. A couple of them went to the same gym, but beyond that, they'd come up dry. Sometimes these sickos had the weirdest quirks that drew them to pick a particular victim. Trying to figure out why they'd targeted Mason could still be an impossible task unless she figured out how to think like a psychopath.

Scanlon filled in the heavy silence. "Up until Jill Walczak, the connections are so generally military-based, not focused on any one unit, we could have said they're connected just as strongly to me. Anybody I know could be next."

Gallardo opened his mouth for the first time. "I know this is frustrating. Walczak and I have felt the frustrations of the military and civilian community since our job seems to give us a foot in both worlds. But the good news is we have a real lead on this guy now, one we hadn't foreseen."

Barrera tapped his pencil on the table for emphasis or attention, but either way, it drew all eyes toward him. "Our people are refining his profile every day.

Each new crime paints a more precise picture."

Gallardo leaned in. "And each crime brings him closer."

Jill had worked with her boss too long not to recognize the glint in his eyes, the hard determination and the absolute commitment to law enforcement, whether he worked on the police force or contracted for special duties in Area 51.

Gallardo gripped the edge of the table. "With luck and a little prodding, maybe this sick bastard will try to get Walczak again."

TWELVE

What the hell?

Mason bit back the words. Shouting wouldn't go over well with this vault crowd. It was one thing to be cool about Jill staying behind a concrete barrier in a parking lot to avoid runaway cars. It was another thing altogether to stand by while someone used her as bait for a serial killer.

There had to be another way. He searched for the right argument, any way to jump-start the discussion to a different direction—

"Gallardo," Lieutenant Colonel Scanlon leaned forward, "I have another bit of information to add."

Thank God. Having the boss chime in would add oomph to the argument, a good thing, since Jill would likely be the toughest to convince to back down. "Please, go ahead, sir."

"I'm not so sure this guy is going after Smooth's friends. All five of these people had a beef against you, not with any great cause that I could see, but a couple of them took it to an extreme."

Jill bristled visibly.

Mason couldn't blame her. That wasn't where he'd seen this going at all, and he wasn't sure he even agreed. "I would say that's more than a little harsh, especially considering they're dead."

"Now isn't the time for their glowing eulogies. Their mamas and daddies aren't around." Scanlon turned in his seat to face Mason full-on. "Annette Santos insisted you stole a promotion from her. Rumor had it around the squadron that Lara Restin broke it off with you because you didn't ask her to marry you by the second date, and then she stalked your every move for two months afterward."

Jill sat up straighter, her face devoid of all emotion, too much so. He hated like hell that she had to hear something so derogatory about her dead friend.

Barrera quirked a thick eyebrow. "I take it we can put that one in the hate column."

Scanlon nodded. "Now, it was no secret that Craig Walker disliked you. He couldn't stand the way you always got the best of him on the ball field. Remember the time he was pitching, and he clocked you upside the batter's helmet?"

"That's just sports, sir, nothing personal."

"There you're wrong, Sergeant. It was definitely

personal to this guy who had a serious Napoleon complex. To him, you were Waterloo."

Barrera tapped his notepad. "The barber—Heidi Green—was rumored to have disliked everyone. What made Sergeant Randolph different?"

"When Mason came in, he talked a lot." Scanlon looked back to Mason. "She cut your hair faster to get you and your conversation out of the chair quicker."

He scratched his forehead right at his cowlick, a nervous tic. Damn it. He crossed his arms over his chest. "Have I been walking around in a freaking bubble?"

Scanlon pulled off his dark-framed glasses with a heavy sigh. "No, Sergeant, you're just a genuinely nice guy."

"What about Erin Murphy? She and I were friends a while back."

"Friends? She told it differently."

"According to squadron gossip again?"

Scanlon put his glasses back on. "As a squadron commander, it's my job to keep my ear to the ground. Her husband works over in the base fire department. Word has it there was trouble in their marriage, and he blames it on her feelings for you."

Barrera jotted a notation.

Jill cleared her throat. "I knew Lara Restin. We met in the mess hall a few times when I pulled shifts out here."

That made sense. Lara had participated when some

of the exercises out in the field required a nurse on hand. Mason shifted his attention back to Jill's explanation.

"We became friends, hung out when we were at loose ends, shared the occasional pint of ice cream when we needed to vent." Jill looked at Mason, unsmiling. "She really did hate you, like he said."

"I take it that means she shared my more negative qualities with you."

She winced. "In detail."

"Great." That explained how hostile she'd been when they'd first met.

"But Mason was out of the country when a couple of them died. We already figured that much out. Not to mention you were both in quarantine when the fifth victim was killed. So you have a rock-solid alibi."

His chair got all the more uncomfortable, but this was Scanlon's call to make on what could be shared about their test project.

The investigator tapped his pen end on end. "You could have hired someone."

Mason shoved back his chair an inch, needing breathing space, ironic while locked in this tightly closed room with no escape. He'd never been a fan of round robin discussions of his flaws, a family-preferred format for years. Hell, he'd enlisted in the air force partly just to ensure a fair fight of future enemies. "Sure, as could a lot of people, but I did not kill these people."

"Of course you didn't." Jill leaned on her elbows,

her face intense in his defense. "And Mason also doesn't have the money to hire that kind of hit."

Mason had to be honest. "I used to, though."

Scanlon swept off his glasses again. "Are you trying to land in jail?"

They would find out anyway once they looked into his past. Scanlon would already know, since he'd seen his file, complete with background checks. "My family is loaded, but I don't have any of their money. I live off what I earn."

Barrera closed up his pad and slid it back into his jacket. "Thanks for the heads-up. We'll look into your family's finances, and yours, of course, if you have no objection."

It wouldn't matter if he did. Yet again, he was glad he'd never taken a penny from his parents since he'd walked out their front door with his new bride. "Go ahead and look."

Barrera smiled for the first time, and damned if it didn't seem genuine. "It's just a formality, since you already have an alibi."

Ah hell.

Scanlon scooted his chair back, his face resolute. "Let's assume for a moment that there was a plane about to be unveiled next week that could travel fast enough to bust those alibis."

* * *

Rex pulled off his glasses and sagged behind his office desk. Talk about a shit day. He'd been so focused on the flight, he'd been completely blindsided by the whole serial killer issue. He pitched his glasses on his desk beside a stack of performance reports waiting to be reviewed.

Thank heaven he'd gotten the clearance to tell the basics about the hypersonic jet to a select few investigators. Hell, more was actually out there on the Internet, hypothesized in articles written by unofficial sources. Still, it rankled having to reveal even part of the project ahead of schedule.

Bottom line, lives wouldn't be lost by telling a couple of investigators four days early. But lives could be lost by holding back information that could be vital. He'd paired up the cops' time lines with the TDY schedules on the three dozen people who'd worked on the craft, including flying in the cargo hold and running maintenance. At least Mason Randolph could be officially crossed off the list, since he actually had been out of the country, incontrovertibly, when two of the attacks occurred.

So far there were three who could use another look, but his gut told him they were as honest as they appeared. Except in this case, it wasn't up to just his gut. It was in Barrera's investigative hands.

So why not go home?

Because his gut was also still kicking up a storm over one simple second during the interview in the vault. He couldn't stop thinking about when he'd offhandedly said the link to Randolph was so flimsy the people—the next victim—could be tied to others on the base, including him. An image of Livia Cicero had flashed to mind, hard and fast and as vivid as the woman herself.

He pulled out his cell phone. He'd tucked Mason and the lady camo cop in the distinguished visitors' quarters on base, rooms reserved for visiting colonels and generals. Not your typical Residence Inn sort of setup, but more of a luxury apartment with the added protection of being within the protective walls of a military base. The rooms would be secure and not a place someone would look for a sergeant since the particular space was reserved for senior officer members. He'd even had one of his people round up a change of clothes for both of them.

He could see the wisdom behind Barrera's idea to use the two of them as bait when the time was right. Randolph and Walczak were both trained and hired to protect. But damned if Rex would give his thumbs-up to some half-cocked scheme.

Thank goodness Barrera and Gallardo had seen the wisdom of taking the time to devise a solid plan. This could be their one shot to catch this killer. Meanwhile, Randolph and his new girlfriend would stay tucked safely away.

Once he'd seen to that, he'd run a call-out to check on everyone in the squadron, under the guise of a practice run so as not to arouse any suspicions. Everyone was safe and accounted for. His thumb stroked over the keys. Almost everyone. Why not check on Livia? He had nothing to lose by calling and a helluva lot to regret if something happened to her.

He dialed the number he'd programmed into memory back during a trip to Turkey when he'd been in charge of keeping up with the Italian diva. While the phone connected, he creaked back in his chair, surrounded by walls packed with hangings. His diploma from Virginia Military Institute was framed, along with going away gifts from eight bases, usually a sketch of the plane with a squadron patch, the matting signed by people he'd worked with. Could this be his last base? The last place to add to his wall collection?

The phone rang for the fourth time, and he started to disconnect, reconsidering—

"Hello?" a groggy voice answered, a husky female voice with a distinctive accent.

"Sorry. I didn't mean to wake you up." His eyes fell to the sofa where he napped with a pillow from his Virginia Military Institute alma mater. He'd caught a lot of ribbing down the years over the kangaroo mascot, but his boys had enjoyed playing with it every time they'd come to visit. Heather had brought them up often, along with supper when he'd worked late. More often than not. How well would he have known his boys if she hadn't made that effort for him?

"This is Rex Scanlon," he added belatedly.

"I know your voice." A mattress creaked through his earpiece, spiking his pulse rate. "I wasn't sleeping that deeply. I have trouble making the time zone adjustment. Now that you called, I'm not restless and bored."

"We certainly wouldn't want you to be bored."

"Oh, Colonel," she tut-tutted. "Why did you call me if you are just going to be grumpy?"

He spun his glasses around on his desk and thought of the time in Turkey when Livia Cicero had boldly asked him if he'd ever considered wearing contact lenses—or at least new frames. "I, uh, wanted to make sure you're all right."

"I could use a decaf double latte, but other than that, I am much the same as I always am."

Time to stop toying around. He nudged his glasses aside. "There's a serial killer on the loose."

Her sigh shuddered through the phone. "That's horrible, but you already told me that when I came by your home."

"He struck again." Thank God Randolph had been with Jill Walczak.

"Dio mio!" Any flirtatiousness evaporated from her voice. "That poor, poor person."

"No one died this time, thank God, but there's evidence it's the guy." He traced the folder Barrera had given him. "I wanted to make sure you're on alert."

"Because I am so reckless about my safety?"

"Because I was worried about you, damn it," he blurted, then winced at how loudly he'd spoken. At least he'd closed his door, even though there were only a couple of diehards in the squadron this late.

"Ah, you are grumpy when you care."

He winced again. There shouldn't be anything wrong with caring about people. Rex adjusted the cube photo holder on his desk. Images of his sons growing up filled the six blocks, the last one taken two years ago when they'd learned to ski. They'd sent the framed cube for his Christmas gift, telling him they hoped he was ready to have family pictures in his workspace again.

His boys didn't look that much younger than Livia. "Maybe you should hang out at Chuck Tanaka's."

She went silent.

Suspicion nipped. "What? Is he there now?" He closed his eyes, embarrassed as hell. "Sorry to have bothered—"

"No one is here," she spoke quickly, as if she genuinely cared that he was an instant away from hanging up. "He is busy with his new girlfriend and his physical therapy. I am completely alone in my hotel suite."

Now there was an image he didn't need. "Is your door locked?"

"Locked, bolted, and chained." Her voice went soft. "I didn't come here just to see Chuck."

"That's right. You're accompanying your family friend to the gathering next week." Hey, wait. Chuck had a girlfriend? Rex focused on Livia's voice.

"Again, the general is not my main reason for being here, although it gives me a convenient excuse so I do not feel like an idiot if other plans do not work."

This woman's convoluted conversation was giving him a headache on a day that prompted the headache to end all. "What other plans?"

"I was hoping that you and I could go on a date."

The phone almost slipped from his hand. "You're joking."

"Not a very nice thing to say when I put my emotions on my shirt cuff, Colonel."

"Shirt sleeve," he corrected, delaying, damn it.

"Thank you, but I believe you understand my meaning. And your answer?"

She was dismantling his walls fast, but defense was his specialty. "You're only interested in me because you think you can't have me."

"If that is true, then your best way to get rid of me is to accept my offer for a date."

He laughed, brief and hoarse from lack of practice. Who could defend against a sense of humor? "You have some twisted logic."

"What's your answer?" A hint of vulnerability slipped into her tone. Accidental or a deliberate ploy to sway him?

Either way, it worked. And there was one way to make sure the woman stayed safe. "I have a full day at work tomorrow, but I can pick you up at six."

"Oh, that's perfect. I don't eat supper until later anyway."

"Six in the *morning*, for *breakfast*. Take it or leave it." His invitation was so rude, even he was ashamed. But not embarrassed enough to say anything more.

This was about keeping her safe, then scaring her off. Nothing more.

Her husky laugh mocked him, utterly feminine and knowing. "It's a date."

* * *

What a bizarre date with Mason.

Jill curled up on the sofa in the temporary quarters at Nellis Air Force Base where they'd been sequestered for safety, a guard dog from Uncle Phil curled up at her feet. He'd insisted on the extra protection and refused to let her tell him anything about her plans. He'd said it was safer that way in case any aliens were in search of her location to take them up to their mother ship.

The two-year-old Rottweiler-mystery mix stirred under her hand as she patted his head. He sniffed the air, checking from side to side before he settled his muzzle on his paws again with a huff.

Jill looked through the open archway into the kitchen, where Mason stood at the microwave in his flight suit and socks. "I can't believe you got them to agree to having a dog in here."

"I didn't tell anyone."

"Can't you get in trouble for that?"

"I could, but it's not like our names are even on the registration, and we hung the sign out there for no maid service."

The place looked nice, a fully decked-out three-bedroom apartment designated for visiting colonels and generals. Sure, it wasn't the Ritz, but it had some pretty colonial-looking pieces of furniture in a dark cherry-wood. Definitely a step up from the industrial furnishings she'd come to expect in any government-funded building. "As long as you're certain."

And as long as they were safe. No one but the OSI and his boss knew where they were. They had a guard and watchdog. She had to admit, it chafed being protected rather than providing that security. She'd always imagined herself as the one dispensing justice with her service revolver in hand and a knee in the guy's back. She'd never pictured herself as the helpless bait trotted out to tempt a psychotic murderer.

Although she had to admit, she was starting to get a feel for the "helpless" thing as her eyes wandered over Mason's shoulders encased in his flight suit. The magnetic pull of the man was going to be hard to resist when they were, in a sense, quarantined together all over again.

The microwave dinged and he pulled out two blue ceramic mugs. "You assured me the dog is well-trained. I hope you weren't lying."

"Rottweilers get a bad rap because they look so scary people have used them as guard dogs—some have even abused their strength and used them as attack dogs." She stroked her canine protector's silky ears. "But they can be very loyal friends. They're also very smart and trainable in the right hands."

Mason opened a dark wood cabinet, appearing totally at ease in the kitchen, a charming dichotomy as testosterone oozed from his flight suit–clad body. "I assume Uncle Phil had the right hands?"

"He worked with him from the time he was a puppy. I named him Boo because of how his brown and black markings make a little mask."

"I'm sure a badass like him appreciates the cutesy name." He stirred one mug, then the other.

"Yeah, yeah, whatever." She hooked her arm around the dog's neck and nuzzled his shiny fur, sneaking a peek at Mason's lean legs showcased in the long lines of his flight suit. "From what your boss said earlier, it sounds like you're not flying until they have some answers on the serial killer."

He set both mugs on a teakwood tray. "That's my decision, too. I can't leave you here to face this alone, not when it's my fault the guy's tracking you in the first place." He plucked a rose from the welcome vase and placed it on the tray alongside their drinks. "If I thought staying away from you would help . . ."

She couldn't resist being tugged by his need to keep her safe, even how he seemed to blame himself. She couldn't let him shoulder it all, even putting himself at risk.

"I understand your need to protect, but don't forget to watch your back." The dog lifted his head as if sensing the tension in her voice, and she forced herself to relax. "If this guy is targeting you through these people, it won't be long before he comes after you. Psychopaths like this can't ever fully satisfy that twisted hunger inside themselves. That's why the violence and the frequency ramps up. Eventually he will turn his attention to you."

"You're a ray of sunshine." He padded toward her, his feet in socks making only soft thuds on the carpet, and placed the tray of mugs on the coffee table in front of her. "Maybe this will cheer you up."

He passed her a mug, their fingers brushing.

She inhaled the steam to steady her pulse, smelling tea and raspberry, then tasting. Perfect. "This is awesome. It's just what I needed."

"I thought you might like it." He sat beside her, reaching past her to rub the dog's nose, his arm warm against her leg.

"How did you know?" She blew into the mug and sipped.

"You have a teacup collection."

How sweetly observant of him, especially in the middle of such chaos during the break-in at her place. Although he didn't have to sound so surprised. What had he expected? A gun collection? "I may be a cop, but I'm still a woman."

He slid his arm across the back of the overstuffed sofa. "Believe me, I noticed."

There hadn't been a second to breathe since the break-in, much less think about where the kiss they'd shared might be going. Already the attraction simmered to life again, and right now, in this pocket of time, she had the luxury of seeing where she wanted it to go. She just needed some kind of sign.

She traced the rim of the mug, the heat steaming from inside nothing compared to the temperature spreading through her at his simple touch. "I never intended to start a collection, but I got a cup and saucer from my grandmother. It looked so lonely all by itself, so I bought one that seemed to go with it, and then another." She shrugged, which only served to rub her shoulder against his hand. "The next thing I knew, I had to buy a curio cabinet to display them."

"Keeping that cup is an awesome way to remember her."

"I like to think so. My grandmother didn't own much. She was a single mom back in the days when there wasn't much in the way of support and understanding. She was widowed young with three kids and precious little money, but she took care of what she had, cherishing that one lovely teacup and drinking her tea out of it every afternoon to keep the tradition of her own English grandmother alive." The heat of the mug between her hands warmed her as did the memory. "She put out biscuits instead of scones, but it was an event nonetheless."

She blinked back sentimental tears. The whole roller-coaster day was pitching her emotions left and right without relief. "Okay, enough about me. Tell me something about yourself."

His green eyes turned somber. "I was married."

Married? But even more important . . . "Was?"

"I'm divorced."

"You'd damn well better not be married, given the

way you kissed me." Her attempt at humor went flat.
Some things were too serious to joke about. There
wasn't anything funny about finding out if he was still
carrying around baggage from his ex, not to mention
that this completely shifted the way she'd viewed him
as a no-commitment bachelor. "How long have you
been divorced?"

"We were married at eighteen, split up by twenty-
one."

"That's young." For him to commit so early went
against every playboy image of him she'd imagined.
"Really young." And what about his ex-wife? What
kind of woman was she? Curiosity bit deep and hard.

"That's what my parents said. They didn't approve."
His mouth went tight, his voice hard. "We told them to
shove it, so they laid down an ultimatum. If we got
married, we were cut off. So I left home and enlisted in
the air force."

Things he'd said came together in her mind. "That's
what you meant earlier when you were talking about
growing up rich."

"I said my family was well off. Not me. I live on a
tech sergeant's paycheck."

"None of your parents' money comes to you?"

"I didn't earn it, so why the hell would I want it?"
He said it so simply, a man with a strong work ethic
and sense of honor.

"I'm impressed." And she was. Truly.

A one-sided smile tugged at his mouth with a wry—
but appealing—self-awareness. "Before you give me

too much credit, back when I decided to leave, I sure did want to keep the sports car. But, well, ultimatums rarely work well with eighteen-year-olds."

He downplayed it all, but she could fill in the blanks well enough. He'd made a difficult choice when his parents tried to manipulate him with money.

"Why did they object to your fiancée?" She couldn't help being curious and a little jealous of this woman who'd snagged Mason's heart.

"They wanted me to go to medical school."

"Ah, now I get your fascination with otoscopes back when we were quarantined at the hospital."

"You're observant. And yes, Dad was teaching me the names of medical equipment along with my colors and shapes." His brief smile faded. "They thought she was after their money, but Kim didn't give a damn about money. She did care about spending more than a week out of every month with her husband. At least she left before we could start a family. She said she wanted kids who would recognize their father as more than a telephone daddy."

"How sad for all of you." She hitched her feet up onto the sofa and hugged her knees. She could understand both of their sides, and that made things a helluva lot tougher than if she could have just labeled this Kim a bitch. And a total bitch would have been easier for Mason to get over.

Damn. Jealousy had deeper fangs than curiosity.

He wove a strand of her hair between his fingers, tickling the end along her neck, the light touch mirroring the surprising way he gave her space, never pushy in the brash player fashion she'd expected. Her nerves tingled in response, leaving her hungry for more.

"On the plus side," Mason said, "I never would have thought to join the military otherwise, and I would have missed out big time. This is what I'm called to do."

His focus, his drive impressed her. *This*, she understood, and in that moment she felt connected with him in a way other than the undeniable sexual pull.

She rested her chin on her knees, flexing her toes in her sock feet and hugging her knees tighter in counter-pressure against the ache building in her breasts. "Have you ever regretted not going to college?"

"You're making assumptions in thinking only officers have a degree. I paid for college myself and completed the coursework through an online program. I was on the road too much to enroll in as a resident student."

"Oh, I'm sorry for assuming." Her hand fell to rest on his leg, instinctively reaching out in her apology. Their eyes met. She carefully slid her hand away. "What did you study?"

"Restaurant management," he answered. He grinned at her obvious surprise. "It seemed a good way of combining my cooking obsession with something potentially marketable if this air force gig doesn't play out."

Now, that really surprised her. "I know you choose unusual foods, but why the passion for cooking?"

He stared into his own mug for a pensive moment. "I grew up with a first-rate chef and ate at the best of restaurants. When I left home, my budget couldn't support those kinds of tastes, but I missed the food." He lifted his mug in a toast. "So I figured out how to take care of my own palate."

His no-whining, fix-his-own-problems approach appealed to her, definitely different from what she would have expected from him. "My frugal grandmother most definitely would have approved."

"High praise indeed."

Another thought niggled at her. "Are you planning to get out of the service?"

"Not in the next twenty years or so, if I can help it. But things happen. People get hurt."

His face went so dark she searched for something, anything to say to steer the conversation back to lighter territory. "Restaurant management, huh?" She leaned forward to set her mug back on the tray and picked up the rose. "I thought all you fliers were some kind of engineers or math majors."

"You would be surprised. We're a mighty diverse group. I knew a guy who majored in opera."

"Then why not be an opera singer?" She swirled the flower through the air with a theatrical flourish.

"The call to serve is louder."

"What called *you* to protect and serve?"

"Initially it was all about the need to support my new wife at eighteen years old. Then I deployed overseas to help out with earthquake relief." His fingers slid from her hair to cup her neck, massaging gently, seductively.

She struggled to focus on his words, but his fingers melted her knotted muscles. The flower dangled between her suddenly weak fingers.

"Growing up, I prided myself on being down-to-earth in spite of all my parents' money. I considered myself quite enlightened for thumbing my nose at it all to join up. But until I saw firsthand how totally stripped bare a person could be of everything in a fluke of nature . . . I was on a cargo plane delivering fresh water and food, just the basics, but I knew. I'd found my calling."

She leaned into him. "How does that work with what you do now?"

"I'm figuring out more efficient ways to help and protect." He smiled wickedly. "And I have to confess, the toys totally rock."

"That plane your boss talked about, the one that can travel around the world in a few hours, sounds amazing."

His fingers slowed, and his eyes took on a faraway look. "You have no idea."

"Hey," she tapped him on the chest with the rose, "I'm sorry you're not flying with your crew because of me."

His gaze came back to her, hooked, and held. "I'm where I want to be."

Desire, need, and a deep, deep ache threaded through her with tenacious roots. She couldn't fight any longer. She wanted Mason. He wanted her.

She and Mason had a window of time here—and too

many hours on their hands. And if this were all Jill had with Mason, she wouldn't overlook the gift of this man in her life tonight.

She knew a damn good way to pass those hours.

Jill stood, twirling the rose between her fingers. "This is where you want to be? That's interesting, because I'm thinking there's an even better place where we could be together."

His pupils widened. "And where would that be?"

She tore a petal off the rose, dropped it at his feet, and backed away. She tossed a second petal to the floor, inching farther away. "Follow me and find out."

THIRTEEN

Mason stared at the rose petal on his foot, the next on the carpet, another falling from Jill's fingertips as she backed deeper into their temporary lodgings on base. He indulged in a slow gaze up the luscious body of the woman plucking the next tempting marker for the trail leading him to her.

As if he needed a map.

Her ankle boots had him aching to take them off and stroke the sensitive arches of her feet she'd kept so well hidden. Just seeing those boots turned him inside out thinking about her heavier work boots. There was something infinitely sexy about a lady with lush curves who could kick serious ass.

He appreciated the way she could take care of herself while never sacrificing her femininity. She may have confessed some of her childhood vulnerabilities to him, but she'd most definitely grown into a strong and confident woman.

He enjoyed the view, without question. But he'd shared some heavy stuff with her, too. No one else here knew about his failed marriage, beyond those who were privy to a peek at his security file. Yet, for some reason, he'd told Jill things he'd never shared with friends he'd gone to war with.

She'd triggered something inside him he wasn't sure he understood yet. He didn't know whether she was feeling the same thing, but there was no mistaking the desire in her eyes or the determination.

Okay, then. He knelt to pick up the flower petals she'd dropped. "Lead, and I will most definitely follow you."

And when they got there, her form-skimming jeans were going to be history.

She backed up a step and let another petal flutter from her fingertips. He advanced. She tore another and another, moving closer to the master bedroom dimly lit by the lamps on both nightstands. The king-sized bed sprawled invitingly behind her. Honest to God, he couldn't see much else other than her as he walked past each fragrant marker.

Mason shut the bedroom door, leaving the dog keeping watch by the only entrance, and closing himself into the master suite of the base quarters with Jill. She continued her tempting trail past the TV armoire they most definitely would not be using. Her knees bumped the back of the tightly made bed.

Her legs folded, and she dropped to sit on the edge of the mattress. She pitched all that remained of the tiny bud over her shoulder. The expanse of paisley comforter spread behind her, lamps on low, with a small welcome basket of nighttime snacks—for later.

Much later.

He stopped, standing between her knees. "I didn't expect this with you."

"You don't have to dredge up a load of romantic bs for me." She leaned back on her elbows. "I don't want that from you."

He gathered up a handful of petals and sprinkled them along her chest, down her stomach, and lower into her lap. "Are you questioning my sincerity?"

She flicked her hair back. "No, I think you're just trying to give me what you think I want or need."

Her words hurt, damn it. "If you believe I'm such a bullshit artist, why do you want to sleep with me?"

"I want this—you—very much." She sat up and crossed her legs. She rasped her fingernail up his flight suit zipper, flicking the tab at the top up and down provocatively. "I just want to make sure we're on the same page."

"I can't tell for sure if we're even in the same library, because you confuse the hell out of me." He threaded his fingers through the sensuous glide of her hair.

She tucked her cheek against his palm, her lashes

fluttering closed for a second. "I don't want you to see me as one of those idiot women who turns all giggly when you walk by."

"Giggly is the last word I would ever use to describe you." He combed his fingers through her shoulder-length of hair, hands falling to rest on her shoulders. "That's meant as a compliment, in case you were wondering."

"I was, actually." Her chest rose and fell faster, her pupils dilating. "Wondering, I mean."

"Good. Then maybe we're both at least in the same novel if not on the same page yet."

Her gaze fell to his mouth.

He retrieved the stem from the bed and trailed the small remaining bud along her lips. "Maybe I should be worried about your expectations of me. Are you here for some kind of super sex? Because if so, I'm afraid this reputation you seem to think I have may leave you sorely disappointed. I'm a regular man who's not into acrobatics or kink."

"What *are* you into?"

He was more interested in her preference. Although he sincerely hoped it had nothing to do with turning off the lights, because he was enjoying the hell out of the warm glow from the lamp on low by the bed, showcasing Jill's curves as well as the flare of desire in her eyes. He intended to use those expressive eyes to gauge just what sent her higher.

"Right now," he teased the rose along her cheek, releasing more of the floral perfume, "I'm big time into you."

"Now that was totally the right thing to say." She took the flower from him and pitched it away.

He cupped her face and kissed her long and deep and exploring, sitting beside her on the rough tapestry comforter. He reached behind her and swept the spread away until it trailed the floor, leaving crisp sheets and fluffy pillows.

She smiled her appreciation against his mouth. She tasted like raspberry tea with a hint of mint from her toothpaste, and he wanted more. Without breaking contact, she eased back on the bed, her head settling to rest on the plump pillows, wafting the scent of fabric softener—his new favorite erotic smell, right up there with roses.

He almost groaned his relief at finally being able to stretch over her, their bodies crushing petals, releasing a fresh swell of perfume. Feeling the way their bodies fit together in a preshow of things to come. Her foot skimmed down his calf and up again, ramping up his desire.

Tunneling his hands deeper into her hair, he nipped along her lower lip. "You're so beautiful. I can't even tell you how many times I've watched the light play off your red hair and fantasized about taking it down. Seeing it against the pillow is definitely fantasy worthy."

She laughed against his mouth, husky and low. "It can't have been that many times, given it's been less than a week since you parachuted into the desert."

He levered up on his elbow. "I'll make a deal with you. How about we both toss away preconceptions about each other?"

"That sounds like an excellent idea." She tugged him closer again insistently. "What were you saying before my insecurities interrupted?"

"I was telling you how beautiful you are"—he kissed her mouth—"how sexy you are"—he kissed her jaw—"how much looking at your long legs turns me on." He sketched a hand over her hip and down her thigh.

"Clothes," she whispered, her voice husky with passion, "we have too many clothes on. I want to see more of you."

"I'm not going to argue with you over that." He scrunched her shirt in his fingers.

She swept aside his hands and tossed aside her own shirt to rest by a stray rose petal. "Time for you to stand up."

Her words took a few seconds to sink in, since he couldn't process more than the sight of the creamy swell of her breasts in her copper-colored lace bra. Then his brain kicked into high gear. Getting both of them naked soon took top priority.

"Damn, you're bossy." He held up his hands. "But hey, I'm not one to argue with a chick who carries her own gun. Although I wouldn't object if you put it on the bedside table."

He stood, and she pulled her gun from the holster clipped to her jeans waistband. She passed him the

9 mm, a sign he understood full well was her way of displaying her trust—here in the bedroom anyway. He set the weapon on the end table. She stayed back on her pillow, reaching to tease at the tab of the long zipper that extended down the front of his flight suit.

He folded his hand over hers, and she sat up, swinging her legs to either side of him. She inched the zipper down, inch by torturous inch. The woman was a helluva temptress. She pushed the uniform over his shoulders until it bunched around his waist, taking her sweet time as her hands teased over his T-shirt before finally sweeping it over his head. With a sassy flick of her wrist, she sent it sailing. He kicked away his flight suit, leaving him only in his boxer shorts.

"Valentine's Day underwear. You wore cupids in the desert." She teased her finger along the waistband. "Conversation candy heart designs this time. Hmmm . . . *All-star. Loverboy. Awesome.*"

His stomach muscles went taut against the taunting tease of her caress so damn near where he needed her to touch. "Can we read my underwear after?"

"Of course, *Loverboy,*" she teased. Jill rose to her feet, her wrists draping over his shoulders. "Do you celebrate all holidays this way or just the lovers' day?"

"Guess you'll have to stick around long enough to see my bunny rabbit boxers this spring."

He made fast work of her jeans, all the faster as she shimmied the denim down and away. He kissed her again, and the next thing he knew, finally, finally they were naked. Her skin was smoother and softer against him than he could have imagined, made all the sweeter by the tantalizing way she arched closer, her curves imprinting themselves on him as fully as in his memory.

Angling back, he lowered her to the bed in a controlled glide, a whole lot more controlled than he felt inside. In fact, before he lost what little ability he had left to reason, he needed to take care of . . .

"Birth control. In my flight suit." He reached down to the floor. "I'll be back before you can . . ." He slid over her again, small packet in hand. ". . . before you can miss me."

"Hmmm . . ." She nipped his ear, stole the condom, caressed it in place until his head fell to rest by her ear with a groan.

Drawing in a ragged breath to steady his control, he kissed along her shoulder, lower, lower still, until he drew her nipple into his mouth and rolled the tip with his tongue. She grew tighter in his mouth, her fingers digging into his back until he could feel the pierce of close-clipped nails leaving little half-moons.

He touched her, just touched and stroked and fell into the sensation of learning everything about her, her feel, her taste. Best of all, her wants. Part of him wanted to rush, to be inside her now, but another, stronger part of him needed to make the most of this night.

From the start, Jill had made it clear he wasn't her

sort of guy, so he might well not have another chance. Although he would be doing his damnedest tonight to persuade her to show up for an encore.

He'd meant it when he said he hadn't expected this with Jill, and he damn well wasn't squandering a second of his time with her. And afterward? They'd both come so close to death over the past few days, living in the now seemed the wisest course.

He eased his mouth away and kissed along her chest, charting his way.

Her hands played along his back. "What are you doing?"

"Playing connect the freckles, my new favorite game."

"I think," she gasped, "that I like this game a lot."

"You only think? I'll have to work harder then."

Her hand tucked between them, and she stroked him. "I don't think you can get any harder than this."

His eyes slid closed, and she caressed again. His forehead fell to rest against hers, and his hands shook as he swept back her hair. Her fingers climbed around to grip his hips. He positioned himself over her, against her, nudging. Her nails dug in deeper, sinking into his flesh, urging him deeper as she bowed up. He thrust inside and damn near came apart like an untried teen. He clenched his jaw and held back, held still, held himself in check until he could hold her again.

And then he moved, and she moaned, moving with

him. Her legs locked around him, lean and toned, holding strong in the moment. He couldn't stop taking in everything about her—her sighs of pleasure, the way her jaw tensed and she bit the tip of her tongue.

He tamped down his release, determined to make this last as long as possible—or at least until she finished first. Something that seemed increasingly imminent if her breathy gasps and soft, writhing body were anything to judge by.

Her orgasm pulsed around him, massaging him over the edge. He drove into her body, taking her as high as he could until they both shuddered against each other in the after-waves.

Mason slid from her body and rolled to his back. His head dug back into his pillow, his chest heaving for air. He inched one hand over to brush his knuckles across her hand, about all the movement he could muster for the moment.

He damn well hadn't expected this with her, and no way could he have seen how being with her would rock him on some level he'd never felt before. He'd never been so into the moment, into this particular woman. Already he wanted to have her again, to learn what made her tick and deliver it right to her doorstep.

But he couldn't escape the sneaking sensation, the question of what could this strong, intensely confident—and competent—woman ever need from him?

* * *

Sitting on the counter in the kitchenette while Mason made breakfast, Jill needed space. Soon.

However, space was in short supply while locked up in a little condo on base with a watchdog and the hottest man she'd ever met. Of course, he was the very reason she needed breathing room. She'd been with men before—not a lot by most measures, but enough to know that something different had happened last night. Mason was different.

She wrapped the sheet closer around herself, tucking it tighter under her arms. The scent of roses clung to her "sarong," reminding her of how long they'd rolled together in those petals while they'd loved each other with their bodies, their mouths, even their eyes.

Never had she been with a man who was so completely and totally focused on *her*. He'd said he wasn't into toys or gymnastics, and he didn't need to be. The man's total and undivided attention provided enough stimulation to send any woman into orbit with a pleasure so intense she'd forgotten to breathe.

Sex was about the physical and the mind stroking. And without a question, Mason's mind, his attention, his focus had caressed every inch of her, inside and out.

Was it this way for him every time? If so, no wonder he had women falling at his feet.

His currently bare feet. He stood at the stove in his jeans only, with the top button undone. His buffed chest rippled as he shuffled pans and ingredients in his breakfast prep, making the most of the basic food products prestocked in the refrigerator, cabinet, and fruit basket. The stubborn cowlick in his hair ramped up, still damp from their time washing each other.

She wanted him all over again, even though every well-worked muscle in her tender body told her they'd both maxed out for a few more hours at least. Her mouth watered, and it had nothing to do with the delicate crepes he cooked in the pan, the scent of brown sugar, nutmeg, and cinnamon teasing her nose.

She tore her attention away from him and eyed the black leather combat boot with doggie teeth marks along the edges of the soles. "Sorry about your boot."

He shifted back and forth in front of the stove with unmistakable ease, a paisley hand towel draped over his broad, naked shoulder. "I thought Phil said he was trained."

"Phil apparently hasn't taught him everything." She stroked Boo's head with her toe as he sprawled on the floor, chewing away happily on a knotted sock. "Or maybe we left him alone too long last night. That walled-in patio where we let him out to do his business doesn't provide much room for exercise."

Mason shot a sideways glance her way, his green eyes deepening to the same gem tone she'd seen when he moved inside her. "That could be. Hopefully we won't be contained like this for too much longer."

She sipped her mug of raspberry tea she'd found by

the bedside when she'd woken alone to only the sound of him in the shower. "What's on the agenda for today?"

He slid a pair of banana crepes on a dish, spooned warm sauce over them, and topped them with a dollop of whipped cream. "As much as I'd like to spend the whole afternoon here with you, Agent Barrera will be by to pick us up in a couple of hours."

"He'll have a plan in place for us to bait the serial killer?"

"That's what he's hoping." He filled two small juice glasses with OJ.

"And what are you hoping?"

"What I want doesn't always matter in these cases." He spooned up a bite of banana crepe and brought it to her mouth. "Now eat. It could be a long day."

Her lips closed over the spoon and . . . Oh. My. "You really can cook."

"Those crepes aren't only about looking pretty."

She swallowed down the bite, taking the spoon and plate from him and feeding a taste to him. Mason probably wouldn't appreciate being compared to a plate of pretty crepes, but she couldn't miss the parallel as she learned there was a lot more to Mason than just his looks.

She leaned over the plate to kiss him. He tasted of caramel and a light sheen of his perspiration, the perfect balance of salty and sweet. "Amazing."

"Yes, you are."

She laughed and leaned back to take another bite. "I

still can't believe you used all those healthy cooking tricks in something so decadent."

He tugged the towel off his shoulder. "You weren't supposed to notice that. When folks hear something's healthy, they expect it to taste like cardboard, and expectations are half of the eating experience."

She shoveled in another bite. "My taste buds are too busy having orgasms to think that deeply."

"Food orgasms? I'll have to remember that."

She dug into a second crepe, hating that she'd even thought about the calorie count. "I know firsthand that not all low-cal food tastes this good." She tried to bite back the words bubbling up, then decided, what the hell? She'd grown beyond those years sitting at the school lunch table alone, whispered about on the bus, picked last in gym class. "I was an awkward preteen. I wasn't just clumsy. I was the chubby kid."

Mason stayed silent, his silence giving her the room she needed put her thoughts together. "Uncle Phil really supported me, helped me look beyond Mom's hurtful asides. He never asked me if I really wanted that Twinkie. Or would I like to take a nice bike ride instead of reading another book? He just accepted me as I was and taught me how to blast a strobe light across a mountain."

He stared at her intently. "Acceptance is a rare gift."

The intensity, the insightfulness of his eyes made her uncomfortable. She'd bared enough of her body and soul for one day.

Jill cleared her throat, dabbing a napkin along the

corner of her mouth. "Uh, where did you learn a healthy heart recipe? I've seen you eat, and you most definitely are not counting fat grams."

He swiped the cloth along the counter. "One of the guys I fly with—Jimmy Gage—is engaged to a diabetic with a serious sweet tooth. I passed along some recipes to Chloe. She gave them two thumbs-up, so I thought you might enjoy them."

"I hope you didn't serve them to her the same way you dished them up for me."

"Jimmy would kick my ass. I'm still walking, so you can safely assume I've never hit on Chloe."

His fingers stroked along her bare arm. "Are you having regrets about last night?"

"No." *Not much.* "I went into this with my eyes open. We're both consenting adults in a high-octane situation. It's only natural we would ride an adrenaline wave that could lead two single people, who were already attracted to each other—"

He kissed her silent.

"What was that for?"

"You were about to give me the brush-off."

"Or give us an out."

He passed her the plate again. "Eat your breakfast." He drained his glass of juice. "We don't have much longer here in safety. Don't bring the outside world in to wreck it."

She looked away from the intensity in his eyes she didn't know what to do with. "Okay, for now." She eased her plate back to the counter. "But I need to give Boo some water, and he needs another trip out onto the patio."

Mason's hand fell to her arm. "I'll let him out. Enjoy your food."

He walked to the table, reached into the bag of supplies Phil had sent for the dog, and pulled out the bottle of vitamins Phil insisted Boo needed for some condition or another. He shrugged his leather jacket over his naked chest while slipping his bare feet into his loafers. He could stand in the open patio doorway and watch both the dog and Jill at the same time. "Come on, big guy."

He slid open the patio door and twisted the bottle to squirt a few drops into the water bowl just inside.

Boo growled low.

Mason's body tensed. He scoured the small patio, looked at Jill and back out again. "It's all clear," he reassured her, then snapped his fingers for the dog. "Come on, fella. It's just your vitamins. See?"

Mason held up the eye-dropper.

Boo sprang forward and body-slammed Mason's legs. Jill gasped at the dog's uncharacteristic aggression and hopped off the counter. Mason extended his hand to keep Jill back. Boo headbutted him again. Boo nipped at Mason's jeans and tugged, snarling. What the hell?

The bottle of vitamins fell to the carpet, the liquid spilling out and bubbling along the carpet.

The bubbling increased to a frothing volcano that steamed an acrid stench. The carpet melted away under the liquid.

Jill's chest went tight with horror.

Tears stinging her eyes as hotly as whatever seared the carpet, Jill raced across the room and hooked her arm tightly around Boo's neck, fear stinging like acid over her nerves. "I don't think we're going to be able to explain this away to housekeeping."

FOURTEEN

★ ─────────────────────────────────────

Rex rolled open the silver server on the breakfast buffet at the Officers' Club, probably not the wisest place to have brought Livia Cicero for their "date," given the crowd, a very *curious* throng of people in uniform along with the occasional civilian family member, most of whom recognized his famous breakfast companion. But he'd been more concerned about keeping things with Livia low-key and quick. Breakfast wasn't even lunch, which was certainly less of a relationship statement than dinner.

Unless people assumed breakfast followed a night together.

Damn, he wasn't any good at this kind of thing. He'd only ever been with Heather. Not that this was a date. This was about turning a page and moving forward with his life.

His work plate was even fuller than the warmed stoneware in his hand—currently piled with eggs, sausage, hash browns, and a side dish of pancakes. He often missed lunch and ate supper late, if at all, so he always doubled up in the morning. Or rather, Heather had gotten him in that habit after realizing how often he skipped meals so he could cram in more work.

He dipped the ladle through the heated syrup and poured it over his stack of pancakes, added some melted butter, and done. Nothing left to do but return to his table for two. He balanced his plates and turned back toward Livia.

She perched on the edge of her chair with her fruit compote and tall latte, linen tablecloth brushing the top of her bare knees. She almost managed to hide a yawn behind her napkin. Livia obviously wasn't a morning person, not surprising, since he would guess music industry people worked more in the afternoons and evenings.

Or maybe she just preferred pampered snooze-ins.

Regardless, she'd sure made the effort to look nice this morning. Her sleek black hair brushed her cheeks as she yawned, oversized gold hoops peeking through the strands.

Wearing a beige baby doll sweater dress, she could have been a kid home from college out for breakfast with Dad, which made him feel like some kind of pervert for checking out the way the crocheted overlay along the top of the dress accented the gentle swell of her breasts. If he looked at her long length of legs stretching from the short hem, he would be toast. He eyed her gold knee boots—no heels—and reminded himself that leather covered scars. Her crutch was propped against the wall. She was frailer right now than her temperament would indicate. He needed to remember that.

Shaking his head, he snagged a biscuit and headed back to his table. Maybe this meal would finally convince the diva to move on. Meanwhile, he might as well eat to pass time until his oh eight hundred meeting with Special Agent Barrera to move Mason Randolph and Jill Walczak, then he would head straight into mission planning for the final test flight to clear before the big unveiling. They would have to bring in another loadmaster from the squadron, which made his gut clench with frustration, but the change couldn't be helped. He only hoped that with one near-fatal accident in this test, he wasn't tempting fate by changing up things just to stay on schedule.

A very high-profile schedule with billions of defense dollars riding on the outcome.

He angled sideways, weaving through the closely packed tables, nodding at the occasional called-out greeting, and ignoring the inquisitive expressions. He took his seat at the table across from Livia, and his boot started tapping before he could even pour hot sauce on his eggs. This was a really crappy idea. She had to see that.

She blew into her steaming latte, her glossy lips pursed in a display that sent his pulse into overdrive.

His foot tapped faster. He averted his eyes. Across the room at a corner table, he saw Annette Santos, the woman Livia had said was dating Chuck Tanaka. But she wasn't dining with the wounded airman. She stood at the omelet chef's workstation with Tanaka's physical therapist . . . Rex searched his memory. He'd learned to be good with names, a must in his job. Garrett Ferguson. Right. The guy was a civilian contracted to work at the base hospital, since the facility was short-staffed.

What was Annette Santos doing with Chuck's physical therapist? Neither made any overtly romantic moves, but of course this wasn't the place for PDAs—public displays of affection. The woman damn well better not be stepping out on Chuck. He'd been through enough already.

The couple took their omelets and returned to sit with Vince Deluca and his fiancée, a nurse who worked at a local free clinic. The meeting probably had something to do with Chuck's care. Rex made a mental note to ask Deluca—a gossip hound anyway—for the scoop later. And later would come sooner if he got this breakfast over with.

He jabbed his fork into his eggs. Maybe if he could get her talking about herself, they would be through with this ill-advised idea once and for all, and he could put Livia Cicero in his past. "What made you want to be a world-famous singer?"

"What made you want to fly airplanes?" She sipped her latte, leaving a light pink gloss lip outline on the bone-white china.

"It's what I do."

"Exactly." She forked a strawberry with mangling force, and when he didn't speak, she finally continued, "Actually, my mother was an opera singer."

So Livia came by the diva personality naturally. "Have I heard of her?"

"Likely not. She is quite the star of Italy, but she never quite made the leap to international fame." She shoved the smashed fruit into her mouth.

"Unlike her daughter." He doubled over a sausage link on his fork.

Livia dabbed her glossy lips, looking down and away. "Ah, but I am not a true artist. I am what you in America would call a sellout."

Now that wasn't what he'd expected in sharing time. He'd figured she would regale him with overly dramatic tales of her life of success. Instead, she hung her head.

Seeing this in-your-face woman's spirit cowed pissed him off. "That's a crock."

He slathered grape jelly on his biscuit.

"A crock?" Her napkin slid away to reveal a hesitant smile. "I assume you mean that word in my defense."

"You assume correctly." He leaned forward on his elbow, butter knife still in his hand. "You've achieved fame and fortune beyond what your mother did. You deserve to be proud."

She set her napkin by her crystal dish, smoothing wrinkles on the linen tablecloth. "Classical artists don't always see it that way." She glanced up. "Needless to say, the whole Las Vegas possibility has horrified my mother."

As a life rule, he made a point of playing things cool, tactful, but he couldn't hold back. "Your mom doesn't sound like much of a parent. Parents are proud of their kids and make sure they know it." Like he'd done with his sons, who he spoke to about once a month?

Shit.

He stuffed half a biscuit into his mouth.

Livia shrugged, drawing his eyes straight to her breasts moving enticingly under her sweater dress. "Music is her passion. My father, her family, everything else comes second. I understood the rules when I made my choice for the popular music."

His gaze snapped up to her face, where it belonged. He placed the rest of his biscuit back on his plate. "I heard you sing back in Turkey, that time you did some warm-ups with your friend Chloe playing the piano. It sounded to me like you've had classical training."

"My mother insisted on it from a young age."

"So you *could* have gone the opera route."

"Perhaps. My mother always said I needed to work more if I wanted to break in. Now I'll never know." She finished her coffee.

"Do you want to?" He touched her elbow, forcing

her to look back at him, not brush this off. This was her life, damn it. She shouldn't let her mother intimidate her—granted that the woman must be one hell of an intimidating human being if she could overshadow Livia. "I don't know a lot about music, but you're still young."

She tossed aside her twisted napkin, her arm inching away from his impulsive touch. "There's not going to be a Las Vegas deal. There is no deal anywhere."

The sounds of the dining room faded as his focus narrowed. He heard the starchy pride, the prickly defensiveness in her voice.

Ah hell. He'd wanted to be wrong about the vulnerability he saw in her. "I'm sorry to hear that, Livia."

"Actually, that's not entirely true. I was offered a tryout for a show, but I know the truth. Even if I do manage to recover from the injury to my leg, I do not have the vocal cords I used to. The damage from smoke inhalation during the explosion in Turkey was too much."

His throat closed up so tight he could have sworn he tasted the smoke. That mission—his mission—had done this. His fists clenched on the table. "I'm so damn sorry."

For more than he could ever say.

"Perhaps my voice would still be considered good enough for some small venue, but I'm not content with that." Her chin tipped with a Roman bravado. "I can't be a shadow of who I was."

"Believe me, lady, there's not a chance of you ever being a shadow."

Her eyes went wide, long dark lashes sweeping up, and now that he looked closer, she wasn't even wearing makeup beyond her lip gloss. She was just that damn beautiful, dynamic.

Hot.

She smiled again, apparently as good an actress as she'd once been a singer. "None of that matters now. It is what you would call mute—wait." She held up a French-manicured finger. "That is not the right word."

"You're close." He couldn't hold back the grin at her vocab quirks. "Moot."

"Like boot. I have it now." She sniffed regally. Or was that just a cover to mask holding back tears? "Mute is the word for no voice, so I guess that is right, too. I have no voice anymore. I have no direction."

No wonder she'd spent so much time hanging out with Chuck Tanaka. She'd experienced her fair share of loss, even if the outward wounds weren't as apparent.

"There's one thing I know for sure." He kept his hands planted on his side of the table this time but infused conviction in his voice if not in a comforting touch. "You will find your voice again. You'll find a new direction and pursue it with every bit as much passion as you put into your music."

Her eyes sparked with anger, her famous temper

flecking shards of white ice in her eyes. "What if you couldn't fly any longer? Would you just be able to pick up some new passion?"

"I didn't say it would be easy. In fact, I think it would be hellishly hard, but I believe—I know—you're that tough."

Her temper faded as quickly as it had sparked. She smiled. But damn, *smile* seemed such an inadequate word to describe the way her beautiful face lit up over a few words he'd just tossed out there.

"Thank you, Rex Scanlon. That is probably the most lovely compliment anyone has ever given me."

"Uh, you're welc—"

She leaned across the table and kissed him. Right there in public with God and everyone else in the Officers' Club watching, she pressed her soft, sweet lips to his, holding contact in an unmistakably sensual moment, even if she kept her hands firmly planted on the table by her uneaten compote.

He needed to ease her away in a manner that wouldn't embarrass her—well, any more than they'd both already embarrassed the hell out of themselves with her impulsive act. But damn, she tasted good. Felt good. Stirred him so hot, hard, and fast he was damn glad the table masked his response. One simple kiss, and she had him buzzing with desire.

Buzzing?

Shit. He was hard, all right. But the buzzing was his BlackBerry. His work. His job. Something this woman had made him forget, even if only for a few drawn-out seconds.

Rex slid his hand down her face for a selfish second before he gripped her shoulders and carefully urged her away. "I'm sorry."

Sorry for more than just the damn interruption. Sorry for things he didn't even know how to put into words.

He unclipped his BlackBerry and clicked on the message—from Special Agent Barrera. He scrolled through the e-mail:

There's been an attempt made on Randolph and Walczak. Call in immediately.

* * *

Mason paced around the squadron briefing room, a space too small for him to stand a chance at working off his nervous energy as he waited for Jill to finish her interview with Barrera, Scanlon, and Gallardo.

Things had moved fast once that hole burned through the carpet in their temporary quarters. God, he didn't even want to think of what could have happened if the tainted vitamins had made it into the dog's bowl, or, heaven forbid, if some of the corrosive acid had sloshed onto Jill. Boo had stayed by Jill's side ever since. Barrera hadn't even bothered objecting to the guard dog's constant presence.

While Mason was thankful for the dog's presence, *he* wanted to be the one by her side, and nothing less would suffice.

His boots plowed tracks through the industrial carpet as he made his way back and forth past the long table with eight swivel chairs. At least he wasn't facing this alone. Aside from the official detail in with Jill now, Mason had the support of his crew buddies who were trying to take his mind off how damn much he hated the plan of using Jill as bait for a killer who always seemed to be two steps ahead of them.

Vince and Jimmy both waited with him, Jimmy having run straight over from the gym and Vince cutting out on breakfast with his fiancée. Both men now sat at the briefing table with their laptops open, working on mission planning notes for the upcoming final test flight—the flight Mason wouldn't be flying.

"Hey," Vince said without looking up as he clicked the down arrow through pages. "Did you hear the colonel's now a groupie?"

Mason stopped dead in his tracks. WTF? "I appreciate that you're trying to take my mind off things, but that's a little out there. Even coming from you."

Vince minimized his computer screen, a goofy-ass grin on his face. "I couldn't make up shit this good."

"You're going to have to explain that one."

"Shay and I were having breakfast with Chuck Tanaka's girlfriend and his physical therapist—the guy asked to meet us to get some insights on how to better motivate Chuck. So anyway, we went to the Officers' Club, and no shit, who do we see but Colonel Scanlon sharing eggs and sausage links with a certain visiting dignitary. None other than Livia Cicero."

Jimmy slammed his computer shut. "You're yanking our chains."

Okay, so that was the last thing Mason had expected to hear, either, but who the hell cared right now? Not him. Not when some whack job had painted a target on Jill's back. "He was probably just escorting her."

"The colonel as an *escort*? Okay," Vince bobbed his big, shaved head, "I'm not even going to touch that one. Besides, by the end of the meal, they were sharing more than food. The whole club saw them in a full-out PDA."

Even über-chill Jimmy choked on a cough. "A no-shit public display of affection? In uniform? In public? Colonel Scanlon?"

Vapor grinned. "None other. She laid a lip-lock on him that had the general's wife spewing orange juice out her nose."

Jimmy drummed his fingers along his closed laptop. "So, does that make the pop star a military groupie? Or maybe the colonel's actually a roadie."

Vince scrubbed his head. "Either way, coulda knocked me over with a feather."

Jimmy backed away from his bulked-up crewmate. "Would have taken a damn big feather."

"Yeah, yeah, whatever." Vince waved away the comment. "I'm just wondering how the colonel and the singer kept this all quiet back when we escorted her on that USO trip to Turkey last spring. He's even better at keeping secrets than I would have imagined."

Jimmy cut a sideways glance at Mason. "I thought you were putting the moves on her at one time, Smooth."

Some of the bottled frustration leaked free and he snapped curtly, "Good God, I don't chase every woman that crosses my path."

He was cranky and knew it, but he certainly didn't need this sort of crap floating around for Jill to hear right now when things were so unsettled—but so damn hot—between them.

"Ease up, pal." Jimmy leaned forward, elbows on knees. "I'm asking because if that serial killer thinks Livia Cicero means something to you, she would make for one helluva high-profile target."

"Fuck," Vapor hissed. "I hadn't thought of that."

Mason mentally kicked himself because it hadn't crossed his mind either, and it should have. If these guys thought there was a connection, someone else—a killer—could as well. Damn it all, he would find this person. Determination jelled with his bottled rage. This bastard didn't know who the hell he was dealing with.

Jimmy ducked into his line of sight. "So, dude? Did you?"

Mason shook his head. "I never asked Livia Cicero out. I was already seeing someone at the time. There are plenty of bad names you can call me, but 'cheater' isn't one of them."

The door clicked a warning just before it opened. Werewolf, Gucci, and the contractor Lee Drummond strode in, reminding Mason of the mission planning scheduled for this morning. By the middle of the night, they would be flying the final test flight—without him. This time Werewolf and Gucci would pilot the Predator in practice for their part in keeping a security watch during the hypersonic flight for the visiting dignitaries.

Werewolf tapped the back of Mason's head. "Somebody's cranky today."

Mason spun his chair to face Werewolf. "Having someone kill the people around me tends to do that."

Werewolf dropped into the seat beside Gucci. "Sorry, dude, my mouth runs ahead of my brain." He pointed to Mason's gnawed boot. "What's up with that? The boss is a stickler about uniform standards."

There hadn't been time to get replacements. It had been futile to hope that no one would notice.

Dr. Drummond slid into a chair at the head and began unloading her portfolio, lining up her PDA, her leather binder, her pen, and her water bottle with her normal precision. "Doesn't Jill Walczak have a dog now?"

"I do believe she does," Vince said, even though he knew full well since he'd seen Boo with Jill a half hour earlier. "That must have hurt your leg having the dog chew on your boot like that. Shay's hairy mutt did that to my favorite pair of shit kickers once. Lucky for me, her little yipper has tiny teeth. Oh, hey wait, you must have had your boots off when the dog chewed it. In fact, the boots must have been off for a *long* time, given how gnawed up that boot is."

"I fell asleep on the sofa with my boots on." Let them "chew" on that answer.

Werewolf winked at Gucci. "Okay, he's so cranky, that's proof positive he's not getting any."

Gucci sighed, flipping open her pink legal pad. "You men can be such pigs—and before you ask"—she tucked her silver etched pen behind her ear—"I'm cranky because my boyfriend didn't let me get enough sleep."

Vince pulled a granola bar from his flight bag. "I gotta agree with Gucci. That cranky thing isn't much of an indicator. I'm feeling crabby because Shay keeps pushing these tree bark bars on me thinking I'll give up doughnuts. Gage is perky as a cheerleader even though Chloe is out of town, and we know he's not screwing around on her." Vince pivoted fast in the chair. "You aren't cheating, are you?"

"You're joking, right? Chloe may be small, but I wouldn't recommend pissing her off. She's well on her way to her brown belt in karate."

Werewolf opened and closed his fingers in a "talk, talk, talk" symbol. "Fine. Everyone's happily hooked up, enough so you're even willing to eat tree bark."

Gucci traded Vince the granola bar for a Snickers she withdrew from her monogrammed lunch sack. "So how do you know when the hookup is the real thing? Enough so even Vapor's willing to eat tree bark?"

Vince grinned, peeling back the wrapper. "It's like the best Harley ride ever on a wide-open road—"

Werewolf pitched his pencil at Vince, while Dr. Drummond smiled silently. "You've been dating the woman for a few months. Get back to me when you've put a diamond on her finger."

Jimmy straightened his chair. "I actually bit the bullet and bought a ring for Chloe."

Vince's jaw dropped. "No shit?"

Mason's neck itched.

Jimmy grinned. "No shit. Don't say anything though. I'm taking a weekend off for a getaway with her when we wrap up this test. I'm proposing then."

Werewolf waved dismissively. "Engagement." He harrumphed. "Doesn't count without the vows."

Jimmy narrowed his eyes at Werewolf. "So, fine then, how did you know, Married Guy?"

Gucci and Dr. Drummond both looked at him. Werewolf stayed silent.

"Come on." Gucci elbowed him. "Don't hoard all the state secrets for yourself. Share the wealth."

Werewolf shoved to his feet abruptly, charging through the door, even ignoring the fact that Colonel Scanlon stood in the opening with his arms crossed. How long had he been there?

Scanlon slowly shifted his attention from the mercurial Werewolf back to Mason. The commander's thumb rubbed over his empty ring finger. "You know when you can finish each other's sentences without even thinking."

The widowed commander's answer sucked the air

out of the room, right along with any inclination to razz him about kissing the Italian singer. Mason stared at his chewed boot, an image of Jill cuddling the pooch with obvious maternal love making his neck itch all over again.

He was in deep.

Scanlon cleared his throat. "Smooth, Barrera's ready for you. He's investigating a solid new lead on a perp."

Chairs creaked throughout the room as everyone sat up straighter. "Just tell me what to do, and I'm there," Mason said.

Scanlon waved Mason out of the room with him and started down the hall lined with aircraft photos, pictures of past commanders, and of the current president. "Barrera still wants to use you and Miss Walczak as bait. But it's going to take some work persuading your friend."

Mason struggled to envision Jill getting cold feet. She had every reason to be scared, but she'd been driven to nail the man who'd killed her friend since even before Mason knew about the case.

"Jill will do whatever it takes to bring this guy to justice." He knew it as well as he knew she collected teacups and was a sucker for dogs. He wondered if that was the first step toward finishing each other's sentences . . .

"I'm sure she will," the colonel acknowledged, gesturing toward the meeting room on the right. "But she isn't happy about the latest direction of the investigation."

"As long as we've got a lead—"

"A lead that points too close to home." Colonel Scanlon glanced right then continued, "To put it mildly, she's more than a little upset to hear our new primary suspect is her stepfather."

FIFTEEN

Lee Drummond readjusted the alignment of her PDA and notepad on the briefing table, checking her slim silver watch. The aviators all huddled together, reviewing flight data before the brief in their flyers' club way that seemed to zone out the rest of the world. She smiled when they pretended to be interested in asking her opinion, vaguely registering what they said.

She had bigger issues at hand.

The mission planning brief with Vince Deluca, Jimmy Gage, and their replacement loadmaster should start in another ninety seconds if the colonel would finish his business with Mason Randolph in a timely manner. Werewolf and Gucci would be flying their Predator by remote control in prep, since they would be on hand for the big show in front of the three visiting generals and their own general in only a couple more days. As part of the secret test squadron, Werewolf and Gucci had the clearance to know exactly what they were protecting—which would make their job simpler.

The boss certainly had a lot dividing his attention. Lee twisted her hands together tightly to hide the revealing tremble of excitement. Good. More chances for things to go awry. This morning's testosterone huddle would prepare for the last test flight set to occur at oh two hundred. Of course it would go flawlessly. *Tonight's* flight was not the issue. The next one, the one in front of the visiting generals, would make for the perfect time to finish exacting punishment.

What good was her scheme without an audience?

Her body hummed with anticipation from the mental stimulation of bringing all the pieces together. Finally Mason would pay for his arrogance in asking the colonel to replace her with another contractor during earlier work on the jet. She'd tried to explain that the plane wasn't perfect, that more time was needed for honing. Sergeant Randolph had dared to imply she micromanaged to a degree that hampered production, and her expectations were unrealistic, unachievable given current-day science.

The colonel had actually been planning to follow on the sergeant's recommendation to remove her. Her fingers twisted tighter in her lap. But life had intervened in the form of budget cuts, and they'd been too short-staffed to let her go. Everyone else seemed to have forgotten the incident from a year ago, or at least they were pretending to play nice, perhaps even laughing behind her back. But she never forgot a single detail, and she most definitely did not believe in playing nice.

At least her life was anything but boring right now, although tampering with the dog's vitamin drops had been easier than expected. She worked with chemicals, after all. Slipping a little cash to a delivery boy who never saw her face had taken care of the rest.

Plans to put Mason in the police's crosshairs as a suspect in the killings hadn't quite gone as planned, but other things were still working to her advantage. Authorities on and off the base were so busy chasing their tails, much of their focus had been siphoned from the upcoming unveiling of the hypersonic jet.

Perhaps they might even catch that annoying Killer Alien. She even had a sneaking suspicion who the psychopath might be, but tipping off the police would then leave everyone free to focus on the flight again.

Security was still tight, but those tiny cracks in resources spread too thin would give her all the opportunity she needed. She loosened her fingers from their death grip and toyed with the ID dangling from a lanyard around her neck. That little square of laminated plastic provided her unsupervised entrée to the most secret of places on base. So she could easily waltz through unobserved and scope out the best way to plant explosives on the flawed plane, set to detonate during the big flight for the visiting generals.

No one would ever know it was her—she was that good, that smart. Smart enough to make it look as if Mason had somehow screwed up the drop again.

The crew might or might not make it out alive. And the blame would fall squarely on Mason Randolph.

Dead or alive.

* * *

Desert sun streaming unrelentingly through the windshield on Mason's truck, Jill refused to believe her stepfather could be a psychopathic serial killer. She'd first gone into law enforcement to vindicate Phil after the way he'd been ruined by gossip that he was responsible for a prostitute's murder—gossip that all later proved to be unfounded. There was no way the man she'd always had so much faith in could have deceived her at such a deep level.

She'd wrapped her brain around plenty of implausible scenarios during her career, but this, she could not accept. All the more reason for her to follow Barrera's instructions about interrogating Phil undercover with a wire. At least then she would have a chance at proving Phil's innocence.

Mason wasn't as supportive of her unconditional faith. She bit her lip to keep from pleading Phil's case the deeper they drove into the desert. There was no budging him. Her tender lover was nowhere in sight.

He'd transformed into her protector. She respected that on a professional level.

But they'd moved way into the personal when they'd climbed into bed together, and for the first time, she was torn.

Mason sat behind the wheel of his truck, driving down the narrow, mile-long driveway to Phil's, listening devices on Mason's belt and in her bra. Barrera and his people were in place behind and ready to act if needed. So she certainly couldn't talk about anything so private with him now, not with Barrera's people listening in.

If only Mason would give her some kind of sign—a smile, a simple touch while no one was looking. She wanted to think he was only edgy because his crew was mission planning without him—a top secret fact she'd stumbled on during the transfer from Barrera's questioning.

Instead, he kept his eyes trained on the dusty desert road, the truck plowing through tumbleweed as they drove deeper into the mountain valley. "You've heard the old saying about a doctor not treating his own family. You can't be objective when it comes to your stepfather. You need to be realistic about that. We both have to keep our objectivity here." His piercing green eyes drilled through her. "No emotions."

She heard him. She understood. But something had shaken loose inside her when they'd made love, and she resented that he could put it all aside to regain control so easily. For that matter, the warning not to have emotions on today of all days felt like a dig after what they'd shared last night.

"You don't know Uncle Phil. I do."

"Can you at least accept the possibility, if not for your own safety, then for the safety of all the other women at risk from this serial killer?"

His words sounded reasonable enough, but it was impossible to turn her back on the man who'd been her only real consistent support over the years, her only real parent figure. She settled for a vague, "I will be careful."

His fists tightened around the wheel. "You're not answering my question."

"Damn it, Mason," she finally snapped, "of course I'm going to do my best to make sure no one else dies. Nothing comes before that."

She'd been on the police side so often, and even with Lara's murder, she'd been able to channel her focus. Now for the first time, she understood the panic that drove victims. When the water had burned through the carpet, they'd called Barrera immediately. She'd been stunned to hear that Barrera suspected her stepfather because of the tainted vitamins and a few thready connections to the victims.

Those old, unsubstantiated accusations in the unsolved murder of a prostitute, accusations that had ended his career early, had come back to haunt him. Whatever happened to innocent until proven guilty?

For the safety of the other dogs—on the off chance

Phil wasn't to blame—Barrera had agreed to let her call and "warn" him about the vitamins. She had to lie and say Boo had taken ill. No longer would she be able to use the pet for protection, because if Phil was the killer, the dog would be useless to her. He would obey Phil's commands over hers.

She'd hated lying to him about the dog most of all. Phil had sounded devastated hearing Boo was ill. He loved his animals. Jill would bet her life on that.

Barrera had made sure she heard that those could very well be the stakes.

The truck bounced closer to the double-wide trailer with no neighbors other than the dogs and a big fat Joshua tree. Barren mountain ranges surrounded the acres of land, providing a world-of-its-own feeling. A tire swing he'd hung on a gnarled tree branch for her many moons ago twisted in the harsh desert winter. Rows of kennels stretched in back with dog runs and a circular fenced playground that resembled doggie heaven with toys, climbing rocks, shelters, and a constant flowing spigot for clean water.

This day had turned everything upside down.

And the man beside her had bolted on her emotionally, leaving her high and dry when she'd never felt so utterly adrift. She searched for the steely will and cool reserve that had gotten her through so much more than the years of hard physical training to be the best at her job. Today, she was coming up damn empty.

"Mason," Jill whispered. "You don't have to scare

me away from you. You can just tell me how you feel."

He put the truck in park and turned to face her, arm draped over the steering wheel. "This is not the time or place to talk about . . . us. We have business to take care of."

"Yes," she said, stung by his matter-of-fact attitude. "Of course we do."

He frowned, leaning on the steering wheel. "Does your uncle have another vehicle?"

"He has a truck." Jill looked around the yard and found a white industrial van parked back near the kennels. "That's not his. Maybe someone is here looking at a dog?"

Uncle Phil ambled from around the corner of the dog shelter, a tray of medicine vials in his arms. Jill shuddered as she stepped out of the Chevy, her ankle boots puffing dirt.

Phil hefted the crate onto the trailer hooked to his 4x4, then anchored his panama hat against a stiff, cold wind. "Hello, you two. Thanks for that heads-up call about the tainted batch of vitamins. Thank God, I hadn't given this new batch to any of my other animals yet."

Mason shook Phil's hand in greeting with such ease it chilled her inside how easily he could guard his real intent. She hugged Phil quickly, not so sure of her own acting skills.

Mason placed his hand on top of the sealed crates. "So you haven't dumped any of them out?"

"Hell, no! I don't want some toxic waste dump pit in my yard, much less risk some wild animal drinking it at night." He pulled off his work gloves and tucked them in his coat pocket. "I gotta admit I'm confused, though. These came from my regular supplier, and I've never had any trouble before."

That's what the cops had told her. They suspected he'd set her up.

Phil swiped a bandanna over his forehead. "I'm not taking any risks with my puppies, though, until I get the professionals out here." He gestured to the stark but clean trailer. "Want to go inside and have a Coke?"

"No thanks. We're good."

He leaned against the trailer. "How's Boo?"

"The vet says he'll be fine." Jill winced at the lie and changed the subject fast. She pointed to the van. "Where did that come from?"

"Ah, yes. Thanks to your friend Mason here, I think Roscoe's found a new home. A pal of yours from base heard about my doggies, and that kid Chuck Tanaka came by to check out my pack the other day. Now they're here to pick up the winner." Phil pointed up the road. "I never adopt out a dog on the first day. Gotta make sure it's not an impulse thing. Everybody loves them on sight, you know."

Mason nodded, his body angled perfectly for the listening device clipped inside his belt buckle, under his leather jacket. "A companion will be perfect for him, and the dog will sure have a lot of his attention while he's waiting to get back up to speed to work."

"That's true," Phil agreed. "But Roscoe can be much more than that. He's a highly trained Labrador-collie mix. He can fetch items your friend can't reach yet. He can also open doors and bark for help if his owner takes a fall. It's a good match." Phil waved for Jill and Mason to follow him. "Come on. They're around back."

She followed her stepfather around to the other side of the kennels. Chuck Tanaka leaned on both crutches today, a long-haired gold dog sitting at his feet. The physical therapist—Ferguson—stood off to the side, eying their third companion kneeling by the mutt.

Livia Cicero nuzzled the scraggly canine, cooing in Italian, threading her fingers through the long yellow fur. The group was too taken up in getting to know the mutt to notice that anyone else had arrived.

Stopping ten kennels down, Phil whistled low and long. "Nice of Chuck to bring his friends, huh? Can't deny the truth. That's a fine-looking woman. I don't care for her music much, but I know who she is." He grinned. "She likes dogs, too. I think she took a shine to little Peanut." He pointed to a miniature poodle plus mystery mix, half-shaved while recovering from a skin disease brought on by neglect from his previous owner.

Phil's besotted expression couldn't be missed. It didn't have to be twisted obsession. His reaction could be as simple as appreciating a person who took an interest in one of his more pathetic-looking creatures.

That's all it was. She couldn't be wrong. She already hurt enough because authorities were listening in on the conversation, and covert cameras were searching around the place while she kept him occupied.

She looked at Phil. Something made her ask, "Are you okay?"

He shuffled his cowboy boots in the sand. "It's probably nothing. Doesn't even matter really."

"Tell me anyway." She hated pressing for answers, abusing his trust of her. Mason, standing next to her, kept his face impassive.

"I just don't like the PT guy—Ferguson. He's a tough customer. Didn't even wince when he passed poor Peanut there."

She looked back at the poodle with the shaved coat and skin red and raw from infection. Her arms ached to scoop up the little scamp.

Phil shook his head. "Never have trusted a person who doesn't like animals. I was kinda surprised to see him. He doesn't strike me as a military sort."

"He's not," Mason interjected. "He's a contract worker at the hospital. Rumor has it he wanted to enlist but didn't pass the physical."

"How sadly ironic," Jill said, "given his career field." She shifted her glance to the physical therapist holding a leather leash looped in his hands and idly snapping the strap while he waited for Chuck to finish greeting his new pet. "Uncle Phil, I thought you said it was Ferguson's suggestion to get a helper dog."

"Oh no. It was Tanaka's idea. Ferguson just came along to offer input." Phil rocked back on his heels, eying the group as the physical therapist hooked the leash onto Roscoe's collar. "Well, girl, it was kind of you to come out and see if I needed any help, but my doggies and I are doing fine. As a matter of fact, I need to take care of settling Roscoe with his new family."

He gestured to Tanaka walking with both crutches and Livia Cicero with one crutch, picking her way along after him in her flat-heeled knee boots and cream-colored mini–sweater dress. Ferguson followed, giving Roscoe's lead a firm tug.

Firm or harsh? Difficult to tell from a distance. Regardless, the dog would be Chuck's, not the other guy's, so no worries for Roscoe.

Phil knelt to wriggle his fingers for Peanut in the kennel and looked up at Mason. "Thanks again for stopping by so I could see Jill's okay with my own eyes. You keep my girl safe now. You hear?"

"Absolutely. She and I are going back to her place tonight, and we're locking down tight." Mason fed the bait Barrera hoped would lure a killer. "You like that Chinese place, right?"

He'd rolled out the line smoothly enough, letting Phil know where they would be at her duplex. Anyone could pose as a delivery person or break in while someone else was distracted at the front door. The bait was out there. Now they had to wait to see if Phil took it.

She kissed Uncle Phil's cheek. "Love you."

He kissed the top of her head. "Love you, too, Gingersnap."

Her eyes stung with tears. Jill blinked them back hard and fast. She couldn't afford for Barrera's people to say she'd done anything to tip him off. She just prayed he would forgive her later.

She turned to join up with Mason.

The dog—Roscoe—let out a yip and yanked free from Ferguson, bounding across the sandy yard.

Tackling Jill flat on her ass in a pile of dirt.

* * *

Mason paced around the living room in the base quarters where they'd stayed last night—a lifetime ago since he'd made love with Jill. She was showering while he met with Agent Barrera.

After the dunking, they'd called the interview session a wash—so to speak. Her listening device had been submerged, and even if it had survived intact, they couldn't risk the wires being visible through the wet and clingy clothes. He'd draped his flight jacket over her ASAP and hauled her back to his truck. Agent Barrera had been waiting two minutes down the road.

Now, Barrera was working his cell phone and BlackBerry with ambidextrous skill, tying up last-minute loose ends. Once Jill finished her shower, they would make their official move to her place and cross their fingers that the killer made another attempt—now that her place had been completely security-proofed with alarms and video cameras. He had a job to do.

While his crew flew the final test flight of their hypersonic jet.

Not only were they flying without him, but now Scanlon was off the flight as well. His crew rest had been busted by the latest development. Since he was an extra pilot, they'd sent up the flight with Vince, Jimmy, and the sub loadmaster—and without Scanlon—rather than scrap the whole mission. Keeping this test on schedule was critical, but good Lord, they were spread thin.

Scanlon cleaned his horn-rimmed glasses on a dish towel from the kitchen. "You're going to wear a hole in the carpet with those chewed-up boots of yours, Sergeant."

"I hate not being on that flight. *If anything happens . . .*" They were a superstitious lot, following routine, working as a unit, nervous about surprise changes. During war situations, it wasn't unusual to fly while sick because you couldn't send your crew up without you.

Incontrovertible fact in their world: survivor's guilt crippled fliers.

Rex clamped him on the shoulder. "I understand, but Smooth, you're doing the right thing."

He had to believe that was true. It was taking everything inside him to stay focused, worried about his pals in the air and Jill here on the ground. "I wonder how Chuck's not losing his damn mind going this long without flying."

"Sounds like physical therapy is keeping him busy."

"Yeah, he's got that new dog to help him out." Roscoe, the Lab-collie mix, had given the physical therapist a run for his money when he'd gotten loose and dunked Jill. Phil's tight-lipped expression had no doubt silently accused Ferguson's dog-handling skills. Something about that whole incident bothered him, but he couldn't put his finger on what. "Jill's pretty upset over not being able to take Boo with us."

"He's safe at the base kennel. Hopefully this will all be over soon. Once they have the sadistic bastard behind bars, everyone can resume their lives again."

That niggling something in the back of his brain started sparking, snapping, demanding air so it could flame to life. "Sir, what did you just say?"

"Life can go back to normal once we have this sick bastard in custody."

"No." Mason's heart pounded faster, harder, adrenaline kicking through him. "You used a different word." *Sadistic.* A word he'd heard recently, but in reference to someone else.

"What is it, Sergeant?"

Such a small coincidence. "It may be nothing, and I

may be grasping at straws because I really don't want this killer to be Jill's stepfather."

"What's your hunch?"

"Colonel, do you remember relaying a conversation to me that you had with Chuck in the hospital?"

"Refresh my memory."

"You were talking about Chuck getting out of the hospital sooner than expected . . ."

"Because his physical therapist is a sadistic bastard."

"Chuck said the same thing to me at his apartment. And today, Jill's stepfather mentioned getting a bad feeling about Garrett Ferguson, something about not trusting people who don't like animals."

Barrera closed up his cell phone, eyes sharp, apparently having been listening in the whole time. He shook his head. "It's not much to go on. What else do you know about this guy?"

Mason pushed ahead. "Not much. He's pretty close-mouthed for the most part. Started working on the base a year or so ago. After a couple of drinks one time, he mentioned wanting to go into the army, but he failed the physical on what he called a 'technicality,' so he decided to do contract work for the military instead."

Barrera nodded. "That's a start. He has a connection to the base and has a medical background, which could explain the wounds on the victims. I wish there was some kind of description from the first victim—Annette Santos."

Ah hell. "Chuck Tanaka's girlfriend."

"But they started dating after the attack . . . Still, it's damn coincidental." Barrera shook his head. "And she can't give us a description of her attacker. She was chloroformed from behind." His face cleared. "You're right that it could be nothing, but it's worth a second look. I'll hook up with Gallardo and see what else we can dig up on his background. You wouldn't happen to know where Ferguson went after you saw him at the kennel?"

Mason replayed everything that had happened and had been said in the mayhem after Jill was tackled into the water by Roscoe. "Ferguson had driven his van to transport the dog more easily. He was going to drop off Chuck and Roscoe, then he was going to . . ." Oh hell, his instincts sparking higher, his gaze snapped up to Colonel Scanlon, aka the pop star's roadie. "He was going to take Livia Cicero back to her hotel. He said something about giving her some tips to help her get rid of the crutch sooner."

"Shit," Scanlon cursed.

Barrera snapped to attention. "Get Jill Walczak out of the shower and on the phone with Gallardo. I'm going to see if I can track down the Cicero woman. God, I hope she's not one of those inaccessible star types."

Mason sprinted through the bedroom and pounded on the bathroom door. "Jill? Jill, we need to get a move on. There's been a development."

No one answered, and the shower wasn't running

any longer. How big was that bathroom window? Could someone have gotten inside?

He felt like his fucking head was on fire. To hell with privacy.

Mason shoved open the door.

SIXTEEN

"Jill?" Mason's voice bounced around the tiled bathroom walls.

Damn. Shivering, Jill tucked herself deeper into the corner of the shower behind the half-drawn curtain. She scrubbed her wrist across her eyes and scrambled to regain control before she faced Mason.

God, she didn't want him to see her like this, hugging her knees and crying long past when the steam had evaporated. But once the water had begun pouring over her, the true waterworks had started. Even when she'd shut off the real shower, she hadn't been able to control the flow of tears—for her murdered friend Lara, for all those victims, for Uncle Phil's past that wouldn't let him go.

And yes, she'd even sobbed some selfish tears for herself.

She wasn't any better than all those women she'd labeled idiots in the mess hall because they'd fallen for Mason Randolph only to have him pull away. Her only consolation? He wasn't shallow. He was just too damaged from his divorce to let himself get close, truly close to another woman. Crap. Now that she thought about it, that wasn't any consolation at all.

She stood, tucking the plain white shower curtain against her as she peered around the edge. "Mason," she hissed low, "give me a damn towel and then get out."

He thrust a fluffy white towel into her outstretched hand. "Jill, we've got a new lead. Barrera's calling in an APB now, and we're heading out. Get dressed before we hit the door if you want to come along. There's no time to waste."

By the time he'd finished his sentence, she'd already pulled on her jeans and was hooking her bra. He shoved a shirt over her head, and she grabbed her boots on the fly. "Who?"

He followed right on her heels. "We're checking out Tanaka's physical therapist. He's now a suspect. And he was last seen with Livia Cicero."

Oh God. Her wet hair turned prickly icy against her scalp.

Agent Barrera stood by Scanlon, who had his cell phone out. "You actually have Livia Cicero on speed dial?"

Scanlon waved him quiet and turned his cell on

speakerphone. Jill sat on the arm of the sofa and tugged on her boots.

"Buon giorno," Livia answered, her husky voice subdued.

"Livia, it's Rex."

"Si." Her voice shook. "I saw your caller identification."

"Are you all right?" Rex pressed.

Livia hesitated on the other end of the line. "Why would I not be?"

"You sound . . . tired."

She sounded scared as hell to Jill, just about as scared as the stalwart colonel looked. His face had gone so pale his black-framed glasses stood out in starker contrast. But he didn't lose his composure, ever the in-control commander. "Livia, are you still there?"

"I do not mean to be rude or grumpy," she answered, her voice picking up speed, her accent thickening. "You know how I wear my emotions on my shirt cuff."

"On your sleeve," he said, his eyes narrowing with the hint of some kind of awareness.

What was she missing here?

"Si, of course, but what does that matter? It is a mute point." Livia's breathing came faster. "I have to hang up."

"Are you sure?" he pushed, tendons visible in his hand as he gripped the phone. "I could bring you a decaf latte."

"No thank you, please, Rex, you know I do not like

those. Just leave me alone. I need my rest—" The line disconnected.

Scanlon charged straight for the door. "She's been taken."

Jill darted a look at Mason, but he was already in step with his commander, no questions, no doubt on his face.

Barrera followed. "How can you be so sure?"

"We'll talk in the car," Scanlon shot over his shoulder. "She used two incorrect English phrases we'd already discussed correcting, and she damn well adores her decaf lattes. She was sending me signals."

Barrera reached for his BlackBerry. "I'll put out an APB and try to get a warrant for his house."

Jill grabbed her phone. "I'll find Gallardo."

Damn, but she really wished she still had her dog.

Mason paused at the door and held out his hand. "Give me the keys. I'll drive while you make your calls."

Scanlon started to take the keys from Barrera.

Mason kept his hand out. "Sir—"

Scanlon nodded. "You're right. You'll be steady. Drive." He turned to Barrera. "Do you have Ferguson's address?"

"Yes," he hedged. "He's got a small ranch out in the desert."

The perfect out-of-the-way place to take and torture victims. Her eyes slid shut as if she could somehow squeeze back the images slamming through her brain at warp speed.

"Scanlon," Barrera warned, "you're staying in the car."

"Of course."

Jill could see the lie in his eyes, and she didn't feel the need to stop him. In fact, she and Mason would be right there with him.

* * *

Rex palmed the dash as Mason Randolph took the corner at breakneck speed, sand spewing from the tires on the dusty back road. Jill Walczak and Barrera sat behind, their voices low and urgent in the darkened car as they worked their phones to get backup and a warrant.

Like he gave a shit about a warrant.

They'd already learned from the concierge at Livia's hotel that she definitely wasn't in her room. She'd never come back after the trip to the kennel that afternoon. This was it. Their only lead.

Everyone else could sit in the car with their thumbs up their rears while they waited for the cops to find this middle-of-nowhere place, but he was going inside. If he was wrong, they could sort it out later.

As they'd left the base, Mason had slapped the bubble light on the roof of Barrera's nondescript sedan but shut it off once they neared Ferguson's ranch house in the desert. No siren, though, since they didn't want Ferguson to hear them even from a distance. Sound carried so far in the desert.

Mason cut the headlights.

Barrera looked up, his face glowing alien green

from the BlackBerry screen. "What the hell are you doing? It's damn dark out here without any street-lamps."

Rex laughed hoarsely. "We can see anything you need. I've landed in Iraq with lights off, no runway, and instruments on the fritz."

Mason nodded. "That's what I was thinking, sir."

"Okay, then," Barrera conceded, stroking his seat belt and checking the latch. "It's your funeral."

As long as it wasn't Livia's. Damned if he would take flowers to another grave of a woman he cared about. He swallowed down a wad of fear he'd never expected to feel again.

Slowly his eyes adjusted, but he didn't need to say a thing to Mason. The sergeant had the car firmly in hand. If Ferguson was their guy, and he had Livia out here, their window for surprise would be short, since other authorities would be arriving soon—and loudly.

This had to be the place. He had to be right. Ferguson's lonely desert ranch house was the logical location for him to take his victims.

Logical?

What a damned incongruous word to use in connection to a serial killer.

They neared the long, one-story house with a barn to the side, the shapes clear enough to a man accustomed to making his way through the dark. Shadows shifted across the yard, a large silhouette walking toward the open barn door with a lamp dangling in the middle. Rex squinted, trying to make out the figure.

"It's a man, hunched over, and he's got someone over his shoulder."

Please God, someone alive. Livia alive. He couldn't make out the blurry form being carried other than to tell it—she?—wasn't moving.

The shadow paused. Shifted. Turned toward the car and straightened. He'd seen them.

Shit. "Blind him with the lights," Rex ordered.

Mason activated the headlights without hesitation. The wiry guy's eyes went deer-wide.

Ferguson.

The unmistakable form of a slender woman was draped over his shoulder, her silky dark hair hiding her face. But Rex remembered the white sweater dress well from breakfast. And he didn't know another woman who would pair it with gold leather knee boots.

She wasn't moving. She wouldn't have even been able to run with her injured leg. His eyes burned.

The stunned look on Ferguson's face faded, and he sprinted toward the barn.

Rex rammed the door handle. "You don't need a fucking search warrant now."

He bolted out at a dead run. The barn loomed ahead, double doors wide to reveal a gleaming setup of work-out equipment inside. He didn't even want to know what kind of twisted shit went on in there. But he certainly intended to make sure it ended tonight.

"Ferguson, stop," Rex shouted, calling up his best commander tones and hoping it would buy him even a second's hesitation from the other man. "There's no chance you're going to get away. There's nowhere to hide, and you're outnumbered. Cops are already on the way. It's over."

Ferguson slowed, then stopped running altogether, standing backlit in the barn door. He turned to face Rex, with Mason, Jill, and Barrera all approaching slowly.

"Then I guess I'm going down in style." He hefted Livia more securely on his shoulder, a far too vulnerable and effective shield. "The headlines will double if I take a famous star with me, now won't they, Colonel?"

Rex stepped forward.

Ferguson pulled out a hunting knife, his eyes full of insanity, and worse yet, depravity. "Nobody moves a muscle unless I give the order, understand, Colonel? *I'm* in command tonight, like I should have been from the start if all you high-ranking tight asses had let me join up like I wanted."

The silvery blade glinted from the bare bulb in the barn, jagged teeth angry and bloodstained. If any of that was Livia's blood . . . Rex's eyes flashed to her inert form, searching for any signs of injury, difficult as hell to tell for certain in the dark of night.

"I understand." In fact he understood more than Ferguson probably realized.

Years of training for battle, fighting in wars, assessing the enemy came together in his head, and Rex knew. This man was now on a death mission. No reasoning, no waiting would help Livia—if she was even still alive. He would have to take Ferguson down now, before he had a chance to use that weapon to slice up his next victim in front of them.

Rex didn't doubt his decision, and he didn't have time to deal with regrets—like the fact that he hadn't called his boys in nearly a month. Or that he hadn't kissed Livia senseless when he'd had the opportunity.

He could only hope he would have a second chance. Rex eyed his opponent, measured the distance between himself and the knife.

And charged forward.

SEVENTEEN

Rex estimated he had three long strides to reach Ferguson's arm and put himself between the blade and Livia. Number one rule in a knife fight? Be prepared to sacrifice a body part.

One step. He was partial to his organs.

Two steps. His face wasn't much to look at, but he preferred it stayed intact.

Three steps. His arm was going to have to take the brunt.

Rex lunged at the roaring psychopath, grabbed a fistful of Livia's dress with one hand and threw his other forearm up. He flung Livia aside. The knife came down. His leather flight jacket slowed the blade for a heartbeat. Then fiery heat seared through his skin. He held back an agonized roar and put everything he had into crashing the guy backward into the barn. His glasses fell off and hit the ground with a crunch, but he was close enough to see clearly the spittle frothing rabidly in the corners of Ferguson's mouth.

A pop sounded.

A gunshot.

Rex waited for the flash of pain . . . And nothing.

Ferguson's eyes went wide. His grip on the wooden handle loosened. The knife thudded to the ground a second before the crazed killer toppled backward, blood blooming from the middle of his chest.

Rex scooped up the blade, crouching, prepared in case Ferguson lurched up from playing possum or scavenged some crazed final burst of maniacal purpose. Acrid smoke from the discharged weapon hung in the air.

"Colonel?" Mason's voice sounded from behind him, but he didn't touch.

Rex flinched anyway, his heart thudding. He shook his head clear and glanced back. Jill Walczak stood with her legs planted, a revolver in both hands, her eyes still steeled over with professional purpose.

Rex passed off the knife to Mason and raced to Livia. He'd been so damn steady a few seconds ago, and now he couldn't even keep his feet under him. He fell to his knees beside her and rolled her to her back. He searched for signs of life, of a heartbeat when he wasn't even sure his own was still pumping.

Dimly he registered the sound of sirens, radio chatter as he pressed his fingers to the side of her neck . . . and felt the flutter, the warmth. The life. His head fell to rest on her chest in relief, and yeah, so her sweater dress could soak up the two tears squeezing out of the corners of his eyes. He coughed the rest back and gathered her into his lap protectively, making damn sure no one would get to her without going through him.

He glanced up. Sometime while he'd been losing his shit, Mason had started hog-tying Ferguson, and Jill was holding her gun while placing a call on her cell phone.

Thank God for the backup of these two top-notch defenders. Rex looked at Jill, the most kick-ass camo dude he'd ever run across. "Thank you."

She tipped her mouth away from the receiver. "I couldn't have managed it without you, sir. You distracted him just in time."

"You saved my arm."

"We all did our jobs."

A siren wailed in the background, increasing and swelling into a whole freaking symphony of police enforcement. Rex cradled Livia closer, her heart thudding softly, a husky moan rumbling in her rib cage.

He lifted his head. "You're okay. You're safe now."

Her lashes fluttered open, fear flashing briefly before her dark eyes focused on his face. A smile tipped one corner of her mouth. "Where is my latte?"

* * *

Mason locked Jill's duplex door behind him and slid the dead bolt as well for good measure. On a night like this, even with the serial killer out cold in surgery, security felt all the more important. He still couldn't erase the image from his head of when she'd drawn her gun, ready to stand down a man who'd brutally murdered at least four people.

In that second before she'd pulled the trigger, Ferguson had looked at her like he wanted to . . . Mason shuddered, his forehead thudding to rest against the door. He couldn't even let the vision into his brain.

At least Livia Cicero was all right, uninjured other than the chloroform Ferguson had forced on her. She was being held overnight in the hospital for observation until the doctors were sure it had cleared her system. The colonel was keeping watch over her.

To think Ferguson had gone psycho because of being turned down for military service. Of course that was the very reason the military hadn't wanted him in the first place. Barrera had already uncovered that Ferguson failed the psych eval when he'd tried to enlist. However, the boundaries weren't as stringent for civilian employees working on base. It appeared Ferguson was even more off balance than anyone had realized, and he'd found a way to take out his twisted wrath on the military.

Phil had been called and reassured, although he'd still insisted on driving over just to look in her face and see for himself that Jill was fine before he drove away.

Leaving Mason alone with Jill.

He inhaled the pure, clean air of her home and pulled himself upright again, turning to face her. She stood in between the living and dining area, the mellow light of her curio cabinet casting her somber face in shadows. She crossed her arms over her chest defensively, and he knew he deserved it. He'd been a distant ass all day, but damn it, it had been everything he could do to manage to stay focused on keeping her alive.

He'd put up the wall today because their night together had rattled the hell out of him. *She* rattled him in a way no one had in a long, long time.

But now he'd made it through the day, alive, whole, and he couldn't wait any longer.

Just that fast, his hard-won control snapped. He charged forward, plowed his fingers through her hair, and kissed her. She stiffened, but only for a second before her arms looped around him, holding him with a strength and urgency that attested to just how on edge she was as well. Her hands tore at his flight suit, yanking down his zipper. His jeans had been covered in blood, so he'd changed. And now it seemed he was changing again.

Mason tugged at her jeans. "I need you so damn much, Jill, I'm not sure I can make it to your room."

He took a step back toward the sofa.

"Stop talking. You're wasting time." She tucked her hand in his pocket and filched a condom from his wallet so deftly his head spun even more than it already was.

She tugged him down to the floor, her soft but determined hand reaching inside his flight suit to free him, sheathe him. He barely had time to scrunch her jeans down her legs before she guided him inside her, and damn, but he was lost.

He levered on his elbows over her and thrust, rocking his hips against her while she arched up into him, around him. Her needy gasps drove him higher, while her frantic fingers scored his back. Everything he'd tried to hold back from her today poured out into the way his body fit with hers, drove inside her. No finesse or flowers or pretty words, he was all raw emotion, and damn it, but that tore through him.

And then Jill was trembling beneath him, her back bowing upward, her cries of pleasure louder, faster, her nails deeper into his ass through his flight suit, and damn what a time to realize they'd been so hot for each other they hadn't even gotten out of their clothes—

His release slammed through him, knocked him off balance, and he sank on top of her with a final heart-deep thrust that left him shaking as he buried his face in her hair.

She gasped under him, her grip slowly easing as her body went slack. He breathed in the scent of her, the scent of them together and alive at the end of a day that could have turned out so horribly differently.

He held Jill in his arms and fully accepted this for the first time.

This woman scared him shitless.

* * *

Sitting by Livia's hospital bed, Rex scrolled through his BlackBerry, checking for updates on the test flight. He'd dimmed the lights, and the private room was quiet except for the occasional calls over the loudspeaker that echoed in the hall.

His second-in-command was waiting on the flight line for the plane to land, since Rex had been getting his arm stitched. He would have to head over before long. Soon. After Livia woke, and he could reassure himself one last time that she was really alive and well.

He worked his stitched arm while reading through . . . The plane had landed safely. All appeared a go for the unveiling in two days. He cranked and stretched his elbow, determined to be in that plane for the big show, no matter how much it hurt.

And it did. But he'd survived, and so had Livia. His thumb slipped off his BlackBerry, and he drank in the sight of her sleeping. Her silky black hair fanned across the bleached white pillowcase, her exotic perfume overriding the antiseptic smell. Somehow she made even the dingy flowered hospital gown look elegant, her chipped manicured nails gripping tight to the sheet with residual tension.

Thank God, she hadn't been harmed beyond the

chloroform Ferguson had used to subdue her. She hadn't even known what was happening until she'd woken on their way to the barn. Thank heaven Ferguson had forced her to take that call in hopes no one would go looking for her at the hotel. While Rex was just damn glad she was alive, he'd breathed one helluva sigh of relief when the doctor had informed them Livia had not been sexually assaulted.

However, she was being held in the hospital overnight for observation until they were sure the drug had cleared her system. That was fine with him, because she was safe here. He still hated hospitals, but he could deal with it for now. He took comfort from the regular check-ins from the nurses to reassure him she was still okay.

Her head rolled along the pillow, and she moaned. He bolted to his feet. She blinked fast, tried to talk, but her lips were dry. He passed her the juice cup from beside her bed.

"The nurse said you're supposed to hydrate as much as you can." He put the straw to her mouth.

She sipped down the last of her orange juice, then passed the empty cup back to him. "Thank you."

He placed it on the rolling tray and sat in the recliner by her bedside again. "Not a problem. Would you like some more?"

"No, I am good for now." She inched up higher on the double-stacked pillows. "And thank you for saving my life. I'm so sorry you were injured."

His arm throbbed like a son of a bitch, and he would sport a scar, but overall he had a lot to be thankful for, since the blade had somehow missed any muscles or major arteries. "I'm fine. A lot of people had a hand in figuring out that Ferguson had abducted you."

"You were the one who understood my hidden message on the phone."

"It's a part of my training to listen for distress words and cues." Yet he knew full well he'd been tuned in to her voice, her fear on a level way beyond anything he'd picked up in technical training.

"Well, thank you all the same." She tapped his temple. "You aren't wearing your glasses."

"They broke." When he'd tackled Ferguson. When he'd been consumed with rage at the man and fear that Livia was dead. "I can see okay without them when I'm walking around. I have an old extra pair for driving. I guess this is a sign it's time to make a change. You told me once I should replace those chunky frames."

She laughed, her voice raspy with a reminder of what she'd lost. "You remember that?"

He simply nodded.

She sank back into her pillows, her brow furrowed. "Why were you so resistant to change them?"

"My wife liked them." He tamped down a wince, his emotions too close to the surface on a day like this.

She touched his hand lightly, her nail resting on his bare ring finger. "How long has she been gone?"

"It's been a year."

"That is not so long as you try to make it sound."

He glanced up sharply. How did she know? Understand? Everyone else seemed to think twelve months was some kind of magic number. Hell, he'd even been trying to convince himself of the same thing.

Livia smiled gently, her lips still glistening from the juice she'd drunk. "Thank you for a lovely breakfast, Rex, but I believe I am going to have to break up with you."

Would this woman ever quit turning his life upside down? He squinted to detect the nuances of her expression or perhaps to make sure she wasn't still delirious. "I'm not sure what you mean."

"I know full well I forced you into that so-called date, and I have to admit you are a fascinating man. But I see now it will go nowhere."

"Good Lord, Livia, I just saved your life. Doesn't that count for something?" Age disparity and lifestyle differences be damned, he had more feelings than he ever would have expected for this woman.

"You do make me smile. Although answer me one question. Am I right in believing you would have taken this cut if it had been any other person in the same position? Of course you would." She leaned forward. "So I do not owe you sex for the saving."

"You're outrageous."

"*Si*, I have been told that before." She cupped his face. "I have also been told I do not play second violin well."

"Second fiddle."

"Right. You still love your wife." She hesitated as if maybe hoping he would say something . . . anything.

But there was nothing he could say to that other than that she was right. He still loved Heather until it filled him up inside. As much as Livia fascinated him, drew him, even made him want to climb in bed with a woman for the first time in a year, he could see in her eyes that wasn't all she was looking for.

There was a damn good chance he'd had his once-in-a-lifetime already. So he stayed silent.

Her head sagged back on her pillow, her hair a dark splash against the bleached white hospital sheets. "In a strange way, that makes this even harder for me, because, oh, there is something so very intriguing about a man who gives his heart that completely." She scratched her fingernail lightly over the left side of his chest before her hand fell to her lap. "But me, I want to be that woman for some man. I deserve that."

And he couldn't deny she was right about that. She deserved it all.

He gripped the bed rail to keep from reaching for her. "Livia Cicero, I can say with absolute certainty when that man comes along for you, he's not going to stand a chance. You're one helluva woman."

She pressed her lips to her fingers, then touched his mouth. "Thank you, Colonel Scanlon. It has been a pleasure."

He turned away fast before he did something stupid like ask her for some time to sort through his feelings. He was doing the right thing in giving this young woman a chance to live her life. If there were anything more out there for him, it wouldn't be the sort of roller-coaster romance he'd enjoyed with Heather. And it sure as hell wouldn't be a bungee-style emotional free-for-all that came with a woman like Livia.

It was time to move on.

Swallowing a bellyful of regret, he knew his exit line. As the door hissed closed behind him, he could still taste the hint of her on his lips.

EIGHTEEN

Jill sat on the edge of her bed, combing through her wet hair and wishing her feelings were as easy to untangle.

Mason stretched out under the covers already, his hands behind his head. After their cathartic sex on the floor—mind-blowing and even a little scary in its intensity—they'd showered together silently, made love again more slowly, then headed toward the canopied retreat tucked in the corner of her room. They talked, sure, about everything except each other.

It seemed strange somehow to transition into that sharing-a-bed through-the-night stage so quickly and without discussion. Yet he held back the sapphire and silver comforter, smiled at her, told her she was beautiful as he skimmed his knuckles down her spine.

He was charming.

He was solicitous.

He was sensual.

But he wasn't intimate, not on any real emotional level. She couldn't hide from the truth. She wanted something more with him. If she'd learned anything tonight, it was that life could be cut short all too quickly for her to waste time.

She turned to Mason, determined to shake some emotion out of him and find out what was going on in that gorgeous head of his. How to start?

Before she could reconsider, she blurted, "I think that first wife of yours really did a number on you."

Mason's fingers went still against her bare spine. Then his hand left her altogether. "Do you really think it's wise to have this conversation when we're both exhausted?" He clicked off the Tiffany lamp. "We can talk after we've gotten some sleep."

Maybe he had a point, but then maybe she did, too, and he was trying to avoid the discussion altogether. Perhaps she just needed to take a different approach. Jill set her comb on the night table and slid her legs under the Egyptian cotton sheets, her decadent pleasure. Yet they only served to tease along her already heightened nerves that hungered for Mason's stronger touch.

God, she was about to jump out of her skin. "This isn't going to work."

Mason sighed and clicked on the light again. "What do you want to know?"

He looked like he would rather have a root canal.

And honestly, if that was how he felt about the possibility of connecting on a deeper level, why would she push for it anyhow? Disappointment simmered.

"Never mind." She tugged the covers up. "You're right. Forget I even freaking asked." And then she felt petty for snapping when she should be grateful to be alive. Instead, she wanted to scream.

"My *ex*-wife didn't do anything to me. It takes two to make or break a marriage. I'm just as much to blame, as I'm sure you're noticing, since apparently I've done something to piss you off."

Curiosity chased away her irritation. She ignored the last part of his little speech and pressed for her answers now that she had him talking. "Where is she now?"

Mason sat up and draped his arms over his knees, covers tenting over his bent legs. "She's married to a firefighter in California."

His bare chest and muscled arms called to her fingers, but she kept her hands twisted along the top of the sheet. "How do you feel about that?"

"I don't love her anymore, if that's what you're asking. Do you really want to talk about this right—"

"Yes, I do want talk about this now. Right now," she finished his sentence.

He studied her with oddly intense eyes before looking back at stripes on the comforter as if they held some mystic pattern. "Fine. I meant it when I said I don't love her, but she's a good person. She was a strong person, could even put up with the dangerous nature of the job—hell, look at how she's in a successful marriage with a guy who fights California fires, for crying out loud." Frustration leaked into his voice.

She inched closer to him, feeling closer for the first time since he'd shut her out earlier. "That must have hurt, seeing her move on."

He looked sideways at her. "I told you. I don't love her. We made a stupid, young mistake. She couldn't handle the long separations. She said it felt like she wasn't even married after a while. Most of the spouses around here would agree the job has that effect on relationships. Have you heard what you want now?"

Mason might as well have left the room for all the emotional distance he'd put between them again. He'd said his piece, and he'd found a way to march through life without dealing with it, without moving on in any real sense. She hurt for him as much as she hurt for herself.

"So that's it." She thumped him on the arm lightly. "You have your pat answer in place for why you can't be a part of any relationship."

"My feelings are my feelings," he answered in a flat, emotionless voice.

"Your feelings are a crock."

"How considerate of you to let me know what I'm feeling." He crossed his arms over his chest. "Maybe I should just sit here, and you can fill in the blanks, since you can finish my damn sentences for me."

She recognized his rude words for exactly what they were. Mason was a man running scared. "For a suave ladies' man, you're really being a jackass." Jill yanked the coverlet from the bottom of the bed and wrapped it around herself. "You're right about not talking. Too much has happened too fast. There's no reason for you to worry about protecting me anymore. I think you should go."

And damn him, Mason snatched up his clothes and didn't even argue on his way out the door. She'd always expected things would end this way if she ever dared act on her attraction to him, that her feelings could run deeper. She just hadn't expected it to hurt this damn much over the possibility of losing something so brief that had rocked her world so hard.

* * *

Two days later, Mason stood with his crew in front of the futuristic transport plane that would revolutionize airlift operations. If it went well today, by sunset they could finally put this hellacious week behind them.

Put Jill behind him?

He didn't know what to say to her. He'd left her a single message, checking, just to say . . . nothing much at all actually. Of course he'd copped out and placed the call at a time he knew she would be working. Damn straight he needed space.

Her questions had dug too deep, too fast. He preferred his life light and uncomplicated—not words he would ever use to describe Jill Walczak.

And he needed to figure out something before much longer, since Jill stood in her camos with Dr. Lee Drummond and the security team guarding this private unveiling of the hypersonic jet for generals from Canada, the U.K., and Australia. The Predator had already launched ahead of them, circling for a bird's-eye view to ensure no unwelcome visitors. Once they all landed, there would be no avoiding a face-to-face with Jill.

For now, he peered through his sunglasses at the airplane. Until today, it hadn't often been out in daylight during its testing. He exhaled in awe. He'd almost forgotten how amazing it was. And untraditional.

Real visionaries back in the early stages had stepped outside the box to come up with this one. From the very start, it defied regular expectations. The nose looked more like a wing, even changing its angle and shape to increase aerodynamics as the aircraft reached hypervelocity. The rest of the aircraft resembled the "lifting body" experiments of long ago, with a wide, flat bottom and shorter wings that turned up at the ends.

Damn amazing that they'd made it to this day with so much working against them. But even the horrifying distraction of a serial killer couldn't stop this mission. It appeared that DNA would link Ferguson to all four of the killings and perhaps even some earlier crimes, including the questionable death of a prostitute that had cast such shadows over the end of Phillip Yost's years in law enforcement.

As for all the supposed ties the victims had to Mason? They'd known the links were thin at best, and it appeared his friend Chuck Tanaka had crossed paths with the victims as well, which brought them to Ferguson's attention. The fact that they bore supposed grudges against Mason was apparently irrelevant. Ferguson's MO had been targeting people with ties to the military, plain and simple, inflicting pain at a higher level than he could as a physical therapist.

Strangely, though, as loose-lipped as Ferguson got when faced with figuring out a way to dodge the death penalty, he still denied attacking Annette Santos. He said he'd gotten the idea to add the alien twist from hearing her discuss her attack with Chuck and when she shared the details about the weird swirl in the dirt.

So who'd attacked Annette?

That was for the likes of Barrera and Gallardo and others in law enforcement to determine. Mason had his own battles to fight. Right now, he wasn't sure what felt like a more colossal task—flying a mission with the potential to send him pinwheeling through the sky again, or trying to convince Jill they could have a relationship without flaying each other's emotions raw.

"Sir, here they come," Mason said out of the corner of his mouth to Colonel Scanlon, nodding toward the blue SUV nearing the craft. The vehicle transported the visiting generals for their up-close.

"Look sharp, boys," Scanlon said softly, prescription aviator shades shielding his eyes. "No grab ass, and don't go all chatty if they ask questions. Keep it short, and let's move things along." He made eye contact with the crew, one man at a time.

The blue SUV pulled up in front of them. A driver and an aide in uniform jumped out and opened the back doors. Out stepped the commander of the Air Force Flight Test Center and air vice marshals from Canada, Australia, and the U.K.

"Damn," Mason mumbled, "that is a shitload of flag officers."

Jimmy and Vince hid smirks behind their hands. Scanlon shot them a quick, stern look. Strangely enough, after all the emotion the colonel had shown when saving Livia Cicero, the woman was nowhere to be seen. Colonel Scanlon had simply informed them she'd left for southern Florida to recuperate from the trauma. His closed expression had brooked no further questions about any relationship with the Italian singer, even for guys used to needling each other about women. Some lines you just didn't cross.

The colonel stepped forward, saluting each general in turn. "Welcome to the desert, gentlemen."

The officers returned his salute, but they weren't staring at him. Their eyes were all pinned on the bizarre gray aircraft behind him.

Scanlon smiled for the first time. "She is a little odd-looking, but she really gets the job done fast."

The Australian officer replied, "It better, because this sheila will surely never win a beauty contest."

Scanlon chuckled. "No, I suppose not. If you will follow us, my crew and I will give you a walk around."

Twenty minutes and about a million questions later, they had completed the viewing with the VIPs. The American general gave the crew a nod as they got back into the SUV.

Colonel Scanlon turned to the crew and said,
"Mount up, boys. Time to earn that flight pay."

Mason hefted his flight bag and stole one last look
at Jill in the same uniform she'd worn when she'd
taken him down after his hellish descent into the desert.
While he certainly hoped this mission would finish on
a more positive note than when he'd been nose-first in
the sand with a gun at his back, he wasn't so sure he
and Jill would end up any better off.

And the hell of it all? He stood a better chance at
understanding how to work this multibillion-dollar test
craft than he did at navigating his way back into the
good graces of this one particular woman.

* * *

Tired, confused, and a little overwhelmed by the mag-
nitude of what she was seeing, Jill stood on the tarmac
with Dr. Lee Drummond, who'd apparently been a major part of the testing team from the civilian angle. History was being made. Mason was making history. And
she grieved that things were so messed up between
them, they couldn't even look forward to celebrating this
awesome moment together.

She and the stylish engineer, Dr. Drummond, stood
off to the side. Other security forces were posted stra-
tegically throughout the viewing area. The four generals confabbed a few feet away, protocol somewhat
falling away. They couldn't hide their awe as the unrelenting sun showcased the large gray beast.

She still couldn't believe her own luck at having

viewed this aircraft, something the regular public wouldn't even know about for years to come. Ab-so-freaking-lutely amazing. And her heart ached so much, she couldn't even enjoy the wonder of the event.

Other than a select few present and ground crew, the flight line was totally deserted and silent. Even the normally busy airspace above stayed empty but for a couple of birds. Air and land had been cordoned off to keep prying eyes away.

She leaned toward Dr. Drummond. "This must be such a proud moment for you."

Dr. Drummond smoothed back a strand of wind-whipped hair. "Plenty of people had a hand in this over the years."

"Still, I admire the genius you're reputed to bring to your job. Those different insights from civilian science help fuel military progress at the most competitive level. I really respect that kind of cooperative effort to propel technology forward."

Dr. Drummond's eyes took on a faraway look as she watched the aircraft . . . no, wait. Her gaze seemed to be following Mason as he boarded the aircraft. She toyed with her silver necklace. "Some are more committed than others. It all comes down to who is the most dedicated to perfecting the science and carrying it through, as opposed to those who are more concerned with flitting through their lives with no regard for other people's contributions."

Something about the fire in her voice, the bitterness in the upturn of her lip combined with the enmity in her glare at Mason set off alarms in Jill's mind as the engines roared to life, more of a low-drone whisper actually. This woman had a serious grudge beyond just professional tension.

And it appeared directed squarely at Mason.

Jill sifted through what she'd learned about the woman. Not much. The doctor was noted to be a genius and worked closely with them on secret test projects, such as this one. Dust swirled on the tarmac, gusting over them as the jet taxied toward the runway, lined up, hitched to a stop, and then. . . .

Whoosh, the plane swept up and into the horizon.

Exhaling, Jill tried for a neutral, more conciliatory tone with the woman standing transfixed next to her. "At least everything is coming together well today, so we won't have a repeat of that awful accident last week."

Dr. Drummond dusted off her clothes, even though she looked darn near perfect, given the gritty outdoor viewing area. "Sometimes it's a win to discover the flaws in a test plan, even if it means the project fails."

"I guess I understand in theory. But isn't there a point when good is good enough?"

"Imperfections must be weeded out with all due diligence." She adjusted her necklace obsessively again. "Nothing short of perfection is acceptable. You have to understand it's all about precision. It's my job, my mission to ensure every detail lines up. I right wrongs. I bring logic and balance to life."

Okay, Jill was starting to get a little creeped out. This woman was seriously wired too tightly, her need for perfection obviously going beyond precisely slicked-back hair and a perfectly centered silvery charm necklace.

"I should go check in with the rest of security to see, uh, if there are any updates."

Dr. Drummond clutched Jill's arm in a skeletally thin grip. "Honestly, I used to admire Mason, not romantically, but as a decent human being. He never led anyone on. It's obvious he's still torn apart over his divorce."

Surprise stalled her. "How do you know about his divorce?"

No one else around here had ever said anything about Mason being married before, which must mean they didn't know, or she certainly would have heard the gossip.

Dr. Drummond arched a thinly plucked brow. "Apparently he told *you*. Now, that should tell you something."

The observation stopped her cold. She'd been so caught up in what he hadn't said, she hadn't considered that for Mason, he'd already said a boatload more than he'd told others. "How did *you* find out?"

"Google, of course. Sometimes the simplest answer is the smartest. A good portion of his life is there on the Internet, thanks to his wealthy parents' frequent appearances on the social pages. He's rich, you know."

"His *parents* are wealthy. He doesn't take anything from them." She admired his proud independence. She admired a lot about him.

Lee rolled a shoulder dismissively. "Giving away all that money from his folks? I guess he's not so smart after all."

Something more than curiosity kept Jill from walking away. Professional instincts perhaps? Or just a genuine defensiveness for Mason when someone judged him so harshly? Too harshly. "If he didn't hurt you romantically, what did he do to make you dislike him so?"

Dr. Drummond's blasé facade faded in a flash as she turned venomous eyes toward Jill. This wasn't dislike. It was downright loathing. "He tried to torpedo my work a year ago." Her chin lifted with condescension. "I can't share all the details with you because of the classified nature of our work. Suffice it to say, I had invested my heart and soul into the project, and if my name's going to be attached, it damn well better be perfect. It's not fair they wouldn't listen to me."

Not *fair*? Lee sounded more like a six-year-old who got a smaller piece of cake at a party. Could all those brains and advancement ahead of time have left her emotionally stunted? Jill got the unavoidable sense that Lee's adult genius had become a dangerous weapon when paired with childish pettiness.

Jill's eyes hitched on the necklace, a round charm with circles etched smaller and smaller with a diamond in the middle. A swirl. *Like circles in the sand.*

She resisted the urge to bolt the hell away.

A coincidence, right? Just a fluke that this woman wore a piece of jewelry with a pattern so similar to a signature marking Ferguson used. A marking he said he'd stolen from a random attack on Annette Santos. God, could Dr. Lee Drummond have been the original attacker? Annette had worked as a contractor in the same test squadron with Mason and Dr. Lee Drummond.

The brilliant engineer dropped her charm, keen discernment glinting. "You can stop spinning your theories around, and don't bother denying what you're thinking. I'm smarter than that. I can see perfectly well when someone has decided they're out to get me." Her smile curdled. "Like you are now."

"I don't know what you're talking about," Jill stalled, inching away, her hand sliding to her gun holstered to her waist. There were people all around them, even if they were too far away to overhear what was being said. They were on a military base, for heaven's sake. There were security forces everywhere—granted, they were all more than twenty yards away, busy guarding generals and machinery. But it wasn't like Lee Drummond could just up and leave. This woman couldn't harm her.

Could she?

Dr. Drummond closed her arms over her tightly belted turquoise leather jacket. "Go ahead and try to call for help to stop . . . whatever it is you think I've done, using my secret clearance, a clearance that allows me to go anywhere, touch anything." She leaned closer, her perfume thick and cloying. "And even if I had done something sinister like tamper with that imperfect plane so it won't complete the testing, even set up an explosion perhaps, do you really think anyone would stand a chance of tracing it back to me? I am so much smarter than any of you."

A bomb—in Mason's plane. Her stomach plummeted to her boots.

She forced her voice to stay steady. "I can't believe you're telling me this." Other than the fact that she'd seen crazed killers who reached a point where they needed an audience for their crimes. But it didn't seem wise to mention that right now.

"Why wouldn't I tell you? It's your word against mine, hearsay, actually. In fact, if you run to the police and try to implicate me, I'll vow it could just as easily have been you who set this up. Maybe you're a crazy stalker striking back at him for all those years he didn't notice you." She smiled evilly. "Again, you forget who has the real brains here."

And how damn horrifying to think the woman's plan could actually work. Jill had to hope that need for an "audience" would cause some kind of slip. "How did *you* manage this?"

Dr. Drummond tapped the ID dangling from a lanyard around her neck. "Thanks to this, I can access anywhere, anytime, unsupervised. By the time the 'incident' is sorted through and they rule out terrorism, the evidence will point to Mason having screwed up.

After all, look how he botched that drop a few flights ago. Very coincidental, don't you think? He really should have gotten out of the way a year ago when I tried to tell them craft wasn't *perfect* yet."

Jill suppressed a shiver at the cold blast of evil emanating from the woman beside her. "Then let's talk to them now, explain—"

"Enough. It's too late for that. Production of this plane must stop altogether." Lee assessed Jill's uniform in a dismissive up-and-down sweep. "Now you have your little role to play in my drama. Go." She flicked her fingers. "Go do your job, try to save the day. Telling you and watching you squirm has only made this all the more fun. I should have tried this technique with some other very rude people earlier."

"You're insane."

"Take good care of that new doggie of yours," Dr. Drummond said. "We wouldn't want anything to happen to him."

Fear for Mason iced clear through to Jill's spine all over again. She had to get a warning up to Mason and his crew that somewhere on board their plane, Dr. Lee Drummond had used her expertise and high-security clearance to plant a bomb.

NINETEEN

★————————————————————————————

"We have a what on the plane?" Mason tamped down the nauseating fear and tightened his focus, looking frenetically around the cargo hold for anything out of the ordinary.

With control panels, hanging gear, and packed pallets, there were thousands of possibilities. Even the smallest explosives could do lethal damage to an aircraft at this height and speed.

The colonel replied, "Yes, I said a bomb. I don't understand all the whys or wherefores yet, but apparently somehow Jill Walczak found new evidence indicating that Dr. Drummond has either turned traitor or gone off the deep end. Regardless, she could be out to set you up, make it look like an accident that's your fault. Jill's theory makes a damn frightening amount of sense. Drummond even said something about having given her plan a test run a couple of flights ago, which leads me to believe the bomb must be on the pallet."

His parachuting accident hadn't been an accident after all? And Dr. Lee Drummond was setting him up? Hell, was this ever going to end? "Is Jill all right?"

"Fine, so far as I know, but we'll be able to determine that much better if we land safely."

"Capiche, Colonel." The sooner the better.

"I'm sending Jimmy back to lend extra hands and eyes."

"Roger." Mason swung his attention back to the pallets.

Drummond. If only she'd been removed from the team when he'd expressed his concerns a year ago about her obsessions that bordered on bizarre. But that was irrelevant at the moment. He had a bomb to locate.

He walked gingerly around the pallets, checking, searching without touching. "Colonel, let's just drop the pallets in the desert now."

"We can't," Colonel Scanlon answered over headset. "With the software that's running the airplane right now, we can only get the load out over the range. Ironically, that was put in there for safety. If we off-loaded it now, we would also be sending some sort of bomb out to wherever the wind took the parachute. It has to be in the range as originally planned for the drop. It's faster and safer than returning to base, where we could blow up a crap ton of people."

Mason glanced at his watch. How long before that

thing went off? The aircraft hummed under his boots. Jimmy stepped into the cargo hold, his face somber inside his helmet.

They needed to act fast. "Colonel, any ideas on how the bomb is triggered? Is it on a timer or what?"

"We don't know. Drummond is swearing Jill made this up, and if anything goes wrong, we should blame your girlfriend. We can sort through all that on the ground. Now, ready the load. Unless we learn anything new, we're dumping everything."

Not a chance in hell did he believe Jill was lying about anything. Mason started checking the pallets over, in each crevice, under tarps, but the sheer amounts made the task beyond any minute-long scan. Damn, damn, damn it! It could be anywhere, and it wasn't like he was going to find a red X with a sign that said, Bomb Here.

Damn, he wished he had a second chance with Jill, to say he was sorry for being a jackass. Sorry for not reassuring her that he believed she was the most amazing woman ever to walk the planet, and hell yeah, that scared him. But if she would hang tough, he would sort out how to get past the fear. Because he was even more freaked out by the possibility of being without her, never getting the chance to know more about what kinds of tea she liked and exactly where she enjoyed being kissed.

All of which had become increasingly clear to him in the past two days of silence, and now came crashing down on his helmeted fat head as he faced the possibility of dying without seeing her again.

Think. Stop freaking out, and definitely stop picturing Jill's face. "Sir, I bet it's not on a timer. If the flight had been delayed, it might have gone off on the ramp." He thought back to working with Lee Drummond. She'd always planned for every contingency. She would never take an unnecessary risk. "I assume the bomber would want to get away with it, so it would have to look like an accident." Or blamed on the person who loaded the cargo hold.

"That certainly makes sense to me. What would the trigger be then?"

Jimmy clicked on. "Maybe an altimeter. If we go above or below a certain altitude, it goes off?"

Scanlon keyed up. "I don't think so. It wouldn't look like an accident if we just blew up in flight. The airplane has been tested for years, and if it just blew up while we weren't doing anything but changing altitude or opening the ramp, it would be suspicious. Vapor? Got any ideas?"

"How about airspeed?" Vince suggested from the front. "Like that movie with the bus. Go below a certain speed, and it blows."

Mason eyed the cargo hold quickly, aware of the danger of each passing second. "It would have to be wired into the plane somehow to know the speed. There aren't any off wires back there are there? Jimmy, see anything I'm missing?"

He shook his head. "Nothing out of the ordinary."

Silence filled the airplane for a few moments while Mason—the whole crew—scrambled for options. He thought back to the original drop, Drummond's so-called practice run. She'd targeted him as the fall guy.

What if . . . "It has to be connected to the pallets leaving in the drop. It would just look like a replay of the last mishap if the pallets were off-loading, and something bad happened. Maybe the G forces of the yank from the parachute triggers the bomb."

"Damn," Scanlon hissed low. "I think you're right."

Mason eyed the pallet. "What if we off-load without the chutes? Cut them loose manually and start a climb so that first mini-chute opens later, when they're out of the craft and sets off the bomb then. If they blow up, then we'll know all's clear to return to base." If not, they would have to land in the desert and pray they didn't explode a big crater in the earth.

Even with time ticking down, there was a collective moment of silence as they all calculated the risks of what they were about to do. The sweat that had been beading on Mason's forehead trickled into his eyebrow.

"Okay, then," Scanlon agreed. "You're the boss in back. Make it happen."

Mason cracked his knuckles inside his gloves, cricked his neck, eying the pallets. Heat itched along his back as much as the exertion while he worked with

Jimmy to disconnect the tie-downs he'd so diligently put in place earlier. "Vapor, how long till we can get these out?"

"We're pointed at the range and should be at the drop point in about ninety seconds."

"All set back here." Mason turned to Jimmy. "When we start climbing, these things should start rolling. We might have to give them a push. Shove them straight. If they turn, they might get jammed up. Masks up and oxygen check."

Jimmy nodded and gave a thumbs-up.

Mason tightened his mask into place and tested his oxygen regulator. All over but the crying. "Pilot, back end is up on oxygen, cleared to open the doors."

"Copy, doors coming open." In the rear of the aircraft the doors opened, providing a glimpse of blue sky instead of the inky darkness he'd faced in all other drops from this craft. "Vapor, update?"

"Coming up on the release point," Vince's voice boomed over the mic. "Start the climb, Colonel."

The deck angled beneath his boots as the nose rose. The pallets started a gentle glide toward the open back. Wheels rumbled along the tracks in a slow elephant walk parody of the whiz-bang releases of the past.

Wheels creaked, then stopped.

Shit.

Mason motioned for Jimmy and went to hot mic so he could talk hands-free. "Time to push."

Jimmy might be tall and lanky, but he had a rep for being a lean, mean mother in a bar fight. They could use all of that fight right now.

Alongside his crewmate, Mason leaned a shoulder into the last of the pallets, planted his boots on the deck, and shoved. Harder, until muscles screamed and burned in his legs. His ankle throbbed, a reminder of his accident just a week ago. Thank God he had Jimmy's help. Never again would he pick on the guy for the unrelenting hours he spent in the gym pounding his body into submission.

Finally . . . the pallets gave way. The first rolled downward, closer to the open door, and hit the wind.

Tumbling from the aircraft.

"Ooh-rah," Jimmy's cheer thundered through the headset.

Then—*push*—number two gone. This was actually going to work. Now they just had to pray they'd guessed correctly on the bomb's location—and his gut told him they had.

And—*push*—number three away.

Push—number four. Harder. He strained.

Jimmy's foot slipped on the rollers. The load shifted sideways. Mason launched toward it as Jimmy grappled for a hold. The pallet continued rumbling toward the rear, drifting sideways.

Mason sprinted to get ahead of the errant cargo. Too late. The load wedged into the side of the airplane right next to the door.

Shit. Mason motioned for Jimmy, and they worked to tip it even a little, straining, pushing toward the middle.

It was jammed but good. How much time would they have left to free it? "I'll pull, and you push."

Mason edged around, almost there. His safety line went taut. No more length.

"Damn, damn, damn it!" Out of options and time, there was only one thing left to do. Unhook. "I'm going around."

Without hesitation, he unclipped the line at his waist. There was no way he was letting his crew die up here. No fucking way. He'd lived that hell the week before when he thought their plane went down. Now he moved in front of the pallet and grabbed the netting, tugging until his fingers numbed. The pallet inched, but not enough. He met Jimmy's eyes.

Mason nodded. Yeah, this was how it would have to be. He was going out for another free fall. Hopefully, it would go well, but if not, he needed to let Jill know . . . Know what?

God, it was so damn obvious now. The only thing that mattered now other than keeping his crew alive. "Tell Jill I love her, and I'm sorry."

Mason pulled, throwing all his body weight into the last pallet, even realizing where that would take him—right out the back of the hypsersonic jet. He'd been there before and survived. He could do it again. He *would* survive it again.

The pallet wrenched free and slid toward the ramp. Mason jumped on and held the cargo netting tightly as they slipped into the wind. The frigid air slapped his flight suit against him, the sun blindingly bright. He looked down . . . Shit. Vertigo kicked in as the desert view spun like a muted kaleidoscope of tans and browns.

The pallet tumbled as it went through the engine wash of the plane and then slowed its rotation. Mason regained his equilibrium and risked looking down again. The cargo's chute probably had at least thirty seconds before the built-in altimeter opened it—and maybe set off a bomb.

Of course it was in this load. It would only be a sorta good bar story if it wasn't in the packed cargo. If the bomb was in this pallet, it would be the best bar story ever.

Assuming he survived.

He flattened his boots against a crate and thrust himself away from the pallet. He grabbed his rip cord. Yanked. The pallet fell away as his own chute slowed his descent.

He zeroed in on the load dropping faster and faster. A small chute whistled out of the bundle on top, then the main chutes spouted out.

The pallet exploded into a huge fireball.

Percussion waves rippled upward, fluttering his parachute against the cloudless blue sky. Heat slapped his face like a drive-through sunburn. But he stayed aloft. Grabbing the risers, he steered himself out of the heat and clear of charred bits of debris.

Above him, the hypersonic jet made no sound. No telltale flash of light in the sky. There'd been only one bomb, and it had gone off harmlessly, away from them all.

Damn! This now qualified as a *great* bar story. He would be drinking free forever.

He eyed the empty patch of desert test range, nothing but a couple of rusted-out trailers for target practice, some bubbly round cacti and scrub brush.

And a truck. A really familiar truck. In fact, the same sort he'd seen driven by the sexiest camo dudette ever to walk the planet.

He laughed, loud and unrestrained. There was no one up here to hear him anyway. Life was good and he was alive and best of all, Jill had come to pick him up for the second time in a week. He had the sneaking suspicion this was a woman who would always be there waiting for him when he landed.

Squinting in the unrelenting sun, he didn't take his eyes off the approaching vehicle for even a second. The big blue F-150 screeched to a stop, and the driver's side door flung open, hard and fast.

Jill stepped out.

Even from hundreds of feet overhead, he could tell it was her. The red hair. The perfect curves. And something else about her that just called to him.

She shaded her eyes with her hand, looked up at him—and she smiled.

Oh yeah, this would make for the best bar story ever.

* * *

The bartender looked more like ZZ Top turned surfer as he leaned toward a college-age tourist with a camera around her neck. "You've got your grays and the greens. The grays are your most common breed of aliens. About seventy-five percent of the ones we've seen out here fall into that category."

The gum-smacking coed angled forward with avid eyes, while her boyfriend clicked cell phone pictures of Area 51 memorabilia on the wall. "Gray, as in the short, androgynous-looking ones?"

The seasoned bartender—Aaron—sketched on a napkin, while the other guy setting up drinks raced to and fro behind him. "I guess you could put it that way. . . ."

Jill soaked up the familiarity of it all as Mason accepted another toast from his squadron pals while the jukebox cranked Led Zeppelin. They'd asked him to share last week's parachuting story no less than twenty-five times, and as others retold it, the tale got wilder and woollier.

As if the entire experience hadn't been hellish enough.

Reliving that moment of watching him float to the ground awesomely whole and alive made her eyes sting all over again. There hadn't been much to say when he'd landed. They'd mostly stood there holding each other and kissing and holding on even harder until a half-dozen security vehicles encircled them.

Once they'd been debriefed and Mason was cleared

by the doctor, they'd gone back to her place, made love, and stayed there. Uncle Phil had even brought Boo home to her—the old guy had a lightness in his step as the old rumors fell away, his name, his reputation cleared.

She and Mason had fallen into an unacknowledged routine. His house was bigger than her duplex, but he didn't have much furniture. So every evening after work, he just showed up at her door with another cooking pot to try out in her kitchen before he stayed the night.

The time to talk would come. She had faith in that now as she found more peace and confidence within herself.

Her instincts were good, damn it, with people as well as at work. She knew that now. She'd certainly pegged Lee Drummond. With the remains of the pallet wreckage and the information Jill had wrangled, Colonel Scanlon and a team of investigators were uncovering a long line of tampering connected to Dr. Drummond. Oh, she'd hidden her tracks well as she quietly sabotaged people and projects according to her own twisted agendas. But she wasn't as smart as she thought. Apparently most of what she'd said to Jill had been picked up by some kind of remote-controlled flying listening device that looked like a bird. Thank God, or they could have spent years trying to sort through evidence. Even a crummy lawyer could have made the argument there was just as much evidence that Jill could have been the culprit trying to pin things on Dr. Drummond. The nanotechnology security measures had been employed because of the sensitive nature of the viewing. It appeared Dr. Drummond would be facing serious jail time.

And she hadn't even managed to tank the jet project.

Jill knew she would be in the dark about details from this point until the public unveiling, however many years in the future that might be. But with a simple nod, Mason had assured her she'd done her part in making sure that historic aircraft she'd seen so briefly would one day make it into the military's inventory.

Mason set his empty beer mug on a passing waitress's tray, snapping Jill's attention back to the noisy bar as he turned his full focus on her.

"Well, my friends," Mason announced to his cluster of fans, "it's been a pleasure, but I have a dinner date with a beautiful woman. So, if you'll pardon me . . ." He angled through the throng and hooked his arm around her shoulder as she stood to join him.

Jill slipped her arm around his waist beneath his leather flight jacket. Once they stepped outside into the darkened parking lot, she looked up at him. "Do I need to play designated driver and take your keys, Sergeant?"

"I only had one beer. Scout's honor." He brushed two fingers over his heart and then across her lips— very slowly. "I prefer to recall every detail after I make love to you."

When he chose to talk, wow did he have a way with words. In fact, she liked a lot of things he did with that mouth of his. "Then let's be sure to make it a night to remember."

He tucked her closer against his side, warming her with his body heat and leathery scent. "I may have an idea for adding some extra power to the memorability factor. I was thinking we should pick up Boo and stay at my house tonight."

Her feet stumbled on loose gravel. Sure, they'd been making progress, growing closer, but she hadn't expected him to move quite this fast. She braced her hand against a Suburban and hoped she wouldn't set off a car alarm. "Uh, sure, that's fine by me." She glanced up at his face backlit by a golden moon and spray of stars. "Any particular reason?"

"I've got this great meal in mind I want to make for you, but it takes a double boiler and a . . ." He picked his way nonchalantly around the parked cars, but the tensed muscles under her arm broadcast his nerves at this new direction in their budding relationship. "Well, let's just say I'm not sure there's enough room in my truck for all the utensils and spices I would have to haul over to your place."

He seemed to want to play this low-key, and quite frankly, she agreed. Much more excitement, and her hammering heart might break one of her ribs. "Fair enough then. Sounds like I'm getting the sweet end of this deal if you're cooking."

"You can have the chair." He stopped beside his truck, a coyote howling in the distance.

"Since you only have a chair, a TV, and a mattress," she turned to face him, tugging at the edges of his jacket, "that's mighty darn generous of you."

"Hey, I have furniture."

"Lawn chairs and a table to go with your grill don't count as furniture in most circles."

"Fine, whatever. But I also have a kitchen that rivals the set on *Top Chef* and a backyard big enough for an oversized dog." He pulled the edges of the jacket around to draw her inside and hooked his hands low behind her back. "What do you say we fill up my house with your furniture? I've even got this great corner in the living room just waiting for a cabinet full of teacups."

Thank goodness he was holding her up, because her knees stopped working. "That's moving sort of—"

"Fast?" he finished her sentence. "Sure, but somehow it just feels right." His hands slid up to cradle her face in his hands, the blinking lights of the little bar showcasing the stubborn cowlick above his forehead. "Just so you know, I have never asked a woman to move in before."

She didn't want to ruin this moment, but he'd opened the door this time. The question begged to be asked. "What about your ex-wife?"

His thumbs stroked along her hairline, somehow soothing and sensual all at once. "We were eighteen years old, full of rebellion when we went straight from our parents' houses into a one-bedroom apartment because of ridiculous ultimatums."

"What's your reason now?" She held his wrists, enjoying the feel of him, wanting more but also completely cool with taking their time so they got things just right if time was what he needed. "Why not just take things slowly?"

"We finish each others' sentences."

"Excuse me?"

"You know what I'm thinking before I say it. I may not be a rocket scientist, but I realize that's damn rare." His hands went still, his glinting green eyes as serious as she'd ever seen them. "And because I'm falling in love with you, Jill. I want you to know that the reason I say 'falling' is because I'm already learning that every morning when I wake up, I love you more than I did the day before."

Wow. Just wow. Her mouth fell open, and she searched for the perfect thing to say back to such a beautiful way of spelling out his feelings. It had been more than worth waiting for. "I love—"

"—you, too." He grinned. "I'm really starting to get into this finishing each other's sentences. So what do you say we give this a try? One day at a time, accepting each other as we are while still working like hell to be even better?"

"I think that's a plan, because I am totally and absolutely falling in love with you, too."

He angled down to kiss her at the same time she arched up, their mouths slanting to a perfect fit that sparked her senses with the promise of oh so much more to come later. She skimmed her hands down his arms as they drew apart.

Mason reached behind her to open her door with those old-timey manners she'd come to enjoy. "So what do ya say we pick up your dog and your grandmother's teacup and head back to my place tonight?"

She took his hand and leapt up into the truck cab. "What was it you said you'd planned for supper?"

"Anything you want." He squeezed her fingers and smiled. "Absolutely anything."